Lia Fail – Stone of Destiny

The Four Keys Series (Book 3)

J.C. Lucas

Copywrite

Published by J.C. Lucas, 2021.

While every precaution has been taken in the preparation of this book, the publisher assumes no responsibility for errors or omissions, or for damages resulting from the use of the information contained herein. Lia Fail- Stone of Destiny. First edition. February 2021. Copyright © 2021 J.C. Lucas. Written by J.C. Lucas.

Cover Art by Maria Spada

Editor- Lindsay York

IF YOU'D LIKE TO BE one of the first to know about new releases or sales, click below to sign up for J.C.'s newsletter. Just click the link below, subscribe and you'll get all the news! As a bonus for signing up, you'll also get a free download of the prequel, The Four Keys!

https://landing.mailerlite.com/webforms/landing/h1f5i7[1]

---

1. https://landing.mailerlite.com/webforms/landing/h1f5i7?fbclid=IwAR1rntmBvudk-JTJH7zQQ7fN1zZrEZfZU__LspFhZ8ihLtg-1e4SviFJ9bo

Dedication

This book is dedicated to my Dad, Grandpa and Papa.
These three men, especially my Dad, have supported me so much throughout my life. Dad, thank you for letting me tag along on your fishing and deer hunting trips, for letting me be a tomboy when I was little, then treating me like a princess as I grew older. Thank you for always being my protector and showing me so much love.
For my Grandpa, who instilled in me at an incredibly young age, the love of reading. For taking me to the library with him and letting me bring home piles of books that I devoured. For letting me dress him up in my Grandmother's wigs and teaching me to dance. And most of all for cheering me on no matter what it was that I wanted to do.
For my Papa who took me on adventures. From riding scooters around the neighborhood, boat rides and trips in the motorhome, to listening to me sing at the top of my lungs while I rode the four-wheeler. From watching him read late at night, to watching Heehaw with him, I will always treasure those memories.
I love these men with all my heart.

Chapter One

I stared at my pale face in the mirror and wondered when I had changed so much.

Gray eyes that had experienced way too many heartaches looked back at me, cynical and harsh. My eyebrows scrunched and my lips now seemed to be perpetually turned down. My hair had grown long. Longer than it had been in ages. I had no interest in going to the salon to have it cut. In fact, I rarely went to town.

Disgusted, I turned away, restlessly looking over everything in the small room that I resided in.

Eira and Balwyn were gracious enough to let me stay in the old Oak with them. I couldn't have been more surprised when they led me to a hidden area on the first floor where doors lined a hall, each one sleeping quarters, and each one decorated with magic.

It's been five months.

Five months since I returned from securing the Cauldron, only to find my guardian missing, and we still hadn't found her.

My friends-well, the ones that wanted to be around me still-assured me that Aine, the Queen of Fairy, had scouts out looking for Celeste. They found what looked to be "crumbs" or clues that she had left behind, hoping they would help us find her.

Only she could be so clever. Like Hansel and Gretel, leading us to where the witch had taken her, but this time the witch was Freya.

The clues soon came to a dead end at the creek in the middle of the woods, and the scouts could go no further. Aine continued to assure me that Celeste was alive. That it was only a matter of time before we found her. When I asked how she knew, a steely glint lit her eyes.

She said that the Moon Goddess would be harder to kill than any being, and if Freya somehow found a way to end Celeste's life, we would know.

Her mouth had tightened, and a flash of fear streaked through her eyes as she told me that should Celeste be killed, the earth would shake and the moon would fall. The animals in the forest would flee in terror and the old gods would scream.

It was a nightmare scenario. One we couldn't let happen.

I grabbed my worn beanie off the dresser, slapping it on my head and pulling the sides down over my ears, before turning to open the door that would take me out of my solitude.

The glow from the main room in the Oak lit my way down the hall, and Eira's small voice traveled through the air to greet me. She had taken to singing lately in hopes that the music would ease the dread that seemed to always hang in the air. Balwyn liked to act as though he hated it, always scowling at her when she struck up a new song, but I'd witnessed a softness take over his brow a time or two as he walked behind her, thinking no one was watching.

We were all out of sorts, as if something were missing, and it was. Celeste was our rock, the glue that held us all together, though we hadn't realized how much until she was gone.

I could argue that no one was more out of sorts than me, but I'd be wrong.

The guy who sat sprawled out on the couch in front of me, staring at the fire that crackled in the hearth beat me in that area. From the moment we returned from Murias, he was changed. Quiet and brooding, no amount of prodding seemed to get him out of his funk. Hunter had gone through so much while he was under Freya's spell. How much, I'm not sure we'd ever know. He refused to talk about it, other than when he told me that it had killed him to be imprisoned in his own body. Watching from the inside, powerless as the spelled version of himself tried to kill me.

And that was that.

When he spoke to me, his words were kind, but short and usually yes or no answers. He spent much of his time in front of this fire, staring at his arms and the veins in them that lit up like fire when we touched, as if willing them to do so on their own.

They never did.

Not unless I touched him as I had the first day we arrived at home, and the few times afterward. He began keeping me at arm's length. If he saw me coming, he backed away as I moved closer. My heart twisted each and every time. To know how he felt about me, and for him to know how I felt about him yet act almost as if I were a stranger was too much to bear.

I kept trying to tell myself that he would come out of it, that he was just adjusting and soon things would go back to normal. But they hadn't, and I feared they never would. Just when I thought I had him back, it seemed I was losing him all over again.

Standing in the doorway, I watched him. He sat still as a stone, the flames reflecting in his eyes, his dark hair mussed as if he'd ran his hand through it too many times. Every time I was near him, the pull was so great to go to him and wrap my arms around him that I had to physically keep my feet planted on the ground. I only wished that he felt the same way.

Sensing my presence, he turned his head in my direction, eyes meeting mine without emotion. How long we stared at each other, I don't know.

A throat clearing roused me from his gaze, and Balwyn walked over to Hunter, standing a good five feet away with his arms behind his back. Clearly, he was hesitant to bother him as well.

"Ya'd better get yer things ready ta go. T'won't be long before ya father is here ta get ya." Balwyn nodded toward the door.

He's leaving. Why didn't anyone tell me?

Unconsciously, I stepped further into the room and Hunter's eyes slid back to me for a moment before glancing back at Balwyn, nodding. He didn't say a word but slowly stood up, unfurling his tall body that seemed to take up so much space inside the magic tree.

Without looking again at either of us, he brushed by me. He wasn't in his room long before he came back, pack slung over his shoulder, and walked right to the door without a word. I could see his dad waiting outside, a forced smile on his lips as he watched his son.

My heart wrenched, and silently I pleaded with him to turn around, to say something, *anything*!

His shoulders tensed and he hesitated, before turning, his gaze apologetic as it found mine, his mouth set in a firm line.

"I'm sorry."

The words were quiet, but I heard them.

"Hunter, I..."

He didn't give me a chance. He didn't stay to listen, turning back before I could get anything else out, closing the door behind him.

The tinkling of the gears covered the cry that bubbled up, and my throat tightened with pain as if someone were actually squeezing it.

My hands clenched as I held them to my heart, and I knew that I would replay the moment he left, over and over in my head for a long time.

Why did everyone keep leaving me? Is there something wrong with me that makes no one want to stay?

All these questions flew through my head as I continued to stare at the door that had long since closed.

"You know he cares for you, Andie. Don't let it get to you. He's still adjusting to his new normal, and we don't even know yet what that is."

Eira flew from behind me, landing on a plant that cascaded from the balcony, perching on one of the delicate purple flowers. Her eyes were sympathetic as she looked toward me.

"I know, but it still hurts." I swallowed roughly. The tightness in my throat had only subsided slightly.

Eira flew down, swiping softly at a tear that I hadn't even known rolled down my cheek to my jaw. "He isn't leaving. You know, that, right? He's only going with his father for now. Aine told me that he'll be spending some time with the Weres before he goes to stay with some of the Titans to figure out just what happened to him, and what he is now."

I understood it, but I worried that the longer he was away from me, the more he would forget me. But I didn't need to tell her that. Eira seemed to always know my concerns, my fears, and sorrows. Maybe I projected them, or maybe I was just really bad at hiding my feelings. She and Balwyn were the only ones I felt comfortable enough letting my guard down around lately. They were the ones who got me through the last few months when at first, I went through the motions of living, too consumed in my fear that Celeste was gone for good.

"Let's sit down and chat a bit." She motioned toward the recently vacated couch. "Balwyn! Please bring some cocoa and cookies!" she hollered toward his hidey hole. I heard him grumble, and felt a small smile lift the corner of my mouth. The two of them were best friends and antagonized each other like enemies.

The warmth from the fire surrounded me as I sat down, and the smell of Hunter rose from the blanket that was draped over the back. I breathed in deeply. He always smelled of cedarwood, even though he never wore any cologne. It was a smell all his own, and I wrapped the blanket around my shoulders, encompassing myself in it.

Balwyn trudged over to us before setting the tray down. It was full of several different kinds of cookies, two regular-sized mugs filled with chocolatey goodness and a container that held extra marshmallows simply because he knew I liked to add them as I drank.

He was trying to help in his own way.

"Thank you. This looks wonderful." I smiled gently at him, picking up a chocolate chip and biting into it, even though I wasn't hungry. His eyes lit up before he scowled quickly. Heaven forbid he smile. I bit my lip to keep from smiling bigger.

"I'd some extra treats tat need ta be ate before they go bad. Tat's all." He shrugged and looked away from me.

I knew better, but I wouldn't tease him, Eira did enough of that.

Luckily for him, she was slurping down her tiny cup of cocoa and ignoring his feigned indifference. "Aine wants you to visit her for a bit," Eira said as she chewed a piece of shortbread. "Amarie and the Elves are there, and she wants them to train you for battle."

She said it so nonchalantly that it took me by surprise. "What if I don't want to go?" I said petulantly, aware that I really didn't have a choice.

Eira's dainty eyebrow rose as she looked over her mug at me. She had a way of not even having to say something, but I understood what she was projecting at me.

I groaned. "Fine. When do I go?" I slumped back against the couch, pulling the blanket tighter around me. Both Balwyn and Eira leaned closer to me, satisfaction glowing in their eyes.

Eira pretended to look at her wrist as if an invisible watch lay there. Smiling mischievously, she looked back up at me. "Oh, in about an hour."

Seriously!?

I jumped up, still clenching the blanket, and looked at the two of them while frustration built up inside of me. "How long am I to be there?" I asked through clenched teeth, hoping it would only be a few days.

Balwyn cleared his throat and sat back. He was like the bad cop to Eira's good cop. They always did this, and he seemed to have been picked to give me the bad news.

"As long as it takes fer you ta become a good fighta. If I were ya, I'd be makin' sure ta learn quick like." His shaggy eyebrows were scrunched down low, and he had the most serious look on his face.

I knew he wasn't trying to be sarcastic. He was giving me advice as if he were a father figure, and in a way, that's what he had been lately. Quick and to the point, no-nonsense if not a little brash.

I nodded at him before walking to my quiet and cozy room, closing the door softly behind me.

I wasn't ready to learn how to fight. I liked the little bubble I was in right now, shutting out the rest of the world and its problems. Going to Aine's castle would bring everything back into clarity, and I'd have to face the craziness that was happening, head-on. I was only glad that I didn't have to worry about school at the same time. With the people of Junction still picking up the pieces from Freya and the Fomori's last visit, and the school beyond repair, it had been delayed until they could figure out how to have it safely.

I grabbed my pack and shoved my suit into it, then grabbed a bunch of my regular clothes and shoes and did the same. I was sick of that suit. I wasn't going to wear it anytime soon if I didn't have to.

I looked around the room once more, feeling as though I was missing something when my eyes fell on the small spell book Amarie had given me.

After finding the Cauldron, I had forgotten about it, so immersed in feeling sorry for myself. I grabbed it and threw it on top of my clothes. It would keep me busy while I was hiding out from everyone in Fairy.

I'd made the bed and picked up the room, and once I was satisfied that Balwyn would approve, I walked out to the main room. Neither one of them seemed to have moved, and both awaited me anxiously.

"Who's picking me up this time?" I asked, and Eira laughed. Even Balwyn's eyes seemed to have gained a certain sparkle.

"Killian will be here in about five minutes." Eira clapped her hands. "I've missed that boy so much!"

My heart leapt. Killian was like a brother to me. He was caring and funny, and I could really use that right now. I hadn't spoken with him since he left to go with Aine, but Eira kept me updated and I knew he was finally learning to harness his Titan powers, but they had still not found out how he had been born with them.

Suddenly the flames in the fireplace swirled. Sparks jumped out to land on the wooden floor around us and Balwyn hopped up, stomping them out as wind whistled through the room.

"What tha blazin..." Balwyn yelled as a mist began to settle through the air, coating us in dampness, and a small tornado formed before a loud rush sounded and Killian appeared, squatting on one knee with a hand on the floor.

His blonde hair was shaggy now and grazed his shoulders as he smiled up at our astonished faces.

"Who's ready to go to Fairy?"

Chapter Two

I laughed because he looked ridiculous, and I reached down to help him up.

"Killian! I've missed you."

He brushed at his clothing and a cloud of dust flew in the air around him, much to Balwyn's dismay.

"Well, you wouldn't have missed me so much if you'd come with us to begin with instead of sequestering yourself here for months." He looked me up and down as if making sure I was whole and okay. I knew he was right, but at the time, I just hadn't been able to be around them all. The state I'd been in wasn't fit for company.

"Yeah, yeah. I know. I'm not sure that I'm ready to go now, but I don't really have a choice, do I?" I questioned him.

"Nope! None at all." He laughed and reached for me, hugging me tightly. "It's going to be okay. I promise." He whispered in my ear as his strong arms surrounded me.

Before I had a chance to get emotional, he pushed me back to arm's length.

"Let's go learn to kick some Elves' butts!" He laughed at the expression on my face. "What? You don't think I'm going to let you train alone, do you? Before Amarie knows it, we'll be better fighters than they can even dream of."

I chuckled because there was no way we would ever be better than the Elves. They were born fighters, strong and sure.

"Hey, if I end up even half as good as they are, I'll be happy."

He grabbed my hand and twirled me around, bumping me into the table, the cocoa from earlier sloshing over the side of the tray.

"Killian, if ya don't stop tat carryin on, I'ma show ya how ta fight, I will." Balwyn growled from his perch on the chair.

To make matters worse, Killian leaned over and rubbed his hand over Balwyn's stockinged head, giving him a noogie while Balwyn's short arms fought to get him off. Eira giggled and egged Killian on until Balwyn told them both he'd never give them cocoa again if they didn't stop.

Immediately, Killian's hands dropped, and he looked at Balwyn with fake humility. "I promise I'll be good from now on."

Balwyn couldn't see his fingers crossed behind his back but scowled at him just the same. Before he had a chance to respond, the door to the Oak was thrown open with the familiar tinkling noise, and in flew Charlie, followed by Emric, who kicked the door shut with his Phooka back paw.

"Why weren't we invited to this party? None of you know how to party like a Phooka." He did a little jig as he made his way over. "But I suppose I can't take offense. We're going to party much better than this in Fairy." He gave a disdainful look at Balwyn before chuckling at the brownie's frown.

"Wait. You guys are going with me?" I stared at Charlie, who sat quietly on Killian's shoulder, and he nodded.

"Of course. Where you go, we go," he said stoically. "Just because we didn't stay here," he looked around the inside of the tree, "doesn't mean we haven't been keeping an eye on you."

I had never thought about them keeping an eye on me. I only knew that they wanted to stay at Celeste's house, and I just hadn't been able to stay there. I couldn't. Not when everything in there exuded her essence and made me think about her constantly. I felt a little bad that I'd left them to pick up the pieces, literally.

Ashamed, I looked at the floor. "Thank you," I whispered. I knew they heard me.

Emric patted my leg softly, and then sauntered over to Killian. "Well? Let's get this show on the road. I'm hungry!"

Killian, who had been watching our exchange without interrupting, smiled down at Emric. "I agree. Let's get going."

Eira flew into a flutter of activity, swirling around us and kissing our cheeks, while Balwyn watched in the background.

"Andie, you've got your beanie? Oh, and don't forget your suit! Do I need to pack some food for you? Balwyn, wrap up some cookies!" She chattered on, before taking a deep breath and looked around at the rest of us as we silently stared at her. "What? I just want to make sure you don't forget anything."

"I've got my beanie and suit. Please, no food. I'm sure we'll have plenty at the castle." I tried to make my voice soothing, but it just sounded strained.

"Okay... if you're sure..." Her voice trailed off, and she hugged the side of my face. "Don't stay away too long. I have enjoyed having another girl to talk to." She smiled up at me.

"Me too, Eira. I'm sure I won't be gone long."

Everyone was silent, and I felt like I was missing something, but this awkwardness was getting to me. "Can we go now?"

Killian gestured for me to come over to stand beside him. Charlie and Emric hung onto us as Killian leaned in, his nose almost touching mine.

"This is different than when you go through a portal. You're going to have to hang on really tight because the wind will be almost unbearable. We're going to travel pretty much at the speed of light, so close your eyes."

The speed of light?

He didn't have to worry; I'd have my eyes shut tight.

He wrapped his arms around me, and I did the same, looping my hands through his belt loops. "Don't you dare let me go, Killian. If something happens to me, I'll haunt you for the rest of your life."

He laughed at me. "Nothing's going to happen to you. Now, let's go."

The wind picked up and I saw the vague outline of Balwyn through the cloud that immediately surrounded us, stomping out more sparks. I slammed my eyes shut and tucked my head into Killian's chest, my fingers already cramping from holding so tightly.

I was aware of the weightless feeling before my body felt like it was being swirled down a bathtub drain, my hair flying straight up and the skin on my cheeks stretched. My heart stuttered when Emric howled.

I heard it again, and realized it was the sound of glee, not terror. That dang Phooka! I focused on letting him have it once we arrived to keep my mind off the pressure I was feeling from this crazy flight.

"Andie." I felt Killian patting my back. "You can let go now."

I blinked a few times at the brightness that greeted me and pried my hands off Killian's waist, flexing them to get rid of the stiffness.

We were in the castle's courtyard, and fairies flitted all around. They always seemed so happy. I don't think I'd ever seen any of them upset, but then again, they were *here*. Who wouldn't be happy living in a place like this?

"There you are. I was beginning to think you'd never arrive." Aine walked down the steps from the entrance to the castle, and I did a double-take. Whenever I saw her-except the time she pretended to be my social worker-she'd always worn the finest dresses and jewels. Today she wore jeans with a silky white top and her feet were bare.

She enveloped me in her arms, and I squeezed back. She was the closest thing I had to Celeste, and I knew she cared for me.

We stayed like that for a few minutes, and she rubbed my back gently before stepping away. I gestured to her. "What's with the outfit?"

I wasn't trying to be rude, and she knew me well enough that she laughed and shook her head. "I was trying to make it feel a little less like Fairy, and more like what you're used to. Plus, I think these jeans look rather good on me!" She turned, showing her butt off to the rest of us, and looked over her shoulder.

I laughed, and Emric rolled his eyes as he took off into the castle with Charlie in hot pursuit. Killian blushed and glanced at me before taking off to join the others and leave us to our girl talk.

Aine chuckled too, her dark curls bouncing around her. "Well, I think I look pretty smokin'!" She gestured to herself. "Isn't that the term you young people use nowadays?"

I grabbed ahold of her arm, winding mine through it as we walked toward the steps. "Yeah, I think you look smokin' too, Aine. Maybe you should invite Coeus over and see what he thinks?" I raised my eyebrow at her, and I was astounded to see a rosy stain on both of her cheeks.

"I don't know what you mean. Coeus wouldn't care about that," she stuttered, embarrassed.

"Sure... sure." I just laughed, and she changed the subject.

The castle hadn't changed any. It was still just as fascinating as ever, and my eyes never seemed to know what to look at first. Aine led us to the dining room where Killian was seated, eagerly waiting while Amarie sat across from him, deep in discussion with Kitt. The rest of her clan filled in the remaining seats around the long table, their eyes lighting up when they saw me.

I tried to remember all their names, but it'd been too long since we left them at their home by the river.

"Hey," I quietly said as I joined them. Aine patted my hand before letting my arm go so that I could sit down.

Amarie looked up, eyes full of emotion. I swallowed hard as she softly nodded my way, her eyes never leaving mine. It was as if she were searching my soul, trying to determine my emotional state. Her observance caused my eyes to well up against my wishes, and I looked away sharply, studying a painting on the wall.

It was large, and the figures in it stood tall and mighty, power exuding from them. If I had to guess it was a rendition of Titan gods. One of them was the spitting image of Coeus, though he looked much younger. How had I not noticed it before?

I studied the other figures. Some were men, the other women. All striking and beautiful. Their eyes seemed to stare right at me from the canvas, and I couldn't pull my gaze away. It wasn't until a plate landed in front of me that I glanced around to see our meal floating through the air, and everyone else began digging in.

It seemed that we were to have sandwiches for lunch this time around instead of the fancy meals that Aine was known to host. I imagined this was also in her plan to make me feel more at home. I chuckled to myself.

She could serve all the boring meals she wanted, and dress in common clothes, but there was absolutely no way that she could make such a magical place as this castle and Fairy seem normal or like home.

The conversation flowed around me as my thoughts drifted to Hunter and Teagan. I longed to know how they were, and what they were doing. Presley had visited me a total of one time at the Oak since Teagan had been injured. And she had only come to explain that she'd be staying at his parents' house to help him recover and return to some semblance of a normal life with his now missing leg.

It tore my heart apart that he had ignored all my attempts to talk to him. I had expressed how upset I was to Pres when she was there, but she had waved it off, telling me that he just needed time. She even went so far to tell me how I'd broken his heart, and between that and trying to figure out how to adjust to being handicapped, I'd need to give him space to figure it all out.

That had hurt. Especially coming from her.

She hadn't been rude, but she had looked at me as if I were to blame for it all, though that could have just been my imagination and the guilt that ate at me day in and day out.

A hand falling on my shoulder made me jump and pulled me out of the depressing inner monologue that I was having.

Coeus looked down at me, a soft smile on his lips and kindness in his eyes. I hadn't known he would be here. I just figured that he was off with the other Titans working with Hunter.

"How are you, my dear? I must say that I miss seeing that quick smile that I am so used to. Surely, I'm not that ugly, am I?" He teased with a sparkle in his eyes as he walked over to Aine and bent, placing a kiss of her forehead before rounding the table to sit in the empty chair in front of me.

Their hidden romance fascinated me, and if they weren't already a couple, they really needed to be. Maybe I could play matchmaker while I stayed here. That would definitely take my mind off everything and could be fun.

"Ah... there's the smile I was talking about!" Coeus boomed and laughed jovially. "Care to share what caused it?" His eyebrow arched slightly in challenge. I wanted to groan because he had definitely read my thoughts.

"Umm... not at this time?" I squeaked, my cheeks turning hot as I did my best to not look at Aine. He just laughed at my discomfort and I ducked my head, tucking into the food and stuffing as much into my stupid mouth to keep quiet.

He still wasn't done, though. He was enjoying making me uncomfortable, or he somehow thought I'd help his cause with Aine.

"Oh, but it must be something really good, Andie. I highly respect your opinions, you know." He winked and looked around. "Don't you all agree?"

Everyone nodded vigorously and stared at me, waiting.

I scowled at him for putting me on the spot. *You know what? He wants me to say what I was thinking. Well let's see how he likes this.*

I looked around again, glancing at Aine to see that she was smiling encouragingly.

"Well, I was just thinking about how you and Aine would make a magnificent couple. I mean, you both obviously like each other a lot. Why don't you just get on with it then?"

Dead silence greeted me.

I hadn't meant for the last bit to sound so rude, and I glanced back at Coeus to see both his brows raised.

Maybe he hadn't read my mind after all because this certainly wasn't the reaction I expected. Aine's face was slack with shock, and her head swiveled between me and him several times before she composed herself.

She glanced quickly at Coeus before looking back at me. "We'll discuss this later," she said sternly, and I felt slightly uncomfortable at the thought, but only shrugged.

If they wanted to pretend nothing was happening between them, or that they didn't want something to happen, that was their problem. I was tired of everyone pretending. I'd had enough of that to last a lifetime.

With the way things were going and all the things I'd been through, none of us-not even gods and Fairy Queens-could stand to lose another minute of lost time with those they loved.

I made up my mind right then and there to not be embarrassed to speak my mind any longer. I wouldn't tiptoe around issues, worries, or blame.

Thanks, Coeus.

Chapter Three

After the intense lunch, I'd excused myself and wandered around the castle exploring. There really should be one of those map things like they have at Six Flags that tells you where you are and how to get to other points in the building.

I mean, this place was huge, and I hadn't even seen a fourth of it yet!

Part of that was probably due to how long I spent in each room, studying all the spectacular things that greeted me. How could you not? From ceilings that displayed the blue sky to fountains that dripped gold and silver, each room held magic that would be unbelievable to anyone from the human world.

Right now, the sight in front of me as I stood in a large arched doorway was stunning.

Inside the room, ceilings soared, and a circular metal stairway wound itself up to the top floor. Books and more books lined the four walls, and ladders with rollers rested against the shelves. While I felt like Belle in *Beauty and the Beast*, shocked at the beautiful library that must house thousands of volumes, the thing that really caught my attention was the glass structure smack dab in the middle of the room.

It rose almost as high as the ceilings, the glass rounding at the top. Inside the dome, a cherry tree grew, decked out in beautiful pink blossoms with flowers growing around the bottom of the trunk. Butterflies of every color flew gracefully or perched with their delicate wings fluttering.

Part of me felt sad that these beautiful creatures were trapped inside of a glass house with no one to appreciate them except those who wandered into the library. That they weren't allowed to soar and swoop through woods and valleys, relegated to this one place instead. At the same time, I was grateful that they were here for me to witness their beauty.

Mesmerized, I walked closer, running my hands over the smooth glass, my eyes watching a rather large blue butterfly that seemed to track my movements as I walked around the clear room. That was silly, though. A butterfly didn't have enough sense to follow me.

Did it?

As I walked around the backside of the glass, I spied lines in it and a small silver handle. *So there actually is a way inside!*

I grasped the handle and thought to myself that I really shouldn't go inside. The wings of the blue butterfly intensified as I pulled at the door and it opened with a whoosh. The air inside felt slightly humid, and I quickly closed it behind me lest any of the beautiful creatures get the idea to escape.

As soon as I did, the thousands of different species took flight. Their dance in the air was beautiful, and my eyes tracked them as they simultaneously swirled in a pattern around the dome before slicing through the air to twirl around me.

I was awed. Goosebumps spread across my arms. I knew I was witnessing a beauty like none other, flawless, and magical.

A muffled noise caused me to look outside the glass toward the doorway of the library, and my heart stopped at the same time the flight of the butterflies did. At that exact moment they landed all over me, and when there was no room left, the others perched on the tropical plants that surrounded my body.

Even if I wanted to move, I couldn't. Not even their little legs that tickled my face, arms and ears could have dislodged me from my spot. I was too stunned. Too afraid that if I moved, the figure in front of me would disappear.

He hadn't moved. His eyes pierced into mine, and time stood still.

Hunter's here. And every bit of my soul longed for him. Like a magnet, he drew me in. I'm just not sure if it's the same for him.

I refused to lay my heart out there again. I was afraid it would only lead to more pain.

He grimaced as if he could hear my thoughts and looked away, jaw clenching and fists balled by his side, before coming to a decision.

He stalked toward the glass room until he was on the far side, his eyes not once leaving mine. His hand lifted, and he placed his palm against the glass.

Immediately, the butterflies left me. Their wings blew the air around violently enough to move tendrils of my hair back, as they clustered against the wall, completely obscuring my view of him. Panic gripped me at first, then wonder as golden light lit all their little bodies and pulsed. Like a heartbeat. Like one heartbeat.

-Hunter's.

He was doing this with whatever fiery magic ran through his veins. It was as if he were trying to convey something to me, but I was still just as confused as ever.

The light show lasted forever, and yet not long enough, as one by one the winged creatures departed from the wall, their bodies no longer glowing.

Through the glass I saw that Hunter had left, and the warmth inside the dome went with him.

∞

I didn't see Hunter again that day. I hadn't spoken to anyone about the encounter, but I'm sure they could tell that something was bothering me. Or maybe they didn't. They had gotten used to my surly behavior as of late.

Aine found me as I left the library, excited to show me to what would be my room for the time of my stay. I pretended to be happy with it. I could tell she had gone out of her way to make it as beautiful and comfortable as she could, and she had-really, she had.

It was gorgeous and filled with all kinds of things she knew I liked. There was even a tray on the little table in front of the window full of my favorite snacks. A Keurig on top of a dresser, with various flavored coffees in a basket beside it, and a bookshelf brimming with books.

Any other time, I would have been excited to have a room like this. But right now, I just couldn't seem to get past the depression that consumed me.

She had even given me a laptop and a cellphone. I'd never had either before, and I wasn't sure that I'd even know how to use them. But I would need to figure it out. She explained that Mr. Timmons had gotten in touch with her earlier in the day and told her that school would resume, finally, but that it would all be online.

With Freya and the Fomori still wreaking havoc, they couldn't take the chance of putting students in danger. The witches had put a spell over the city to make it look like a highly contagious virus was going around, and that was the excuse the school used.

I was fine with having online school. That gave me time to deal with everything else and not have to worry about appearing as if everything were normal. The cellphone, though? I didn't know who I'd call. I didn't even know anyone's phone numbers.

As I glanced over to it on the nightstand, voices filtered in from outside the window, and I walked over to look out, pushing the curtains back slightly. The view from the room was amazing.

I was extremely high up, and the back of the castle looked out onto a valley of hills that rose and dipped for as far as the eye could see. Trees of every color dotted the landscape.

The voices sounded again, and I pulled my gaze from the beauty before me to look down at a small patio where Coeus and Hunter sat close together. The deep rumble of Coeus's voice drifted up. Hunter sat with his head in his hands mumbling softly, but I couldn't make out what he or Coeus said. When he placed his hand on Hunter's shoulder, I knew something was wrong, that Hunter was upset.

I wanted to be the one to comfort him, but I knew he wouldn't let me.

As I turned away from the window, I caught a slight movement from him, and walked away as his eyes turned up to where I stood, full of pain and longing.

I couldn't be the one to go to him now. If I was what he wanted, he would have to be the one to come to me. It was the only way.

Just as I was about to flop down on the bed, a knock sounded, and I slowly made my way over, pulling at the heavy wood door. I inched it open and peeked my head outside.

Killian, Charlie, and Emric stood there, all three of them with stupid grins on their faces.

"What's up?" I asked, still not opening the door further, and their eyebrows raised in concert. Normally, I would have found it comical, but right now I just felt annoyed. I wanted to be alone.

"How rude," Emric purred. "Open up and let us in. I personally do not care what kind of mood you're in. This is my room too, and I'd like to be allowed to enter." He pushed through the gap by my feet and I stumbled back, opening the door wider.

"Be my guest," I said sarcastically as I let the wood go and retreated to my bed while Emric jumped up to land at the foot of it. Killian and Charlie followed his lead, making themselves comfortable.

"What's going on Andie? And don't try to lie. We know something's up, and it's high time we talked it out." His face was serious, and I knew he meant business. Charlie and Emric had similar expressions as they stared at me.

"I'm fine, really. I just miss Celeste, and nothing seems right anymore."

I picked at the soft bedspread and looked away from them.

"I've never known you to give up." Emric growled, and my head snapped back to look at him. "Life hasn't been easy for you, but until now, you've always fought. Why are you letting that change now? Don't be juvenile." He looked disgusted, and I was thoroughly shocked.

Do they all think I'm being immature?

"But you don't understand how it feels," I sputtered. "I've lost everyone who comes close to me. In one way or another. And I'm just done with it." I wrenched up the covers and slid my legs under them, pulling the sheet up to my chin and turning my body away from them as much as possible.

Charlie's voice sounded behind me, soft but strong. "You can pretend like we don't understand young lady, but deep down you know we do. You're not the only one who's lost someone. You're not the only one who has experienced pain, and you'll not be the last. And you'll lose more. Your life is far from over, and life has a way of taking and giving. It is a roller coaster, bringing you up and down, and then back again. But you cannot give up. You just can't. We need you too much. Think about it, sleep on it, and fight your way back up out of this darkness. We need your light."

My breath caught, and I hiccupped, squeezing my eyes shut tight, but his words had hit something inside. I knew he was right. I hated that he was right. Nothing would ever be easy, but I couldn't give up.

Celeste, Nan, and my mother wouldn't want me to. In fact, I was sure that the speech Charlie gave would have been something similar to what they might have told me. It wasn't long ago that I received pretty much the same advice from Loxley. I missed that fairy. I missed a lot of people.

It was time to grow up. It was time to get on with life, regardless of what has happened or will happen to me.

I felt two small bodies curl up behind the curve in my back, and I reached behind me, laying my hand against them both. Killian squeezed my ankle before I felt his weight lift, and the light clicked off, the door quietly closing on his way out.

Chapter Four

I woke up the day after with a new attitude. Was I still depressed? Yes, of course. But I wouldn't let it show. I decided to put all my effort into training, school, and moving forward.

The next few days were a whirlwind. Amarie and the Elves trained with me and Killian for hours on end. After the first day of training, my body felt as though it had been beaten black and blue. I was sore from head to toe, but I pushed on. In a way, the pain reminded me that I was alive, and I leaned into it, feeding off the pain to keep going.

In between training, I did my schooling online. It was rather convenient because I was able to get work done within a few hours. So far, my grades were good, and I intended to keep them that way. It wasn't exactly how I expected my senior year to be, but it is what it is. There were far more important things right now than worrying about senior photos, prom, even graduation. Who knew what I would be doing in a years' time? Nothing was anywhere near normal.

I hadn't seen Hunter at all since the incident in the glass room. I knew he had to still be here somewhere since Coeus hadn't left, but it seemed he went out of his way to stay out of my sight.

On the fourth day of training, Amarie and I were working on hand-to-hand combat together, and I was proud of how much I had learned and achieved in just a few days. I felt stronger, more confident in the fact that should a situation warrant fighting, I'd be able to handle my own.

The day was beautiful, with the sun shining down but not hot. We stood in a forest clearing near the castle, and I could still see the courtyard from where we trained. Amarie was showing me how to use my palm to punch up into someone's nose to incapacitate them, when I noticed a flurry of activity at the front of the castle.

Fairies zipped to and fro, excited, and that's when I noticed a group of people walking out of the opposite side of the woods. Some were men, some women, but they were all beautiful. The men were dressed in jeans and button-down shirts, though one man wore a three-piece suit. The women were dressed in a variety of styles. Some in jeans, some in dresses. If they hadn't been all so gorgeous, I would have thought them to be normal human beings.

But power exuded from them, and the way they carried themselves spoke of nobility and confidence. Not even the floating silver balls or fountains of diamonds seemed to spark their interest.

"Pay attention!"

I barely had time to move before Amarie's fist narrowly missed my jaw, and I hopped back, tearing my eyes from the group now ascending the steps to the castle.

"Sorry," I said distractedly, glancing at their backs as they disappeared inside.

She huffed before stalking toward the tree where we had set down our water bottles and took a long drink.

"I wonder who they are?" I voiced my thought aloud, following her before sitting down on the ground.

"There are always visitors to court. But those are Titan gods and goddesses, come to work with Hunter. Now, let's get back to our session."

She reached down, pulling me to my feet, and walked back, turning to face me in a fighter's stance.

I wondered exactly what they'd be doing with Hunter, what they might find out about him and what he had turned into. My curiosity was overwhelming, and I longed to be a fly on the wall.

We fought for another hour, and Amarie kicked my butt *hard*. I blamed it on being distracted, and she confirmed it.

As we walked back to the castle, she looked over at me with impatience. "You can't let yourself be distracted during a fight. What will you do if it happens when you're fighting for your life? You'll die. That's what." She shook her head and walked faster when she saw Kitt and Killian returning from their training as well.

Sighing, I knew she was right.

Get it together, Andie!

I'd fight harder tomorrow. I'd show her that I wouldn't let any distractions get to me.

I ran up the steps and into the huge foyer. A fairy blew by me in a hurry, and I saw many more inside in a frenzy. This group of Titans must not visit very often.

I kept my head down and hurried up the stairs to my room, shutting the door with a hurry. I'd already finished my schoolwork for the day, so I was free to do as I wished.

Despite being tired, I wanted to know more about the group that had arrived, and I couldn't meet them all stinky and dirty.

My shower was done in record time, and I quickly dried my hair, letting it hang loose, and threw on jeans and a T-shirt. I glanced at the makeup on the counter, dismissing it as I had each day I'd been here. The sunglasses that Killian gave me upon my arrival still sat unused on the dresser. He had been so thoughtful bringing them to me, aware that auras were a big problem for me, and caused headaches that were debilitating.

But since arriving here, I hadn't experienced any.

It was strange, but not unwelcome. It was nice to not see a blinding color radiating off everyone who I looked at. It was a relief. At least for now.

Hurrying, I took the stairs two at a time, and hopped to the bottom only to jump right into the path of one of the men who arrived earlier.

His hands steadied me, keeping me from plowing him down as my momentum carried me.

"Whoa!" He laughed, his grin bright white like Coeus. He was tall and broad and his three-piece suit immaculate. He looked to be in his thirties, but I knew he was much, much older than that.

"In a hurry, little one?" He stepped back and looked around, as if searching for something that might be chasing me.

"I am so sorry for running into you. I was actually on my way to meet you all," I said, angling my chin, refusing to be embarrassed.

He laughed again and spread his arms, looking behind him as the others in his group filtered in, followed by Coeus.

"Well, looks like you've found us. Might you be Andie?"

The men and women behind him looked at me curiously, as if I were an oddity or something fascinating, though they seemed much more stoic than the man in front of me.

"That's me. And you are?" I questioned him. I should probably show some awe and excitement at being the object of the Titans' scrutiny, but the new Andie wasn't willing to let herself be intimidated like she used to.

He dipped his head toward me. "I am Iapetus, at your service." He grinned. Turning he pointed to each one of the other men and women as he introduced them. They gave a slight wave or dip of their own head as he announced their names. "Rhea, Perses, Epimetheus, Phoebe, Lelantos, Leto, Metis, and Crius."

Their names were familiar, and I couldn't for the life of me place them with the mythology I'd read about previously on the Titans.

But you could bet after meeting them I'd find out. Google was my best friend right now.

"Pleased to meet you all," I said serenely before Coeus steered them out of the room and into a large study. He turned after they'd all gone in, holding both doors before shutting them and giving me a stern look.

"Behave, Andie."

That was all he said before closing the doors.

I rolled my eyes and turned away, only to see Emric flouncing down the steps, Charlie hot on his heels.

"Behave, Andie," Emric mimicked. "What fun is behaving? Coeus wouldn't know fun if it bit him in the behind." He hmphed.

"No, not a'tall," Charlie parroted before they both ran down a hall opposite me.

"Come on Andie. Let's have some fun!" Emric called as he went around a corner. I hesitated before following them. Fun sounded just like something I needed.

∞

The hall twisted and turned, and I barely kept from running into a broom that was sweeping imaginary dust from the floors. Before long, the hall ended, turning into a huge, cavernous room that housed an enormous swimming pool, complete with a waterslide and waterfall.

Banana trees and palms lined the room, and my attention was taken away from them as I watched Emric belly flop into the water, sending a plume into the air to land all over me. Charlie changed into a panther, following behind him, yowling as he dived.

"Come on in, Andie! You can't have fun if you're only watching!" Emric hollered from the water, his little paws paddling furiously.

I shrugged and took off my jeans. The T-shirt I wore was long and came to mid-thigh, so I wasn't worried about anything showing. Running, I jumped high in the air, tucking my knees in, and yelled, "Cannonball!"

As I surfaced, I was splashed in the face repeatedly, and I sought them both out for retribution. "You're gonna get it now!" I swam over to Charlie, pushing on his head and ducking him under the water before swimming as fast as I could in the opposite direction.

Seeing stairs beside the slide, I headed toward them, pulling myself out and charging up to the top, flinging myself down as water flowed through the tube, jetting me out back into the pool. I laughed loudly and realized that this was the most fun I'd had in a long time.

We played until we were completely worn out. I had long since pulled myself out of the water, fingers and toes wrinkly, my ears waterlogged. I lay on one of the chaise lounges staring up at the ceiling while Emric and Charlie snoozed beside me.

Behind me, footsteps approached, and by the slapping sound the person was barefoot. I didn't look their way until a soft splash sounded.

I watched as they sliced through the water, and then went back and forth between the length of the pool several times before surfacing. When they did, a head covered in a swim cap turned toward me with a bright smile.

"I do hope I didn't disturb you. I needed to get away from all the boring politics going on behind closed doors."

Her face belied her age. She blinked slowly while the corners of her lips turned up in a grin. "Oh, dear, you have no idea how old I am. You couldn't even fathom. But that is neither here nor there. Beauty and youth are irrelevant in this life. What's really important is strength of character, perseverance, and kindness. Oh, and a good sense of humor. You definitely need that to get through it all."

She dove back under the water and swam back over to the stairs before climbing out. She wore an old-fashioned one-piece swimsuit with black stripes and a sweetheart neckline. As if she felt my stare, she looked over her shoulder before walking out of the pool room and waved.

"Come find me later. I think we could both do with a good girl chat." And then she was gone. I hadn't even been able to utter a single word, so caught unaware had I been. It's not every day that you're in the same room as the mother of Zeus.

"Something else, isn't she?" Emric purred beside me. I'd forgotten that he and Charlie were there.

"You should feel grateful that Rhea wants to talk with you later. She is not known to have many friendships with other women," Charlie said in his somber voice.

It made me wonder what it was about me that had changed her mind.

Standing up, I gathered my things and dried off with the towel I'd pilfered from one of the fancy racks nearby. Once I felt I wouldn't drip water over the floors, I slipped my jeans back on and headed into the rest of the castle with Charlie and Emric following. As I made my way through the winding hall, a haunting melody sifted through the air. It sounded close but also muffled.

It was beautiful, and whoever played was masterful on the piano. Melancholy seemed to pour from each note, and I wanted to find out who it was. The curiosity that flowed through me was difficult to stop, in fact my body seemed to have a life of its own, steering me toward the source.

I rounded the corner, and a large white door with silver handles and hinges stood before me. It had to be at least fifteen feet tall. The soft music seeped out, and my curiosity was too much to deal with. I bit my lip and reached for the handle, pulling it down and slowly opened the door.

Soaring ceilings greeted me, and silver columns stretched up, shining against the rays of light that flooded through glittering windows that lined the large hall. There was no furniture, save a lone black grand piano situated on a platform hovering over the middle of the room with silver stairs floating beside it.

The haunting melody was louder now, echoing around the large space. The acoustics in here were better than any concert hall I had been in. And the solitary figure whose fingers flew over the ivory keys was lost in the song, unaware that they had an audience.

I stared unabashedly. I had never known that he could play. That he was so talented. The ache in my chest that had worn heavy on me during my trek through the halls expanded as I knew that he poured all the anger, sorrow, and confusion that was flowing through him into every note. My feet once again found a life of their own, and I glided closer until I was not but five feet away from the stage. I turned to gaze up at the beautiful picture he made.

His dark hair was haphazard, a lock hung over one eye and his eyebrows were drawn down in concentration. His lips were a slash of red, and his jaw clenched, highlighting the sharp angles of his features. His chest rose and fell as though he were running a race, in and out just as quickly as his fingers played each key, and the music began to crescendo.

I closed my eyes as my heart sped up with it, feeling the notes almost as if his music were talking directly to me. Was it a spell? I couldn't say, but I felt unlike I ever had before. Happiness, sadness, anger, and a need for something I couldn't express all rushed through me as the music ended on its final note.

When I felt all those feelings sifting softly away, I slowly opened my eyes and his dark ones pierced into my soul.

His usually passive face was softer, and his eyes seemed to plead with me. I wanted to make it better for Hunter. I did. But I had no idea how.

Smiling tentatively, I reached out a hand, hoping he would take it. *I won't beg.*

His gaze shifted to my outstretched palm, studying it with curious eyes. As if he didn't understand what I offered. He stood, his eyes coming back to look into mine, but with determination this time. They held me captive as he descended the floating steps, making his way over to me.

Time seemed to stand still as his warm palm grasped mine, his fingers intertwining with my own. The fire lit up inside his veins; the gold swirled in his eyes.

We stood together like that forever. I was too afraid to say a word. Worried that if I did, it would stop the magical pulses that traveled between us. That he would go back to being cold and aloof like before.

I didn't have to worry though for he broke the silence.

"You have no idea what you do to me."

A gasp escaped as I tried to comprehend his words. They were unexpected, and I had only hoped for acknowledgement that he cared that we were still friends. That he wouldn't leave me. A million thoughts ran through my head at his admission, and even though I didn't quite know what to say, my mouth opened to respond.

Before I was able to, he placed a gentle finger on my lips. Emotions flickered in his eyes and over his face as he contemplated what he would say next. The moment he came to a decision, his eyes turned serious and his hand gripped mine tighter.

"There is so much you don't know. So much I want to tell you but can't. I realize that I've hurt you over the last few months. I didn't want to."

His finger left my lips to brush roughly through his thick hair, and he glanced away searching for the right words. I wanted to reach out to him, to soothe his fears that somehow I could feel as they coursed from his hand to mine. I wanted to stop those fears, to wrap my arms around him as if that would be enough.

He turned his head, his eyes boring into mine before he dropped my hand and took a step back, clasping his arms behind him.

"Please don't take this the wrong way Andie. I have to distance myself from you from time to time. Touching you... it's just too much. I can feel what you're feeling." He hesitated, taking a deep breath. "And I can hear what you're thinking if I open myself up to it. That's why I kept away from you at the Oak so much. It became over-whelming. I didn't know how to close it off, to stop hearing every-one's thoughts. The Titans have been training me on how to block it out. And how to listen in when needed."

I was shocked. Anger warred with worry at what he might have heard all those times I longed to go to him when I thought he didn't want me to. Indignation that he kept it from me. I mean, surely I could have helped him in some way.

"Why didn't you tell me?" I sputtered. "All this time, I thought you were angry at me. That I had done something wrong. All this time, I've been heartbroken that I found you only to lose you again!"

By the time I was done, my voice had pitched up to a yell, my chest rising and falling fast as my breath seemed hard to catch.

He nodded, a contrite look on his face, and began to reach for me, only to pull his hands back, clenching them, his eyes sparking in anger at himself.

"There is so much to tell you, Andie, but I just can't right now. I've got to train more, become more disciplined. I've got to be better, get better before anything. I don't want to hurt you any more than I already have."

I couldn't believe this. I knew he had a lot going on, so much more than I could ever imagine. But I wanted to help. I would do anything to help him.

Celeste had known that about me, she told me that my heart felt more than others, that I would always fight for my friends, and she was right. I would, especially now. Before I had a chance to say anything else to him, a noise sounded behind me, and I turned to find Rhea standing in the doorway. A white dress hugged her lithe body, and her hair was styled with long curls hanging to her waist.

She smiled kindly at both of us, taking in the situation, and guilt clouded her eyes for a moment as she glanced at Hunter before she turned to me.

"There you are. I think it's about time for our chat. Come with me, Andie, and let's let Hunter be for a bit."

I looked between her and Hunter, waiting to see if he would disagree. He only bowed his head in my direction, walking by first me and then Rhea. I watched him disappear out the door and around the curve in the hall. It felt like my heart had left with him.

"Don't worry, dear. You'll have your moment with him. But right now, I think it's high time for you to know what is going on. Too many people continue to leave you in the dark, thinking that you can't handle everything. We know better, though, don't we? All that you've been through has melded you into a strong woman. I can see that. Strange how the others can't." Her eyebrows rose, and thoughtfulness gleamed in her eyes.

She motioned to me, and I walked closer. I already liked her attitude and forthrightness. She wound her arm through mine, and we walked out of that haunting hall together, but not before I glanced back at the piano only to see it disappear in a glimmer of twinkling lights.

She took me to a cozy room not far from there. When we entered, it reminded me of Nan's living room. A small fire burned brightly in the hearth, and several chairs and a couch were situated around it with fluffy pillows and blankets draped here and there. As we sat down together, a tray floated in, landing on the coffee table in front of us with mugs of steaming coffee and plates of pretty sweet treats.

"I do hope you like coffee. I can't stand that dreadful tea everyone else is so fond of. I had my fill of it after a few hundred years. Once I found coffee, I never went back." She smiled as she blew on the hot liquid before delicately taking a sip.

"No, coffee is fine. I like them both." I cleared my throat, and she looked at me, questioning. "I am really curious as to what you all have been doing with Hunter. I mean, can you tell me what he is, what is going on with him?"

I was anxious to have my most burning question answered, but just as I thought, it wasn't going to be that easy.

She patted my hand and sat back, folding one of her legs under the other, totally relaxed. "We'll get to that soon, but first I must tell you a few other things. Just relax, dear, and listen."

It didn't surprise me at all that she listened into my thoughts. It seemed to be a bad habit of the gods. I had a feeling this was going to take a while, so I settled back, pushing myself to be patient. I was sure whatever she had to tell me would be interesting.

"First, let me start off by telling you that Celeste has been found unharmed."

Shock and elation lit inside me at her words, and I sat up straight again, stunned. "Seriously? Oh my god. She's really okay? Where is she? When can I see her?" The words tumbled out so quickly, and bubbles of excitement trickled out. I felt like a young child again on Christmas Eve, although this time my present was to be the Moon Goddess, my guardian. My adopted grandmother and mom all rolled into one.

I practically bounced on the couch cushion. Rhea's smile was radiant as she watched me. Her white teeth gleamed in the firelight, and her eyes sparkled brightly.

"I thought that might put a spark in you. She is fine. Nothing is at all wrong with her. She is just as eager to see you as you are her, and I imagine she will arrive here tomorrow. She and Rohn are traveling a great distance and have to be extremely careful to avoid any traps that might be in their way."

Wait... Rohn? As in my father? That Rohn? I sat back again in disbelief. *He and Celeste were both on their way here?*

"What do you mean, she's on her way with Rohn?" I spoke slowly. I was excited to see Celeste, but I wasn't sure how I felt about him coming back after he had left the last time, even when I begged.

Sympathy lined her face, and I realized she understood the words that I hadn't said.

"Yes, Rohn. Your father didn't leave you because he wanted to. Not either time. He did so because he is called to help others, to fight this hidden danger that threatens to destroy our world. It's in his blood and something he cannot hide from or deny. Sound familiar?" She cocked an eyebrow at me and took another sip.

I realized that her words were true. That aspect was something that we shared it seemed. But how was I to know? I'd only met the man once before, and then he left. Anxiety and all sorts of other emotions warred within me until it was almost too much to bear. But I wouldn't let it break me. I had pledged to myself to be stronger, more resilient. Grown up.

I squared my shoulders and nodded sharply. "Yes, it seems that I would understand that. How did Celeste and Rohn come to travel together?" I asked her, standing up as I did because I no longer felt that I could sit still.

"Why, Rohn rescued her."

I turned at her words.

"He heard of her abduction and immediately started searching. There's far more that he knows about what is going on in this world, and he has many connections. It seems that Freya wasn't so smart and sequestered Celeste in the same place that she has been hiding her poor mother while she drains her of her powers. Nothing secured the place other than some of her paltry magic. She had no guards, no one to stop Rohn's powers. Freya has no idea he's still alive, and we must keep it that way so he-and you-have a fighting chance. With her not knowing this, he's able to hide and work behind the scenes to thwart her at every corner. But as I am sure you have suspected we believe there is a far mightier being behind Freya and the Fomori. She is strong, yes. But she is not gaining all her power just from her mother. Not the kind of powers she's been wielding as of late. And your father is on a mission to find this being and bring it down."

I shivered at her admission. I'd felt it in my bones that there was someone else at work in all of this, but hearing it outright, that my feelings were correct, caused a deep fear to settle inside of me. I think the not knowing is the worst.

I shook it off as I warmed myself by the fire. Rhea continued on about how the witches and Were shifters were working with all of the other factions across the world, trying to gain more knowledge and warn others, but I barely listened to her.

Tomorrow, my father and Celeste would be here. Hunter had shown some semblance of normalcy toward me, and who knows what would be next? I turned around again, cutting whatever Rhea was saying off.

"Where did Rohn find Celeste and what happened to Freya's mother?"

"He found her in Italy. locked away in a cave under one of the canals. Freya's mother was alive, but her mind is gone. Freya took far too much from her for too long, abusing her to the point of madness. No one could have stood it all those years, even someone so powerful as she. Aine sent the fairies to get her. She will be brought back here to the castle to be tended to. They'll do their best to help her, but they don't expect much improvement." She lifted her shoulder slightly.

The Titans had lived so long that I imagined the decline and death of others was something they were used to, a slight blip on their radar. I imagined it felt lonely at times to live their lives for so long, see so much change and so much death. It would be numbing after a while.

Rhea patted the seat next to her as she looked where I stood. "Come sit back down and we'll finish this conversation with answers to your most burning question."

I took a deep breath and sat back down, her deep eyes looking seriously into mine. She grabbed both of my hands in hers, and I wondered if this was something I really wanted to know.

"It's not bad news, Andie. But it is life altering. Hunter as you know, was changed greatly when you brought him back using the Cauldron. The power contained within it was forged by us, the Titans, many hundreds of years ago. Dagda gifted you with it as he knew the future and what must happen. He also knew how you would use it, along with the fact that it is one of the four Keys. Hunter's path has always been written, along with your own. He was always meant for great things, and many great things he will do. You see, when he was brought back, that Titan magic weaved and wrapped itself inside of him, becoming one with his blood and soul. In doing so, he was transformed into one of us, a god with incredible powers. All the knowledge that each one of us have, so now does he."

I stared at her, unbelieving, but deep inside I knew the truth of it. I tried to pull my hands back, but she held tightly to them.

"Look at me, Andie. His heart is still Hunter, but his mind, body, and soul are Titan. I won't get into what all that entails now. I know that at some point he wants to be the one to explain it all to you, and we've granted that to him. Don't despair. Though he has changed, his feelings for you have not. He just needs time to come to peace with his new identity. And you know what? I think you will help him with that."

Her hands finally let mine go, and I jumped up. Adrenaline raced through my body, and I had to move. Rhea stood up as well, straightening out her dress before looking over at me pacing the room.

"How about we find the others? The walk will help displace that extra energy."

I couldn't seem to form words but hurried to where she stood waiting, and we silently made our way down the hall.

As we entered the foyer, fairies zoomed through the air, and one barely missed running smack dab into my forehead. Luckily, I ducked in time, and I heard a soft "sorry" called out behind me.

Aine stood on the other side of the room talking with the Titans, and Rhea left my side to join them. I wasn't needed here, and the chaos was making me anxious. Turning the opposite direction, I made my way up the stairs and down the hall to my room.

When I opened the door, Emric chuckled and Killian responded with something that made him crack up again. Killian was stretched out on the bed with Emric and Charlie at his feet while he threw a ball into the air, catching it before throwing it back up again.

"What are you guys doing?" I asked, grateful they were here. I didn't want to spend much time with my thoughts alone for once.

"We couldn't take the craziness of everyone down there any longer," Killian said, tossing the ball again. This time before it came back down, I snatched it out of the air.

"Scoot over and make room."

He shimmied to the other side of the bed, and I handed the ball back to him.

"What's got everyone in a tizzy then?"

He looked over at me, a sly smile gathering on his face before he pointed toward the bathroom door. I looked that way and saw a ball gown hanging from it, dark blue in color with silver sparkles going up the side of the full skirt and across the bodice. It reminded me of the night sky and was absolutely breathtaking.

"Uh, what's that for?"

He laughed and shook his head before resuming his ball throwing.

"It's for you to wear to the party Aine is throwing tomorrow in Celeste and Rohn's honor. She sent that dress up here a while ago along with the shoes she put in your closet. The jewelry she wants you to wear is on the bathroom counter. She said, and I quote: "she is to wear this to the party tomorrow, and I will send some fairies up to do her hair and makeup beforehand.""

Killian looked at me again with that same sly smile. "You're going to love that, aren't you?" He chuckled with Emric and Charlie following suit.

"Ugh. Do I really have to dress in all of that? Why can't the party be a normal one? I don't see a reason why we have to dress up."

I rolled off the bed and went to look out the window.

"Well, if it makes you feel any better, I've got to wear a suit. I don't even know how to tie a tie. We'll just be uncomfortable together."

If I was honest with him, the thought of wearing the gorgeous gown and getting dressed up didn't really bother me half as much as meeting my father for the first time. What would I say to him? What would he be like? I don't even remember what he looked like, since the first time I met him, I was half-alive.

As if Emric sensed my anxiety, he twined himself around my legs before hopping up onto the window seat, his head tilted back to look at me.

"His blood runs through your veins, and you must remember that more than likely he is having these same thoughts that you are. You may not know him yet, but you will. Right now, you cannot dwell on the unknowns. You must rejoice in the fact that what you've always wanted is coming to pass."

I knew he was right. I had wanted nothing more. *But I'm still scared.* Maybe it was because I worried that he wouldn't like me, that he would leave me again without a word. I reached down to scratch Emric's crown and nodded.

"I can do this."

Chapter Five

The next morning was a flurry of activity. The fairies wore little flower dresses or leaf pants with daisy crowns as they zipped around the castle, leaving trails of glittering dust in their wake.

Brooms and mops swished and swashed throughout every room. Dusters flew up and down, cleaning every surface, and the entire place gleamed and sparkled.

Aine had retired her casual clothes for a ball gown made of silver gossamer with fairy lights intertwined throughout the fabric, and her crown was made of stars. Actual stars. They twinkled and swirled about her head in a moving halo.

She directed everyone with supreme precision in the main hall. Tables had been set up, and flowers of every color lined the middle of them, created with such beautiful care that it looked as if a rainbow dipped and fell along the length of them.

Glittering lights bobbed and swayed by the ceiling, and there was a table set up on the far side of the room with speakers and what looked to be a sound system.

One of the male fairies hovered behind it, studying the different buttons before landing with both feet on one. Instantly, music blared, assaulting all our ears to the tune of "Baby Got Back". I chuckled at the look Aine cast over to him, and the panic that ensued as he jumped on a different control in his search to turn it off. After different sound effects rang out, I felt the need to go to his aid.

I rushed over, taking pity on the little dude as I noticed his cheeks were bright red and he looked about like he could have a heart attack at any second.

"Here, let me help you out," I said as I studied the multitude of buttons in front of me. They were labeled with different letters, but the volume up and down button was clearly labeled with an up and down arrow. I reached for it, sliding it down, and instantly the music quieted.

"Oh my word. Thank you so very much for your help. Aine would be very displeased with me if you hadn't helped. I've never worked one of these before, but young Killian insisted a party needed a DJ booth, whatever that is, and here we are." He slumped onto the table beside the microphone.

I pulled up a chair and looked over everything again, noticing a small booklet under the control panel. Sliding it out, I opened it to see that it was instructions and all the buttons on a graph that told us exactly what each one did.

So for the next thirty minutes, I went over it with him, and by the time we were done, he seemed much more confident in his task ahead.

"I don't know how to thank you. By the way, my name is Neo, and if you should need anything, anything at all, while you are here, please seek me out and I will be glad to repay the favor." He bowed slightly and smiled.

I stood up, pushing back the chair, and curtsied in return.

"Thank you, kind sir. I'll be sure and do that. And Neo? You're going to rock it today. High-five!" I held my palm down to him and his little palm slapped against mine before he turned to fly off, waving back at me as he disappeared into the other room.

It felt good to get my mind off the upcoming arrivals and to help someone in such a small way.

I pulled out the phone that Aine had given me to check the time. Seeing that there were only ten minutes before I was supposed to be back up in my room to be turned into Cinderella, I quickly pushed it into my jean pocket.

When I looked back up, my heart stopped at the sight before me.

Standing there in a black suit, his white shirt unbuttoned at the collar and his dark hair styled in a messy wave, was Hunter. Dark stubble lined his jaw, and I'm not going to lie, my mouth might have dropped a little. He looked absolutely beautiful. I know, beauty is usually a term for girls, but I couldn't think of any other term to describe him right now that fit like that one did. His dark eyes bore into mine, and my heart raced at the heat from them.

Forcing myself to move, I walked toward him, but I didn't smile. I approached him like a kid approaching a small animal that they didn't want to run away in fright. As I came to stand before him, he looked down at me and reached out to tug my hair, just like he had done multiple times before he had changed, and my heart stuttered. Normally, I would have griped at him for doing it, but all I could do was gulp and look down at my feet.

His finger touched the underside of my chin before he applied slight pressure, pulling my face back up to his.

"Don't do that, Andie. *Please.* I'm still me." His eyes were somber, but a slight grin lifted the corner of his mouth, and I swear I saw a glint of that old cockiness.

My silence seemed to confuse him as his brows lowered, but I didn't dare say a word. If I started in, I was afraid I wouldn't stop. Words would vomit out of my mouth that it wasn't the time or place to say. He seemed to realize this as well and leaned in close to my ear, his breath tickling it.

"Save a dance for me?"

Again, I gulped and nodded as he pulled away before rushing around him and up to my room.

∞

The sight that awaited me was not what I expected. At least twenty fairies were there. They lined up along the edge of my bed, eyes alight as they spied me, excitement rippling off their small bodies. One by one, they took flight, approaching me, and stopped to hover in front of my face.

One of the girls smiled shyly, and her caramel-colored skin sparkled with glitter. She ducked her head before looking at me again, her small voice squeaking with anxiety as she addressed me.

"We are here to get you ready for the party. If there should be anything additional you require from us, you have but to ask."

I studied her, not really understanding why she seemed so embarrassed, but they were here to help me, and I would do my best to make them feel at ease.

"Thank you. What's your name?"

"Druesy, ma'am. At your service." She bowed her head toward me.

"Please, no ma'am, and no bowing. I'm just grateful for your help. I don't know the first thing about hair and makeup and all that stuff. You're doing me a great service by taking care of this for me." I smiled gently at her.

Druesy's back straightened, and I watched the transformation from shy to in charge take place. She nodded at me, all serious now. "Right. If you'll follow us this way, we've got a bath drawn for you. You'll need to wash up first, then we'll get started."

Upon entering the bathroom, the first thing I noticed was the bathtub. It was so full of bubbles that they nearly spilled over the edge. Candles were lit throughout the room and the smell was heavenly. Like coconut and pineapple. As I breathed it in deeply, the door clicked and the fairies left me in privacy.

I relaxed in the bath for as long as I felt I could, and reluctantly, I stepped out, grabbing a towel off the warmer that was close by. I'd have to ask Celeste if we could get one of those.

Fairy is really starting to spoil me, I chuckled. Although the amenities here were wonderful, I missed plain old regular life.

Wiping the steam from the mirror, I stared at my reflection, noticing the changes that had taken place on my face in just a few months. I knew that, in truth, life would never really be normal again.

The door swung open then, the army of fairies swirling in and ushering me out into the room where they rubbed the same sparkly lotion that they wore all over except for my face. Then I was sprayed with something that smelled like the same coconut and pineapple candles and bubble bath that had wrapped me up in its essence in the bathroom. When they seemed content, the dress that had been hanging on my door was ushered over to me, their wings straining from the weight of it.

I relieved them of their burden, and Druesy spoke up. "Once you are dressed, we'll set about styling your hair and makeup."

They flew back to line the bed again, and I quickly donned the dress. The silk and satin were soft against my skin, and it fit as if made just for me. Maybe it had been. It wouldn't surprise me.

Druesy flew over, sighing, her small hands against each of her cheeks. "You look beautiful miss. Look in the mirror and let us know what you think. We knew this color would be perfect for you. The star bursts bring out the silver in your eyes."

Before I turned to see what I looked like, I held out my hand to her and she landed in my palm. I carried her back over to the others and bent down slightly so that we were all level.

"Do you mean that all of you made this beautiful creation?" I asked. They looked to each other uncertainly before turning as a group to nod.

I smiled at them and bowed my head slightly. "I can't tell you what an honor it is to wear something so beautiful. The fact that you made it with your own hands is astounding. You should be extremely proud of your talent. I've never seen or worn something so magical in my entire life. Thank you."

Their faces transformed with happiness, and some of them even preened.

"Well now." I straightened back up. "Let me see if I do your work justice."

I walked to the full-length mirror and did a double take at the image reflected back at me.

Though my hair was still wet and my face makeup free, the dress fit my body perfectly. The silver stars twinkled in the light from the window, and it was simply gorgeous. I'd never had one iota of interest in dresses, but this one... this one made me feel like a princess. As if I was beautiful.

Aine walked in just then, stopping in the doorway, her eyes approving.

"That's because you are beautiful, Andie. You just have never seen yourself the way the rest of us do."

I highly doubted that, but right now I felt it.

"I just came to check on you and see how everything was going," Aine said before moving back toward the door.

"Everyone should be here in an hour. I'll send Killian up to get you once they arrive. And Andie? Just be yourself and don't worry. Everything will work out okay." She gave me a smile as she slipped out the door, and the fairies descended on me again.

A short time later, I stared at the vision in the mirror again. I was sure that they had worked some sort of magic that changed my appearance.

The girl looking back at me was a stranger. Her hair had been styled into long waves, shiny and full. Gray eyes that looked larger than my own with full black lashes and a sweep of silver eyeshadow only added to the luminescent sparkle in her eyes. A light lip gloss had been applied, but somehow her lips looked fuller and just plain different.

How is this me?

Druesy hovered, waiting for me to comment on the job that they did. Not wanting to disappoint, a grin lit my mouth and I looked at her in the mirror as well.

"You all made a miracle happen. Never in a million years would I have thought I would ever look like this. You're amazing!"

The fairies all breathed a collective sigh of relief and began chattering at once before flying off to collect all of the tools that they had used. I called my thanks to them as they filed out the door, and before long, it was blessedly quiet.

I still hadn't moved from the mirror. Aine had set out jewelry for me to wear, but I opted to wear the locket that Rohn had left for me instead of the diamond necklace she selected. I did wear the little diamond earrings that dangled. Between those, the locket, and my dragonfly bracelet, it was enough.

Emric and Charlie had long since left the room once the fairies arrived. They must have decided the coast was clear as Charlie whistled outside the door before a knock sounded.

"Come in," I called, turning away from the image that I hadn't been able to stop staring at.

Another whistle sounded then, and my head swung to the doorway to find Killian stopped there, his eyes wide, and his mouth hanging open.

"You sure do clean up good, Andie."

I could say the same about him. He wore a gray suit with a crisp white button up shirt underneath and a black tie. *He must have found someone to help him with it,* I thought.

"Thanks, Killian. You look very handsome yourself." I smiled at the look on his face.

"You really think so?"

"I do," I told him. "Too bad Pres isn't here to see you. Oh, hey, we can take a selfie and send it to her."

I chuckled at the look on his face and had to explain what that was. I grabbed up my phone and brought him to stand in front of the mirror beside me and showed him how to take a photo. He was amazed by it, and we took a few silly ones too just for fun.

"Okay, so now we just need to figure out her phone number. Then we'll send it to her, and she can see for herself how great you look."

He blushed a little but nodded. "Have you talked to her lately? I feel bad because the last time I saw her was a while ago, and I've got no way to get in touch with her."

He looked at the ground, and I slung my arm around his shoulder. "We'll fix that. After the party, I'll get Aine to find out her number and you can call her anytime and talk to her. Catch up, you know?"

"I'd like that a lot. Thanks, Andie. Now, it's time to go down to the party. Celeste and Rohn are here."

I sucked in a breath and nodded. I could do this.

Just be you Andie, just be you.

I grabbed ahold of Killian's hand. "Let's go. I'm ready to see Celeste. I just hope she recognizes me in all this." I laughed brokenly and gestured to myself.

Killian just shook his head. "She'd recognize you anywhere." He squeezed my hand as we began to descend the staircase.

My gaze landed on the group standing below and my heart beat wildly.

She was the first one my eyes found, and I wanted to fly down those steps and fling myself at her. She looked good. She hadn't changed or been hurt, and the smile she aimed at me told me that all would be okay. Rohn stood with his back to me, but seeing the trajectory of Celeste's gaze, he turned.

My throat squeezed as my eyes met his. He didn't look much different than the photo in the locket. Strength emanated from him, and he was very handsome in his dark suit. He and my mother must have made an incredibly beautiful couple.

When I reached the two of them, I pulled my eyes away from the man who looked so much like me, throwing my arms around Celeste. A whimper sounded from my throat as she hugged me tight.

"I missed you so much," I whispered. "Are you okay? They didn't hurt you, did they?" I pulled back and stared into her turquoise eyes.

"Oh, they tried their best, but what they didn't realize is that I've been hurt many times before, and nothing can keep me down." She smiled gently at me, running her hand over my hair.

She still held onto my upper arms, her gaze traveling down and then back up again, searching to make sure I was whole and well.

"I've been worried about you. It pained me to think of how my disappearance had affected you. It seems my worry was for naught. You look healthy and the same as always. Though I do detect a new maturity in your eyes." She frowned slightly.

I hurried to interrupt as I felt like she might be trying to read me. I didn't want her to know the dark road I had been headed down after her abduction.

"Let's not worry about that. I'm just so glad you're back. We've got so much to talk about."

She nodded slowly, her eyes serious.

"Aine filled me in on Hunter. I know it must have been a relief to find him, but it couldn't have been easy. I know it's still not easy to comprehend what is going on with him." She tsked. "We'll figure it all out in time."

Gesturing behind me to where my father stood, she shook her head. "And we're being rude."

Her hand nudged me to turn around and face the one person who had my emotions in a tangle. I wouldn't show him my nervousness. I squared my jaw and lifted my chin as I looked into his deep eyes again. A serious look covered his face, but a gentle smile bloomed as he looked me over again.

"Andie. I know this all must be extremely strange for you. I realize that you most likely have a lot of questions, probably a lot of hard feelings, but I hope you'll give me the chance to explain everything." He looked down at his feet, and for the first time, I realized that he was as nervous as I was, and also trying to hide that fact.

Just like me.

I nodded slowly. I wanted to give him the benefit of the doubt. I needed to believe that one day we would be a family. That he hadn't left me each time because he wanted to. The fact that he stood before me, somber and serious, was a good start. Not to mention the fact that he saved Celeste. I owed him big for that.

Willing to give a little, I offered him my arm as everyone around us began filtering toward the ballroom.

"Shall we?"

He looked at me, and though his mouth didn't move from its serious repose, the corners of his eyes crinkled up a little. I knew I had put him at ease.

Celeste didn't hide her merriment, though. The grin that stretched across her face was all the proof I needed to know that she was proud of how I had grown over the last few months.

And I'd do anything to keep her smiling and happy.

∞

Dinner was a production I hadn't been prepared for. Upon walking into the large room, we were surrounded by the witches and Were shifter clans. It must have taken a lot of fairies to bring them over.

Of course, I couldn't remember all their names, but my father had known each and every one. While they'd been happy to see me, they were ecstatic to see Rohn. Their excitement was that of fans adoring a movie star or famous singer. It was almost too much, and I'd extricated myself from the fray to find Celeste.

I hadn't realized that all these people would be here. I'd only expected a small group. Boy was I wrong. When Aine said she was throwing a party, she threw a party.

I slipped into a chair beside Celeste where she sat at one of the dinner tables. Her hands twined around one of the daisies that spilled from the rainbow flower arrangement in front of us.

"I didn't expect all these people." I sighed as I turned to her. "I guess I should know better with Aine."

Our knees touched as she turned her body toward mine, the blue dress she wore blending in with my skirt, and it reminded me again of the night sky. Hers the color of dusk and mine of midnight.

"Thank you for giving Rohn a chance." She squeezed my hand in hers. "I know this has been a whirlwind, and I know your fears when it comes to him. But... you don't know the half of it, Andie." She sighed.

"I really wish Aine hadn't thrown this party. There's so much we should be discussing instead of celebrating." She waved her hand around, her lips pursed. "But I've never known her to not do something big when she feels the need to celebrate. And it is definitely not worth arguing with her about. She'll win every time."

Her eyes lit up as she looked behind me, and I turned to see what caught her attention. Striding toward us were Killian, Toni, and Logan. I strained to look behind them to see if Teagan and Presley followed, but they weren't there.

Disappointment tugged at me, but I couldn't expect Teagan to be healed and ready to face me. He had been through a lot and I didn't want to think about the extra pain that I had caused when he saw me with Hunter. Though he had wanted to find him as much as I did, I knew that he hoped I would choose him instead.

As the three surrounded us, I expected Toni and Logan to treat me differently than they had before, but Toni surprised me when she swooped down to wrap her arms around me.

"Oh, Andie, I am so happy to see you. I hope you've been doing okay and haven't let current circumstances get to you." She squeezed me once more before letting go and stepping back. Logan had done the same with Celeste, and then they switched, and I found Logan's large arms around me in a fierce hug. It surprised the heck out of me.

I had expected their loyalty to their son to make them standoffish, but they didn't show any indication of being upset with me.

Logan let me go and looked down at me with sparkling eyes.

"I know you're worried about everything. But don't take on that kind of heaviness. You're far too young to worry about things you can't control." He smiled and maneuvered Toni to the surrounding seats and Killian sat down beside me, smiling.

"He's right, you know. You can't take on the responsibility of how everyone feels. You have absolutely no control over that, and you can't make everyone happy despite how much you try."

I stared at the flowers in front of me, knowing he was right. I could only control so much.

Dinner was a five-course meal, all foods I had never eaten before. I didn't eat much as my stomach still twisted with nervousness.

My father sat across from me. We made small talk, but anytime that we formed more than a few sentences between us, someone else would interrupt, eager to talk to Rohn. That was fine with me because most of the time I had been searching the room for Hunter.

He hadn't come.

I felt for sure at the start of dinner when I'd seen his father walk in with the Were shifters, that he would follow shortly behind. But he hadn't.

Disappointment continued to gnaw at me, but when it came to Hunter, he did his own thing. Never one to follow the rules or do what others wanted or expected.

As dinner wound down and the laughter and conversations weren't as loud, the music began.

I spied the same male fairy at the table where I had helped him this afternoon. Tonight, he was dressed in a small suit, and a little black top hat sat on his head at an angle. He looked comfortable as he slid the volume up and "Calling all Angels" by Train filled the room.

Slowly, couples took each other by the hand and began filling the dance floor, much to the small DJ's delight. He clapped as he watched the dancing, and I smiled at his happiness. When he turned back, I caught his eye and gave him a thumbs up, to which he gave me one back, his grin stretching from ear to ear.

Chuckling, I turned back to the table to see that I was alone. My eyes sought my dinner companions only to find them all dancing together. Rohn and Celeste, Toni and Logan, and Killian with one of the female witches.

It was at that moment when I saw him through the dance crowd.

As the words to the song, *And I won't give up if you don't give up,* rang out, his eyes met mine. Without taking his gaze away, he approached me, and my breath caught as he maneuvered through the dancers.

The suit he wore was tailored and fit perfectly. The black coat unbuttoned, and he wore a white shirt without a tie, giving him a casual look with the first button undone. That scruff that had been on his jaw earlier was still there and gave him an even darker look than before.

I'd say that I held my breath, but that's so cliché. It was more like he held my breath. He had sucked it straight out of me the moment I saw him.

Now he stood before me, his gaze calm and serious. We seemed to be in our own little bubble, the world around us fading.

He reached his hand down to me, and his lip quirked up. "Dance with me?"

I didn't hesitate and slid my hand into his warm one.

Pulling me behind him, he found a spot on the dance floor in the back, further from all the other dancers. In a quick move, he twirled me around once before bringing me back in close to him, his arms loose around my waist, and his chest to mine.

He didn't speak, only leaned his chin gently against the top of my head as we swayed back and forth. I thought about the gloves I had noticed on both of his hands as I had followed him over here and guessed they were to keep the gold fire from lighting him up from the inside.

For some reason that made me sad. The fact that his blood only lit for me was something that I wasn't ashamed of. And I didn't want him to be ashamed of it either.

As we turned in a circle, I saw my father studying me as he turned Celeste. Questions lit his eyes as he watched Hunter and me dance, but a smile danced across his face, and surprise passed over it. As if somehow he knew something I didn't.

When he was out of my view again, I turned my face into Hunter's chest, breathing deeply of the cedarwood smell that I loved so much, and his arms tightened around me. I could feel his heart beating hard, and I squeezed his biceps gently. I wanted to scream how happy this made me. How his being here, whole and safe, filled me with joy. But for now, I'd settle for this dance.

It was over all too soon as the song came to an end and another one began. Hunter's arms slipped from my waist, and I pulled back to look up at him, not caring that everyone else was leaving the floor and younger people rushed onto it, dancing wildly to the beat.

I only had eyes for him.

"Are we okay?" I quietly asked. He didn't nod; his face didn't change other than the slight rise of an eyebrow.

"We've never changed. Only the circumstances." He grabbed ahold of my hand, pulling it to his chest and holding it against his heart, his eyes smoldering.

"You are a part of me, and that will never change. My blood recognizes your blood and it always will." He turned, not releasing my hand, and pulled me off the dance floor and back to my seat at the table.

My heart flip-flopped in my chest as I turned his words over and over in my mind, and a warm feeling ran through me all the way down to my toes.

My dinner companions had returned, and it seemed that every one of them took interest in our interaction. I felt their eyes on me, but I couldn't peel mine away from Hunter as he pulled out my chair, gesturing for me to sit down.

When I did, he kneeled, still grasping my hand, and reached up with his other one to run a finger down my cheek.

"We need to talk. I know you need to meet with Rohn and Celeste after this is over," he gestured around us, "but once you've finished, meet me in the library?"

I'd meet him anywhere he asked. Anytime.

"Yes, I'll meet you there. But I don't know what time I'll be done talking with them," I responded, halfway disappointed that I would have to wait. I'd much rather go with him right now. Even though I wanted to know what happened with my father and Celeste, I wanted to be with him more.

A smile lit his lips. An actual full-on smile that I hadn't seen in forever, and his eyes sparkled before he looked away and then back at me.

"It doesn't matter what time. I'll be waiting however long it takes."

And with that, he leaned in and kissed my cheek before standing up and striding out of the room.

It seemed a collective breath was loosed as he made his exit and I looked around to see almost every eye in the room on me. My cheeks heated and I felt the blush run down to my toes. How I had been so lost in the moment, I would never know.

I just stared back at them all, shrugged, and then dismissed the looks while turning to Celeste.

"Can we go ahead and leave? I'd like to hear everything that happened now."

She laughed out loud, the sound tinkling through the room as she stood up, pulling me with her and nodding toward Rohn.

"Yes, of course. Let's find a quiet room. I know you've got other plans after, but this might take a while."

Chapter Six

A few moments later, we found ourselves in the same room that I had spoken with Rhea. The fire was warm and glittered off the stars in my dress. I was still so impressed with the fairy's handiwork. If I ever needed a dress or outfit for a special occasion, I knew where to go.

Rohn cleared his throat as he sat down in an armchair beside the couch where Celeste and I had made ourselves comfortable. He didn't waste any time getting into it.

"First of all. I know you think I left you. I want you to know that I *never* would have left you if it wasn't imperative." His voice was forceful, eyes beseeching me.

"I loved you before you were born, and I love you still. I lost your mother, and I had to lose you too. To keep you safe. It was the only way. Freya and the Fomori were behind her death, which I found out much later. I knew that if I didn't leave, if whoever had murdered her had seen us together, as a strong family, they would come after you. If you were by yourself, they wouldn't see you as a threat. But together we would have been a force to reckon with, and they would have killed you, just like your mom, had they gotten the chance."

He took a shaky breath, and I could see the strain and the strong emotions reverberate out at every mention of my mother.

"You see, they thought that they had killed the person who would find the Keys when they killed Selene. They had *no* idea that it was actually you. If it hadn't been for Celeste and Aine and the rest of the magical community suppressing your powers, make no mistake, they would have killed you in cold blood no matter your age. When I disappeared, it cemented the fact in their minds that when they killed Selene, they killed the one that would save us."

I don't understand... How would his leaving have given them even more concrete evidence of that?

He raised a finger as I was about to ask.

"What you don't know, what no one has yet told you, is that the legend states the woman who saves us will be tied to her life mate. And in being tied to her life mate, should something happen to her, so too will it happen to her love. Her mate will perish as well should something happen to her."

His eyes stared holes into me, waiting for my reaction.

I was stunned. He was right; I hadn't known that fact, and suddenly it all made sense.

He had been protecting me, making it look like he had also died to perpetuate our enemy's acceptance that they had taken out the one person standing in their way of total dominance.

But they hadn't, and now they knew. And no wonder they came at me so hard and with such vengeance.

He grimaced as he stared at his clasped hands resting on his knees.

"I wish there had been some way that I could have been there. Been a father and experienced all your firsts with you. Been there to wipe your tears and celebrate our victories with you. I can't express how much it hurt here," he hit his chest with anger, "to not be there for you." His voice cracked, and I trembled, wanting to go to him.

Celeste held me back, patting my arm softly. "Let him finish first," she said quietly.

He had risen and stood in front of the fire, his back to us, and I stayed silent.

"All these years, I've been searching for the truth. You see, I just couldn't understand how someone like Freya was able to garner so much power, even with the Fomori at her side. It just didn't make sense. I've been piecing things together, and not until recently was it clear."

He turned around, his hands in his pockets and his mouth tight.

"There's an old power, an old god, that has been using them all this time to rise back up. I'm not sure why no one else figured it out or suspected. I can only guess that it's due to the hundreds of years that have passed. People have a way of forgetting, even the Titans. Life goes on, and no one wants to remember that which caused so much pain."

"What happened and who is it?" I breathed, my chest tight with this new knowledge. How on earth were we to fight an old god?

"His name was Helios, and he was long thought to be gone forever after Kratos killed him. You see, Helios was the Titan god of the sun and Guardian of Oaths. It is said that Kratos killed him when he wouldn't tell him where the Flame of Olympus was. He beheaded Helios in an effort to discover secrets, blind enemies and unlock new paths through Olympus in his search. Later, when Kratos battled Zeus, Helios's head was lost, and everyone assumed it had been destroyed."

Rohn took a deep breath, rocking back on his heels and pulling his hands out of his pockets to hold out on either side of him.

"But they were wrong. I'm sure of it. The clues that I've found in my travels all point back to him. And the things that Freya's mother said to Celeste, whether just delirious rantings or not, confirm it. He is somehow giving power to Freya, hoping she can stop you from finding the Keys that will destroy all the evil set out against us."

I interrupted him then because the question had been burning to be asked for quite some time; I'd just never had a chance.

"And once we find all four Keys? What happens then? What do they do and how do they work?"

Celeste and Rohn looked at each other solemnly. Celeste nodded in assent and Rohn sat back down, leaning forward to look at me with his elbows on his knees.

"When the four Keys are placed together, they become one. They become a power like none other and will search out the evil forces in this world and elsewhere. Evil is like a magnet to the power inside of them. It will seek it out and crush it. No one knows exactly how. And mind you, the evil it seeks is only the kind that wishes to destroy the magical realm, so evil will still exist once it does, just not in that form. And on the opposite side of the coin, the Keys can be used to destroy us as well. It depends on who puts them together. Together, they can be used for good or evil. Destroy worlds even. And that is why it's imperative that we find them. That's all I know from the legend. Anything else is something we will have to find out for ourselves when the time comes."

It was hard to wrap my head around the thought that these Keys, these treasures that I've found, and the ones left for me to find, had such great and unimaginable power. How somehow, I had been the one chosen. I still didn't understand why, and it didn't really matter, because here I was anyway.

I squared my shoulders and ran my fingers over the starburst on my skirt.

"And how do we defeat Helios?" I questioned, looking into his eyes.

He shook his head, concern bright in his eyes. "I haven't figured that out yet. But I'm working on it. And that's where Hunter and the Titans come in."

I glanced at Celeste; her face was as serious as his as she nodded.

"We can't do it without them. We'll need all their power and then some."

I ran my hand over my face, exhaustion weighing me down at just thinking about what lay ahead for us. And in a very un-Andie like way, I smiled and looked at them both.

"I guess we'd better get busy then."

I left the two of them then, staring after me with I'm sure looks of shock. At least Celeste. Rohn didn't know me like she did.

I flew through the halls, passing a few fairies that giggled and flew haphazardly around me. One bumped into the wall before laughing and continuing on. If I didn't know any better, I'd say they'd gotten into Aine's spirit cabinet.

Ahead, I saw a small group of Titans talking, and I walked by them as quickly as I could with my head down. I didn't want anyone stopping and deterring me from getting to the library. Hunter said he'd wait for me, but my conversation with Celeste and Rohn had taken longer than I'd thought.

The corridor to the library was dark save the stars twinkling in the ceiling above and a soft glow that filtered through the open door to the library. As I stared inside at the glass enclosure, the butterflies were still and unmoving. Two chairs sat beside it, and Hunter lounged in one, his fingers trailing over the glass slowly.

As if he sensed me, his head turned and his eyes met mine, the slight light from the butterfly enclosure glittering in his dark eyes.

I approached slowly, heart pounding with each step I took.

Why are you so nervous? It's not like you don't know him.

I shook off the feeling and tried to relax as I sat down into the chair beside his. He immediately grasped my hand with his. He'd taken his gloves off, and the fire lit up his veins, the swirling began in his eyes. It was mesmerizing, and I couldn't help myself.

I reached out with my other hand and traced a vein in his neck. I could actually feel heat emanating from it.

"Do you know what it is?" I asked. I knew I didn't need to say what *it* was. He knew.

His head shook slowly as he glanced down at our intertwined hands.

"Lelantos said they've never seen anything like it. None of them have experienced it before either, so it's not a Titan thing." His brows scrunched. "Phoebe thinks it has something to do with you and is on a mission to prove it, but so far she has no evidence."

I swallowed thickly. "It doesn't hurt, does it?" I'd be beside myself if I caused this and it hurt him.

He quickly calmed my fears. "No, not at all. It's a strange feeling, but it doesn't hurt. It actually is hard to explain how it feels since it only does it when I touch you. It's a warm feeling, a good feeling…"

His voice trailed off, and we sat in silence for a few minutes before he cleared his throat and looked at me again. "I need to tell you what I've learned so far."

"Okay, I'm all ears." And I was. I was eager to know more about what he was now, how he was feeling and what he found out. And I was content to just sit here and listen to his deep voice.

"So, as you know, somehow when you used the Cauldron to bring me back, the Titan powers within it transferred to me and changed me into a Titan as well. I retained the Were shifter abilities-those didn't leave-but they were also enhanced. I'm still learning what all I can do. There's so much, and I've never had abilities like this before. I feel like a fish out of water most of the time. I don't like feeling like that." He frowned but continued on.

"Perses has been working with me on how to harness and explore the powers that I have, but it seems like new ones arise every day and it's a lot to keep up with and stay in control of. And of course, as Rhea told you, I'm now considered immortal. I mean, they said I can be killed, but it would take a lot of power to do so."

He ran his hand through his hair, and I could tell he was irritated.

"Tell me what's wrong, Hunter. Maybe I can help?" I wanted to help him so badly, but I didn't know how.

He reached out and cupped my jaw, his thumb smoothing over the skin of my cheek.

"I don't want to be immortal, Andie. If there was a way you could help me with that, I'd let you. But I don't think there is." His eyes were filled with sadness, and I placed my hand over his and nuzzled my face into it.

"But being immortal isn't so horrible is it? I mean, think of all the things you will see and witness. All the good you can do. And I suppose it will take you forever to age." I laughed softly.

He smiled but it looked pained.

"You don't get it, Andie. I don't want to be immortal because *you* aren't. How am I supposed to live forever without you?"

I froze at his words. I hadn't thought about that, it hadn't crossed my mind at all. And now I felt what he must have been feeling. *Terror.* Straight up terror. And I had no idea where it came from.

His hand gripped mine harder, and it seemed that the fire in his blood burned hotter.

"I already cared a lot about you before I was taken. But now, after you brought me back, something's changed. I can hear your thoughts and feel your pain. It's as if your magic somehow tethered us together, and I can't stop thinking about you, worrying about you. I know you feel it too."

I knew what he was talking about, and I had felt it, but shrugged it off, not exploring it further.

"It's like I know in my heart that we're meant to be together. That you are mine, and I am yours, but how? How can that be when the years pass by and you get older while I stay the same? When you..." He swallowed hard and clenched his jaw. "When you die, and I no longer have you?"

My mouth opened and closed, but I had no assurances to give, no positive words. Giving up on it, I simply stood and walked around the chair to him, sitting down in his lap. I whisked up my skirts and tucked them under my calves so I could curl up in his arms. He held me tight with my head against his shoulder.

"We'll figure it out," I told him, my voice strong. "We will. I promise."

Chapter Seven

I slept fitfully that night. Tossing and turning, my mind wouldn't shut up. Everything that Celeste and my dad had told me, what Hunter had confided. My mind swirled with all the implications.

When I woke up again and looked at the clock on my phone, it was only six in the morning. Sighing, I rolled out of bed, resigned to the fact that it was going to be a long day. I still had training to do, regardless of the fact that all I wanted was to find Hunter and spend time with him. I made a mental note to also seek out Rhea, I wanted to talk with her more about his new life and what all it entailed. I'd gotten the feeling last night that he had left out a lot, and I wanted to know everything.

The dress from last night caught my eye as I pulled out jeans and a tee to wear today. I remembered the way that I had felt wearing it, and the way that Hunter had looked at me. It hadn't been uncomfortable to wear, simply different. Maybe I should hit Pres up when I got home to do a little shopping. As I pulled my converse on, I chuckled. She'd be beside herself. She had been trying to get me to shop with her for months and I always made up some excuse or other.

"Don't you know what time it is?" A voice growled from the window.

Emric blinked sleepily at me and yawned before curling up again, Charlie snuggling into his tail.

"It's polite to at least try and be a little quiet when you wake before others. But no, you've got to stomp around giggling like a schoolgirl. Plus, the fact that you flipped and flopped all night long..." He grimaced at me. "I swear I'm going to find Aine's alchemist to make a potion. And I'll put it in your drink, you hear? Then I might actually get a good night's sleep for once." He hmphed and turned away.

I felt bad, I did. It wasn't my intention to wake them up, but honestly, I'd forgotten they were in here while so much weighed heavy on my mind.

"Sorry, Emric," I whispered. "But if it's that bad you know there are plenty of other rooms you can stay in. You don't have to stay in mine."

His eyes flashed back open. Even Charlie opened one eye wide, like what I'd said was blasphemy. "We'll stay in another room when and only when we want to. You're stuck with us for now."

And with that they both rolled over, turning their backs to me.

Sighing, I tiptoed out the door.

This was the first morning I'd woken up so early, and it amazed me to see all the fairies up and swirling around, taking care of their daily duties.

When they saw me walking down the stairs, many of them stopped and stared, probably surprised to see someone else awake besides them. I imagined that most of the time when they had guests, they stayed up late and woke even later. I'd witnessed it last night as I headed to my room. Shifters and witches were having a fine time, deep in their drinks and conversation. Laughing and dancing and acting as if there wasn't a care in the world.

For them, it wasn't as in their face as the rest of us. They hadn't been through the journeys, seen the evil up close. They had no idea- well maybe an inkling-but not the full picture, of what could happen. I hadn't either until last night. I mean, yeah, I knew the danger of

Freya and the Fomori, but when you throw a god hell bent on revenge in the mix, it was scary.

Since no one else other than me and the fairies were up, I imagined there was no breakfast available, but the closer I came to the dining hall, the smell of bacon and maple syrup tickled my nose. My stomach growled loudly.

I hadn't eaten much last night. Heck I hadn't eaten much the last few days, but it was catching up to me now.

The hall was bathed in soft candlelight and quiet. The sun hadn't risen yet to filter in through the tall glass windows along the walls, and the moon hung over the tree line.

Breakfast food lined the sideboards, and I helped myself to a little bit of everything. I sat at a small table near the window, staring out at the courtyard before me. The glowing balls caught the light from the moon, glistening as they bobbed gently in the air, and the fountains glittered.

I wondered what Hunter would do today, what the Titans were working with him on. My thoughts were interrupted as a hand grabbed my shoulder from behind. Twisting, I turned around to see Toni.

She smiled and came around the table, sinking into the chair before setting her mug of coffee down. She looked tired, but it was early. "I hope you don't mind if I join you. You looked to have been miles away in your thoughts." She smiled gently.

"Oh no, you're fine." I waved my hand in the air. "Probably better that I have company. My thoughts are starting to become annoying anyway."

She laughed, picking up her mug and blowing on it before taking a sip.

"I know how that can be. They can be dangerous sometimes." She glanced out the window just as the sun broke over the horizon. "I suppose you have heavier thoughts than most of us do right now." She looked back at me with sympathy in her eyes.

It surprised me still that there didn't seem to be any animosity from her toward me. I had thought that surely she would be mad about what happened to Teagan and blame me. But strangely, I didn't get that sense from her at all. Curious as to how he had been doing, I cautiously broached the subject.

"I hope Teagan is doing okay," I tentatively said, looking her in the eyes. She nodded, taking her time before answering. Emotions flickered over her face in a quick second, and I realized that she hadn't spoken about him to me last night because it was hard.

"He... he isn't taking it so well. He has a lot of anger inside of him right now." My eyes widened, and she reached forward, grabbing my hand.

"No, no. Not at you. Never at you Andie. He's angry at himself for letting Freya get to him, for not being, as he puts it, 'strong enough,' though you and I both know he's stronger than she is." Toni shrugged, sighing.

"Things happen, though. When we go into battle, we know that these things can and will happen. There will be casualties and injuries. We just never expect it to happen to us. He let his guard down for one minute, and that's all it took."

I sighed, knowing all too well. The picture of him lying on the ground, his leg torn apart, will forever haunt me. She squeezed my hand again and I looked back at her.

"Physically he's doing much better. Mentally, he has a lot to get through."

I nodded, biting my lip. I'd always been able to talk to Toni. She put me at ease, and I didn't feel like I was talking to someone older. She listened and cared, so I decided to put it all out there.

"I feel responsible still. I'm so happy he's healing well, but the mental part? I'm afraid he hates me." The words came out in a broken whisper. I hadn't let myself dwell on it too much until now. Now, I remembered all the times that he made it known how he felt about me. I remembered the soft kiss outside my room. And it was hard. I hadn't wanted to hurt him; I tried my best not to. I even told him! But he didn't listen. Like the stubborn guy he is, he kept on.

"You mean how he feels now that Hunter is back and what all that entails?" she asked gently and I nodded. She patted my hand and then sat back in her chair.

"We always have an idea when we are younger of how things should be. We create this life in our heads as we look to the future and I'm sure as you've experienced, feelings grow, and of course it's easier when your best friends too. It doesn't help that we did what we did when you both were babies. I'm sure you know about this by now, right?" she asked in a no-nonsense voice with a hint of guilt running through it.

"Yes. I know now."

She took a deep breath and forged on. "It was a good idea at the time. So, we all thought. We were young and never once thought of a scenario like the one we find ourselves in now. If there hadn't been the legend for us to fall back on, we never would have entertained making a pact that our children would marry, promising you to each other without your consent. Somehow, we need to fix it."

I was confused, and when she looked at me, surprise gathered in her eyes. "You don't know about that part, do you?"

I shook my head, biting my tongue. This was getting really old.

"Oh, dear. I can't believe they didn't tell you this either. When we made the pact, we cast an extraordinarily strong spell. A spell that would seal the deal, so to speak. As far as we know, it's unbreakable."

My body shook. I didn't know if it was anger or shock that caused it, but a bitter cold settled into my bones. "I don't understand. Are you telling me that I still have to marry Teagan?" I ground out.

"No. That's not what I'm saying at all. We will find a way to reverse it, I hope, and all will be well. But if we don't, it's not so much you having to marry..." She stopped and looked out the window, pain lancing her face. "I'm sorry, Andie. We didn't realize what we were doing. But the spell ties you together. You're linked together unless we find a way to reverse it."

I swallowed thickly.

What does this mean?

Sensing my turmoil, she leaned forward. "Didn't you feel it when you first met? Almost as if you'd known each other forever? That was the spell. I'm not saying that's the only reason for your friendship. I'm just saying it helped."

I slumped in my chair, the food that I had eaten turning sour in my stomach. Over her shoulder I watched shifters and witches pour in, helping themselves to breakfast and chattering with happy voices.

Why did so many people feel the need to meddle in my life, even when I was a baby? Did they only see me as a tool for their prophecy? With no thought whatsoever to my emotions and how I would feel about it all?

Anger rose its ugly head inside of me.

"I understand that none of you thought this through, not even my parents or Nan. But this is my life you've all played with. What am I supposed to do with this information? You said you'd find a way to reverse it, but how? When? I don't see any of you working on this right now." I gestured around to the others, my voice carrying and stopping them all in their tracks to look at the two of us with curiosity and confusion. Logan walked in at that moment, hearing my last words, and stalked over to us with furrowed brows.

"I told you it wouldn't help to tell her about this." He looked down at his wife impatiently, and she looked back, guilt written across her face, before she gritted her teeth and her back straightened.

"She needed to know. She needs to know everything from here on out. She's not a pawn in someone's game, and that's how she has been treated lately. Look what happened! Teagan is hurt. She's been hurt. It didn't help us any, and it isn't doing her any favors. She needs to be prepared to face what's ahead as well as she can."

Toni stood and pushed past Logan, leaving the hall while he looked after her. His eyes tracked back to mine, and a small bit of shame flashed through them before he shook his head and took off after her.

Everyone else had gone back to their food, trying to act as if they hadn't witnessed my outburst and Toni's. It was embarrassing, but I had an inkling that more than likely they were all privy to the information that I had just found out. It wouldn't surprise me anyway.

I stood to leave, only to have my arm grabbed up by Rhea. I hadn't seen her enter. She must have come through the kitchen behind me. "Come with me."

She took me outside, and we wound around a path full of fragrant white flowers. They grew up the surrounding trees and on the branches that spread out over top of us. It was as if we walked through a tunnel of white petals.

Rhea was quiet as we walked, and I spent the time calming down and doing the breathing exercises that Killian taught me.

After a few more twists and turns, the tunnel ended, and we walked out into a clearing. Ahead of us a stream gurgled, and a bench sat before it. There was no one there but us, and it was blessedly quiet. I'd gotten used to the cacophony that constantly plagued the castle except at nighttime. All I could hear were the birds chirping and the water flowing. My shoulders eased, and my mind cleared. Here I could think and not feel as though the world was crashing around me.

Rhea gazed at the water. "It's beautiful, isn't it?" I agreed and watched the water flow around rocks and sticks.

"I came here an awfully long time ago when I needed to find some peace. This morning, I think you do too. So I'm not going to talk to you about all the things that are in the future, or the past. I want you to tell me what you're feeling. Let it all out, clear your heart and mind, and once that's done, you can start fresh on this journey. With a clear head and a plan."

I was impressed by Rhea. She was poised and strong. Most Titans were, but she was also thoughtful and smart.

Kind.

I could only imagine what she had been through in her many years of life. What heartaches she had endured. I only hoped that after getting older, I had the grace she did. I trusted her, and I liked her.

I took a deep breath and let it out slowly, leaning my head back and closing my eyes.

"I feel like I've been swept up in a whirlwind. No, a cyclone. And a million lifetimes have been shoved into a few months. I went from being a normal girl in high school to an orphan thrust into a magical world that no one else would believe existed. I was told I was a part of a prophecy." I snorted. "I never used to have friends. I think I was pretty naive about a lot of things. But then I met these incredible people, shifters and warlocks and gods and goddesses, and they've become the best of friends. I've got two protectors that are animals that speak and change form. And now I've been on two journeys to find two magical Keys. I've been poisoned, cut up, thought I lost people I loved over and over. And now? Now the father I thought I lost is back. I barely know him. I want to know him, but I worry he'll leave me again or that something will happen to take him away. Everyone expects me to be this strong person. I want to be-believe me I do-but I'm having a hard time with it right now. Things keep getting thrown at me, and I'm beginning to wonder if I can dodge anymore."

I sniffled and scrunched my eyes closed. *I will not cry!*

Rhea didn't say a word.

"And now I find this thing out about Teagan. Not only did my parents and his arrange for us to marry when we were of age, but they also had the audacity to weave a spell that tied us together forever unless they find a way to reverse it. And Hunter? What about him? Where does he fit into this all? There's something going on with us, something I did when I brought him back that has us linked somehow. I mean, I can feel his emotions, and he mine. And I don't hate it. It makes me happy, really. But what if there is no reversal of this thing with Teagan? Where does that leave us?" I groaned and opened my eyes to stare at the tree branches above.

Rhea still didn't say anything.

It felt good to voice this all aloud and know someone was listening but not interjecting their thoughts and feelings. This must be what people feel like when they go to a therapist or psychologist.

"Somehow this will get fixed. I don't care what it takes. I can't live my life worrying about the future, but I want to make sure I help shape it. And if that means figuring all this out on top of finding the Keys and staying alive that's what I'll do." I nodded to myself.

"And I think I need to talk to Teagan. We need to air all this out. And Hunter, god, I've got to talk to him about this. Maybe he'll have some ideas."

I bolted upright and turned to look at my companion.

"What about you guys? Can't you help try to reverse the spell? I mean, you're super powerful, so surely you can break a witches spell?" I pleaded.

Rhea pursed her lips and shrugged her shoulder.

"We could, yes. But as a rule, we are not able to step in and break it. We're not able to meddle in pacts. Reversing hexes that weren't agreed upon? Yes. This pact? No."

My face must have been full of fury if it reflected what had bubbled up at her words.

Regret crossed her face. "I would reverse it right now if I could. You must believe me when I tell you it's physically not possible for us. If we tried, the pact itself would only stop us and cause us pain. It would get nowhere."

I stared at the green grass at my feet. It wasn't fair that they couldn't help. It was ironic that the people who had the most power had their hands tied from helping us defeat a power that might eventually take even them down.

I looked over at Rhea and the distress was clearly written on her face. She wanted to help, and it must be frustrating to not be able to. "If you guys can't help magically, then maybe we can figure out some other way that you can. Even just advice would be helpful at this point."

She nodded slowly, then stared back at the water. I could almost see the wheels turning as her mind raced over ideas.

As she did, I stood up, my mind clearer.

"If it's okay, I'm going to head back. I need to get ready to train with Amarie. It's more essential now than ever that I become a good fighter."

Chapter Eight

I met Amarie in the clearing where we always practiced, my resolve that morning stronger than ever.

"I don't want you to take it easy on me today. And I need you to be honest about what I need to work on and what I don't."

Her eyebrow rose as she looked me up and down. "I've always been honest. You don't realize how far you've come in such a short amount of time. But all right. Let's see what you've got."

I bent my knees and lowered into a fighting stance; she did the same.

She wasn't easy on me. Not one bit. The blows were real and violent. But I gave as good as I got. She sported a swollen eye and a few cuts that blood welled out of. I'm sure I looked much worse, but I felt a bit of satisfaction, even through the pain.

We both breathed heavy, and I leaned over with my hands on my knees trying to still my racing heart.

"I think you're almost ready." Amarie took a swig of her water before upending the rest of the bottle over her head, cooling herself down.

Her words surprised me. I didn't feel ready at all.

"Tomorrow will be our last day training, but I want you to practice your defensive moves every day. You don't need a partner to do that."

I agreed and we went our separate ways.

So, if my training was done, did that mean I could go home? I was anxious to go back and scour the Oak for any information I could find on Helios. Information *is* power. If I could find something that would help me understand a way, if any, to defeat him, I'd feel a little less dread.

As I walked through the forest back to the castle, a rustling noise sounded behind me. I glanced over my shoulder to see who it was and was surprised to see Hunter behind me.

I stopped in my tracks and turned to face him, excitement buzzing through my body. "Hunter," I breathed.

His mouth stretched into that grin that I so rarely saw. And I was amazed to see a slight blush on his tan cheeks. He looked down before looking back into my eyes as he came to stand before me.

"I, uh... I was watching you train back there. You've gotten really good." He cleared his throat. "I'm just sorry that I didn't have a chance to teach you like I promised."

I was sorry he hadn't been able to also, but that's neither here nor there.

I waved my hand in the air and frowned. "You would have if I hadn't gotten you into that mess. Don't worry about it. I'm sure at some point you'll be able to teach me even more fighting tricks." I smiled into his dark eyes.

He looked away, toward something in the forest, and his expression turned serious. "I've got to leave with the Titans today."

My heart stopped. I hadn't been expecting that. I knew he would have to go at some point, I just hadn't expected it to be so soon. "How long will you be gone, and will I get to see you again sometime soon?" I bit my lip, working to keep my voice steady and not let any emotions show.

I studied his profile and watched as his jaw worked as he ground his teeth together. When he finally looked back at me, a serious look in his eyes, I worried that the news wasn't what I wanted to hear.

I was wrong.

He grabbed both of my hands, pulling them up to rest against his heart. I don't know why, but just that simple gesture got me every time. Chills raced up my legs and over my arms as the fire lit within him.

"I don't know how long I'll be gone, but I will try to get back to you as soon as I can. This isn't easy for me. I know it isn't for you either. I think it's going to hurt, this separation, more than the others. In fact, at least for me, I know it will. The more I'm around you, the more the pull to be with you every second gets stronger."

He pulled me into his arms then, his warmth surrounding me. I imagined I smelled pretty ripe after my training, but the thought fled as he pressed a soft kiss to my forehead.

"We'll figure this all out. And while I want to be selfish and stay right here with you, we both have a job to do. The sooner all the Keys are found, and this evil defeated, the sooner we can get on with our lives, and figure out what this is between us."

I knew he was right, but at this moment, all I could concentrate were his arms around me and his heartbeat against my ear.

He pulled back too soon, turning us both and we walked back to the castle, his arm around my waist. Every so often he glanced down at me, a small smile gracing his lips, but before long, we reached the courtyard and his arm slipped away.

He was looking toward the steps and at the group of Titans who stood there watching us. I couldn't read any of their expressions save one, Rhea. She looked at me with sympathy, and I could feel the support behind her gaze.

"Well, I guess it's time to go then." Hunter sighed.

I nodded, my happiness deflated. I wouldn't show the group watching us that it affected me, and I knew I didn't have to show Hunter. He could feel it. Just as I felt his.

The group descended the stairs and walked over to us. No one said a word, but Coeus nodded to Hunter and he turned to me.

"I'll see you soon. Please don't do anything stupid," he joked, trying to lighten the mood, and it reminded me of all the times before that he had poked at me. I ran with it; I didn't want to make this harder than it already was.

"Only if you don't."

He smiled slightly, and his dark eyes sparkled, before he turned and walked with the group out into the forest.

His muscular form fit in with the Titans. He looked like one of them, regal in some way. I knew he had changed, but he'd always be the Were shifter I met almost a year ago. The one who had given me such a hard time at first and the one whose soul called to mine now.

I turned too, and with my shoulders firm, my back straight, and my head up, I walked into the castle, intent on setting my path forward on the one that I wanted it to be on. Not what everyone else thought it should be.

I searched for Celeste and found her with Aine in a sitting room, their heads together in deep discussion. As I stood in the doorway, I cleared my throat to let them know they had company. Both sets of eyes turned, questioning before they saw it was me.

And both of their eyes lit with welcome. Celeste motioned me in, and I took a seat beside them. "Well now, how are you doing after all the excitement you've been through the last few days?" Celeste looked at me knowingly and I took a deep breath.

"Nothing like I had expected, of course. But it never is." I blew out a breath. "I wanted to talk to you and form a plan. In fact, I'd like Rohn, umm... my dad, to be here also."

Aine nodded, whispered a few words, and flicked her finger toward the door. I faintly made out a shimmer in the air. "He should be here in a few minutes." Aine stated. "I believe he was looking for you earlier as well, but you'd already left for training. Rather early morning wasn't it?"

She reached for her tea and took a sip before leaning back against her chair.

"Yeah, I couldn't sleep. I had a lot on my mind and ended up making a mess of things with Toni and Logan. Then Rhea and I went for a walk. She isn't what I expected a Titan to be."

Celeste laughed and shook her head. "They're just like us Andie. I mean, you don't treat me any different, do you?" I looked at her and realized what she said was true. I certainly didn't think of Celeste as the moon goddess.

Huh.

"I guess you're right." I would've said more, but Rohn made his appearance then, hurrying through the door, studied the three of us.

"You look thick as thieves in here." He smiled and lowered himself into the chair opposite me. "I received your message." He looked at Aine.

"Yes, dear. Thank you for coming so quickly. Andie wants to talk with all of us about something, and she wanted you here." He glanced at me, eyes serious.

"Is everything okay?"

"Oh, yes, everything is fine. Amarie told me today that our last training session is tomorrow, and I was hoping to get your thoughts about me going back home. I'd really like to study up on Helios and I need to speak with Teagan and Pres. We need to prepare to find the third Key, and I'd like all the information I can get before we start."

They looked at each other a little uneasy.

"What? Why are you all looking like that?" I asked, worried that they would tell me no.

Celeste spoke first, her voice gentle as if she were talking to a small child that she was afraid might burst into a temper tantrum if they didn't get their way. Little did she know about my mission to be more mature. I planned to stick to it, *whatever* they had to say.

"Well, I think that's a fine idea, and of course now that your training is over, you may return home. But... Teagan won't be able to go on the upcoming journey with you. From what I've heard, his mental state is too fragile to endure it right now. His parents are worried about him, and frankly so am I from what they've told me."

Aine nodded in agreement. Rohn didn't know Teagan, but he had surely spoken with his parents as they rekindled their friendship when they were reunited.

How the heck was I supposed to do this without him? He had always been the leader, the strength that kept our team going and me on the right path. He was born to do that.

Confused I looked around at them.

"Maybe I can talk to him and it will help? We've been through a lot together. He probably just needs a friend to talk to through all of this."

Celeste looked at me with sympathy lining her face. "I know you want to help him. But he's got his parents, and Presley is there too. You're going to have to give him time to get over everything. I'm not quite sure seeing you is the best way for him to do that," she said quietly, squeezing my hand.

She was probably right, but I wasn't about to give up on him and the chance that I might be able to get through to him. But for now, I'd let it alone.

"Okay, so when can we go home?"

She seemed skeptical as she took in my acquiescence. "Well, you have one more day of training, so how about tomorrow afternoon once you're done?"

Rohn spoke up then. "And I'd like to come with you, if that's okay?" He looked at me, and my heart overflowed. I hadn't thought about him wanting to come with us, but the fact that he did, that he wasn't leaving again, made the little girl inside of me squeal. Maybe we'd get to know each other better at home where there were fewer distractions. I hoped he'd even teach me a thing or two.

I smiled at him, and the relief was visible in the relaxation of his shoulders. "I'd love that."

The rest of the day was uneventful. Mostly because I sequestered myself in my room. Emric and Charlie were nowhere to be found, and I hoped they weren't up to trouble.

Dinner had been quiet with all the guests gone, and I decided to turn in early. Excitement kept me up as I stared at the moon while I lay in bed, Emric and Charlie snoozing at my feet. It was as if they knew I needed the extra comfort and solidarity, even if it just meant they kept my feet warm.

When sleep finally pulled me under, it was a restless sleep filled with crazy dreams.

I woke the next day exhausted. It was as if I hadn't slept at all, and my body was sore in places I didn't know it could be, thanks to the intense training from yesterday. I hadn't looked in the mirror once since then, but as I studied my face this morning, there were small bruises on my cheeks, and cuts along my neck. Amarie had given me her all yesterday, and I was surprised that the damage wasn't worse. Maybe she was right and I was holding my own well. It gave me a bit of pride to realize that I could take care of myself.

I threw on some leggings and a long T-shirt, throwing my hair in a ponytail and slipped on my fighting boots. I wasn't worried about how I looked today, and most of all I wanted to be comfortable.

I hightailed it downstairs and stopped in the breakfast hall to grab an apple, water, and a piece of toast. Amarie would meet me soon in our fighting spot and I wanted to make sure I had something, even if it wasn't much to give me some energy. I didn't know what our training would bring today, but I was hoping for less damage than yesterday.

Out in the courtyard, Killian stood looking out at the forest. He was still and unmoving, which was strange for him. Normally, he was a ball of energy and always on the go.

"Hey. What's up?" I stood beside him, and he quickly wiped his face, turning to me with a tired grin.

"Oh, just lost in thought, I guess. I didn't sleep well last night." He shrugged. "I heard you were leaving today?" He looked a bit upset as he said it, and I nodded, still watching his face, trying to figure out what was wrong. I knew something was.

"Yeah, this afternoon. I want to get home and see what I can find on Helios. Oh, and there's something that keeps bothering me, and I wanted to ask you about it."

His eyes slanted toward me, eyebrows raised. "Of course, what is it?"

"Well, I've learned more about the Titans from Rhea and Hunter, and I guess I just don't understand that if you have Titan blood in you, why you don't have to go with them too?" His brows scrunched down in consternation.

I rushed to add, "Don't get me wrong-I don't want you to. It just didn't make sense to me. Also, the fact that they let you fight alongside me on our search for the Keys. Rhea said they weren't allowed to intervene, so I don't really understand why you can."

I wrapped my arms around my middle.

He nodded, my words making sense to him, and he looked at me again. "I had wondered the same thing a few months ago and Coeus explained to me that while I have Titan blood, I'm not fully one of them. I'm also fae and-get this-Elvish. How in the world that happened, we don't know, but I'm hoping we figure it out soon?" He sighed deeply. "And to think if you guys hadn't come around and saved me, I would have gone on for the rest of my life-if I'd lived-never knowing any of this." He stuffed his hands in his pockets and rocked back on his heels.

"Have you talked to Presley lately?" he asked, effectively changing the subject. And by the look in his eyes, I realized then what had been bothering him.

"It's been a while, too long really since I've spoken with her. I know she's been busy helping Teagan recover. She wasn't happy with me when we spoke last." And that's when I remembered the selfie that Killian and I had taken before the party. "Hey, we never sent the photo to her!" I grabbed his hand and pulled him with me. "Let's go grab my phone real quick and send it to her. I bet she'll get a kick out of it." I smiled and he followed me to my room. "I just have a minute, though. I've got to meet Amarie soon."

We sat on the edge of my bed and I grabbed the phone, showing him how to send a text message. I'd gotten her phone number from Aine and programmed it in. "Okay, so we're going to add the photo in here like this, and look, you can add these little faces, so we're going to do a smiley face." I typed in a message too her:

Bet you never thought you'd see the day I was in a dress! Killian says hi!

"And now we hit this where it says *send*." I watched the message go through, and then shoved the phone into his hand. "Here, you take this in case she messages back. I've got to get to training." He looked at the phone in his hand like it was a foreign object, not sure what to do with it.

I placed my hand on his shoulder and squeezed. "See ya later!" And I was out the door, taking the stairs two at a time. It was my turn to almost run into a fairy who flew by. I shouted a quick apology behind me and waved at Aine who had entered the foyer as I flew out the door.

Amarie was waiting as I sauntered into the clearing, and to my astonishment, she wasn't wearing her normal fight clothes. She motioned me over. "Feeling okay today?" she asked.

"Yes, I'm fine, despite the beating I took yesterday. Just a little sore." I shrugged.

She nodded knowingly.

"Why aren't you dressed to train?" I asked as I watched her sit on a fallen log under one of the trees.

"Oh, we're going to train today, but not in the way you think. Come here." She tapped the wood beside her, and I did as she asked. "Today we're going to train your mind. We're going to work on your ability to shut others out, because there will come a time when you're faced with a foe who will try to use your mind against you."

I remembered the mirrors and how they had reduced me to a blubbering mess, and what could have happened had Loxley not shaken me out of the stupor I was in.

"Okay. What do you need me to do?" I agreed eagerly.

"I want you to close your eyes and try to tune everything else out. I'm going to invade your thoughts, and give you visions. None of them are real, but my magic will make you believe that they are. It is your job to try and pull out of them, to destroy them. However you feel necessary."

Her voice was serious as she looked into my eyes. "If you can master this, it will be a great help going forward. I'm not saying you'll get the hang of it in this one training session, but when we're done, I'll give you tips on how to do it at home. To exercise your willpower, so to speak."

She pulled her hair back behind her and grabbed both of my hands. "It's imperative though that you squeeze my hands if it gets to be too much. I don't want to damage you Andie."

Okay...

That was a little frightening, but I was all in regardless.

I took a deep breath and nodded. "Let's do this." I closed my eyes and heard her chant a few quiet words before the darkness behind my eyelids receded and I was in the castle again, standing in the foyer.

There in front of me was Rohn. His body was on fire, and moans tore through the flames that surrounded him. Pain lanced my heart at the scene before me, and I looked around for anything I could find to douse the flames. A large vase stood nearby, and I ran to it, reaching to pull out the flowers, but my hands went right through them. And that's when it hit me that this wasn't real. How quickly I had been pulled into this untrue vision was frightening. But how did I get out? The moans turned to screams and I closed my eyes, willing it to go away.

Nothing happened. My eyes flew open to once again land on the terrifying scene that was suddenly made worse with the picture of Freya gliding down the stairs, followed by the Fomori with Killian in her clutches.

It's not real. It's not real.

I reached down within me and found the ball of power that was always waiting when I needed to use my magic. I tugged and pulled on it and literally felt something in me snap and that ball surged up and out and the vison shattered into a million stars, only to fade to black again, and my body fell backward, my eyes snapping open to the branches above.

I rolled over onto my side, my legs still hanging over the log I'd been sitting on, to see Amarie clutching her head. I sat up, grasping for her. "Are you okay?"

She put her hand out, waving the air around us. "I'll be fine. This happens. It's part of it. Just give me a minute and it will go away." She took big breaths, massaging her temples and over her closed eyes while I waited.

It seemed like forever, but eventually she cracked her eyes open, her shoulders relaxed, and she gave me a steely look.

"Well. I don't think it's going to take much training for you. You did exceptionally well. That's only if you can tell a vision from what is really happening. And you must remember that most attacks like this you won't have a warning that it's about to happen. You didn't realize it wasn't real at first, even though you'd just been present with me and expected it. When an enemy uses this against you, it will be when you least expect it. So always be wary."

It was a scary thought. To think that I could be thrust into something like that and not be aware that it wasn't actually happening. And what happened if I didn't pull myself out?

I asked the latter to Amarie.

"If someone uses a vision on you and you can't get out of it, that gives them time to sneak up on you and kill you. Or they could break your mind, and you'd never be the same again."

Chills ran up my neck. I could never let that happen.

She dusted off her pants as she stood and reached down to help me up. "Let's get you back. I hear you're leaving today."

And suddenly my head was back in the game and I was giddy to go get started.

Chapter Nine

Aine had the fairies pack my bag and it was waiting downstairs beside Emric and Charlie who also seemed excited about going home. Celeste and Aine walked in to join us, Killian not far behind. Aine hugged Celeste and kissed her on both cheeks before coming to me and doing the same.

"It was so nice having you here with us. I hope you come stay again soon. Though next time we'll try to throw more fun in and less work." She winked at me.

Killian stepped forward and handed me the phone. I took it and hugged him hard. "Did she respond?" I whispered in his ear. He only stepped back and shook his head sadly. That wasn't like Pres, not at all. I was so sure she'd respond with something snarky. But to not respond at all? Something was up.

"I'm sure she is probably just busy. Hey!" I turned to Aine. "Can you get a phone for Killian too? That way we can stay in touch."

A smile stretched from ear to ear and she nodded. "But of course. We'll get you one today, Killian." She patted him on the back, and he seemed to perk up a little.

Emric wound around my legs and headed outside, but not before I caught him mumbling, "In my day, we'd just use magic to communicate." His furry head shook as he walked out the door. "Kids these days." I chuckled, as did the rest of the group. "If he was able to dial the numbers, I can picture him having a ball with prank calling people."

Aine laughed merrily. "Oh no, I could see him having his own Ticky Tok and making funny videos. Isn't that what it's called?" I was stunned that she even knew about TikTok. I had only stumbled across it one day when doing a paper on social media. She must really be trying to keep up with the times.

Celeste ushered us outside, and a group of fairies swarmed around us. We held hands while Charlie and Emric hung on for dear life and waved to Aine and Killian before being swept through space to land back inside the Oak.

"Bout time ya got back." Balwyn sat by the fire, studying us the only way he could. Eira flew at us, making up for his lack of enthusiasm as she bounced between us, her iridescent wings tickling my face.

"I am *so* happy your home!" she squealed making Celeste laugh and Balwyn scowl. I left Celeste to calm her down and went to sit across from the cranky old brownie. On the coffee table in front of me sat a tray with cookies and mugs of hot chocolate. He must have known we were on the way.

"Why, Balwyn, did you put these out just for us?" I gestured to the snacks. His eyebrows lowered as he scowled again and looked away from me, but not before I saw a slight tilt to his lips. I laughed and leaned forward, grabbing the chocolate drink, and sighed.

"It's so good to be back. I missed you guys."

He hmphed and crossed his arms across his small chest. "Well, if ya hadn't been fritterin' away ya time, ya coulda been here much sooner!" So he missed me? That's what I took from what he said, and just being in the Oak gave me a comfort like none other.

Celeste and Eira came over to us, and Eira landed on my arm. "So, are you all ready to fight? I hear that you did extremely well with your training." She looked at Celeste, who smiled back at me.

"Well, yes, I guess I did. I'm not near as good as Amarie, but I do believe I can hold my own."

Eira nodded seriously. "Good, good," and she looked back at Celeste. "Will you be going home to the house now then?" Celeste nodded and I hesitated. I wasn't ready to go back there. Even though Celeste is back and okay, the trauma I had been through after she was taken would all be brought back to the forefront.

"Umm... would it be okay if I stayed here in my room for a little while? I mean, I need to search for some reading material to study up on and it would be more convenient. I'd get a lot more work done." I looked at Celeste hoping she'd see the pleading in my eyes and understand that I couldn't go back there just yet.

She dipped her head in acknowledgment of my question before smiling brightly at Emric and Charlie. "Well, seems it'll be just you two and me for a bit, though I do want you both to come here and check on Andie every so often." She turned to me. "And if you need anything at all, let Eira know and she can come get me." She stood and bent over to hug me. "I'll be around too, and I do hope you find what you're looking for." Straightening up, she headed for the door, Emric and Charlie behind her.

"Don't be stuffing your face full of those cookies. Extra padding doesn't help in a fight," Emric called over his shoulder, and I rolled my eyes.

"I have a surprise for you, Andie." Eira clapped her hands, her little body vibrating with excitement. "While you were gone, I took the liberty of making one of the guest rooms into a practice room for you. It's warded so that it can't be damaged by your magic. I figured you might need it to practice, now that you've got the physical training done. And well, it's been a few months since you've used magic much. Could be time to start working on it daily again. And if Rohn is going to help you, you'll definitely need a good place that can stand up to strong magic." She flew ahead of me down the corridor to the guest rooms before swirling her finger, her magic turning the handle on the door and swinging it open to reveal a room that looked like something out of a strange dream.

It was dark inside, but the walls, ceiling, and even the floor made the room look as if I were simply stepping into space. Stars glittered, and comets streaked by. It was quiet, so quiet that I heard my own heart beating. It reminded me of the ceilings of the castle.

"It's beautiful... and strange all at once Eira."

She laughed and swirled through the air, the slight light from the stars glinting off her wings. "Yes, but it is exactly what you need. Something that's calming and quiet, no distractions."

I realized she was right. Just standing in here right now, the stress in my shoulders began melting away. "You did a great job, and I really appreciate it." I stepped out of the room and back into the lit hallway, Eira followed. "I may just come in here later and try a few easy spells."

She preened, happy with my response. I followed her back into the main room, stooping to pick up my pack. "I'm just going to get my stuff put away." I pointed in the direction of my room. Balwyn ignored me, and Eira just nodded and waved.

I closed the door to my room, and I leaned back against the hard wood, taking a deep breath. I had so much to do, and I wasn't sure where to begin first. Ultimately, I decided to get my things put away, and then go to one of the libraries to search out books that might give me some insight into Helios.

As I put everything away, the small spell book dropped out from between a pair of jeans. I had totally forgotten to do anything with it when I was in Fairy. Flipping through it, I decided right then that tonight, I'd try a few of these out after warming up. I needed to expand on my spells anyway, and what better way to start then with the new ones in this book.

I searched and searched until my eyes felt like they would cross, and none of the books I'd found yet mentioned Helios at all. It was as if he'd been written out of history, out of the magical world and beyond. What had he done that was so terrible to completely wipe him out from mention?

I knew there had to be something on him somewhere. It just wasn't in this one room filled with books. I realized it might take a while to find what I was looking for. Yawning, I wiped my eyes, turning the light off as I went downstairs. The smell of something delicious hit my nose, and I was once again thankful that Balwyn was so smart in the kitchen.

I followed the smell and found a small table had been set up near the fire, with one chair. A bowl filled with soup and bread on the side sat there waiting to be eaten. Balwyn and Eira were nowhere in sight.

I knew it was for me. This is how they had done dinnertime for the last few months of my residence with them. It was almost as if they thought dinner was a sacred time to eat and reflect and not be bothered by anyone. Sometimes it was nice other times, it had been extremely lonely.

It was lonely tonight. After all the camaraderie at the castle, the quiet left me with way too much time to think.

I finished the delicious soup. I wasn't sure what kind it was, but potatoes and beef made it hearty and the onion made it flavorful. I sopped up the remainder with the bread, and once done, my stomach was full and happy. But my mind kept on with the wandering. It wouldn't stop until I gave it something else to focus on. And though I wasn't really in the mood to work on my spells, I figured it would be for the best.

I dragged myself to the bedroom, grabbed the small book, and then went to practice.

My first obstacle was being able to see the spells in the book. It was so dark in the room that it made it impossible. I cracked the door open a little, with the book situated in the light from the hall. Sitting cross-legged in front of it, I flipped through the pages until one seemed to call out to me. It was a spell that supposedly stopped time. That seemed interesting.

I skimmed through the words and what to do, memorizing them in my mind until I felt that I had it all down right. Then I stepped further into the room, sitting down again amidst the stars. Comets still swirled by, and I focused on them.

Raising my hands above my head, I moved my pointer fingers in a clockwise motion and whispered the words to the spell. Each time I repeated it, I said it louder until the final time was shouted and my fingers stopped rotating.

I had been fixated on a comet that streaked across the wall, and I blinked once when I saw it was still there, stopped in motion but the fire in its trail still undulating.

It worked!

Impressed didn't even begin to cover how I felt at that moment. This spell was a game changer, and my mind raced with all the possibilities. If I could use this spell in a fight, I could stop someone in their tracks. I could stop something bad from happening.

I pumped my hand in the air and whooped loudly. No one was here to see my elation anyway. I could act like a fool if I wanted. Settling down, I went to the book again, to see how to reverse it. Eira wouldn't be happy if I'd stopped her magic in here for good, and I really did like it.

Running my finger down the page, I spotted where it said "reversal" and it was basically the same spell, only this time my fingers would turn in a counterclockwise motion. I ran back and sat down again, doing it exactly the same. When I was done, the comet took off across the room in an explosive burst.

It must have been a strong spell because my body felt drained. It'd been a while since I felt the aftereffects of one, and I'd forgotten how debilitating they could be. Slowly I rose and grabbed the book before leaving the room. Once in my own room, I fell onto the bed, and that was the last thing I remembered before being woken by Eira the next morning.

∞

I felt a tickling on my ear and woke to her telling me that if I didn't get up for breakfast, Balwyn wouldn't be happy. The smell of bacon and biscuits reached my nose, and I tried to clear the sleep from my eyes.

"Come on, sleepy head. You must have really overdone it yesterday. It's already ten in the morning. You're burning daylight!" And off she went, flying through the crack in my door as I sat up yawning.

I couldn't believe I slept in my jeans and still had my socks on. Dragging my feet against the floor, I made my way to breakfast and sat down at the table again, but this time, Balwyn hovered nearby.

"Thank you for breakfast. I'm sorry to keep you waiting. I guess I was more tired than I knew." I looked at him, and he just nodded. No scowl.

Weird.

"Umm... you wouldn't happen to have any coffee, would you?" I asked him tentatively, knowing he preferred to make hot chocolate to anything.

"I gots some."

He turned to go and fetch it for me and when he brought in the steaming mug, the smell alone told me how strong it was. I'm sure he probably had never made a cup of coffee before in his life. I took a sip of the burning liquid and knew I was right. The bitterness of it made me wonder how much of the coffee grounds he had used to make this one cup. But I would drink it, chug it down like a sailor since he'd gone out of his way just for me.

"Ya'd better eat up. Rohn'll be here in a little bit and ya need to be a little more alive when he gets here." Balwyn turned away to go back to his hidey hole.

My dad's coming?

I hurried to eat the rest of my breakfast and then scurried to my room to take a quick shower and dress appropriately. This would be the first time we spent any quality time, just the two of us, and I wanted to make a good impression.

Why? I don't know. But I felt it was necessary. I didn't want him seeing me look weak and not put together.

Once done, I rushed back into the main room and sat on the couch, changing my position this way or that. I couldn't get comfortable and settle down. I leaned forward, elbows bouncing on my knee when my foot wouldn't be still. Balwyn entered the room, Eira behind him. I could tell she understood what was wrong from the look on her face, but she didn't say anything. She just landed beside me and sat in silence.

"I guess I'm nervous," I said honestly. "I didn't have any time alone with him while we were at the castle. And this is all new to me." I sighed, making a conscious effort to stop moving.

Balwyn just stared at me. "Ya've waited for this forever, havn't ya? Quit yer being nervous and put some steel in tha backbone. I know ya've got it," he grumbled before hopping onto the other chair. Before I could respond, the air around us moved and blurred. A shape took place in the blurriness until my father's form filled out and he stood before me.

Smiling.

"Hello Andie." He nodded to Balwyn and Eira.

I stood up and fidgeted with my hands before he walked to me and wrapped me in a big hug. It was uncomfortable at first, but I let myself relax and put my arms around him too. He squeezed me tighter and ran a hand over my hair.

"I can't tell you how long I've waited to do this. How many times I wanted to leave what I was doing and come home to you." He kissed the top of my head and then held me at arm's length. "You've grown into such a wonderful young woman. Your mom would be so proud. I know I am." He smiled at me again, joy lighting his face.

He lifted the locket and looked down at it. "I hope this has given you some comfort. I wanted to make sure you had it for the pictures as well as what it can do." He pulled me to sit down, and I turned to him on the couch.

"It has, thank you. But I'm still not sure what the feather is for. And I've yet to need to use the locket."

He nodded, and a serious look came over his face. "I'm glad you haven't needed to use it yet. But if the day comes, it will be at your disposal. Just don't ever take it off." He steepled his fingers under his chin. "The feather I hope you don't ever have to use. I tried to think of all the ways I could spell something to give you aid while I wasn't around, much like your mom did in the beanie that she knitted you." I smiled because that had certainly come in handy. I hadn't realized that she'd knitted it with her own hands, though, and just the thought of her toiling away at it made it even more special.

"The feather is spelled so that should you ever need to sift, which is what I did just now to transport here, and you're stuck in a magically warded place, all you'll need to do is take it out. Then blow on it, and as it drifts away in the air, you'll be taken where you want to go, even if you're in a place where your magic has been warded. The magic in it will be stronger."

It seemed like a good thing to have. But I really hoped I'd never been in a situation I couldn't get out of. The fact that he had thought of all of this and tried to leave things to help me in his absence made my heart warm.

"Do you think you can teach me to sift like you did? It certainly would come in handy for the future." I asked hopefully.

Again, he smiled at me, and patted my knee.

"Of course. I'll try and teach you all that you want to know. I'm here now, and I'm not going to miss anything else if I can help it." He looked away for a moment, but not before I'd heard the emotion in his voice.

"I promise you: if I have to go away again, it will only be a short while, and then I'll come back to you. We still have a lot of work to do and that might entail me having to go on a mission, but that's all it will be. If I don't have to leave, all the better. I want to be here to help you and protect you when I can."

His eyes said it all. Fierce and emotional before he gathered me to him again in a quick squeeze. I smiled up at him, my heart full, and I felt like this was honestly one of the best days of my life.

"Can you teach me how to sift now? I'm ready."

His smile became wider and he took my outstretched hand. "Lead the way."

Chapter Ten

We worked tirelessly for hours in what I'd dubbed 'the spell room.'

This spell was hard. Not difficult. *Hard.* My frustration with myself was running high, but my dad remained calm and kept pushing me to try again. I'd almost gotten it when the magic fizzled away. We decided to take a break, and wouldn't you know it, Balwyn had water and fruit set out already.

I was grateful to the little dude who'd made it his mission to look out for me while I stayed with him and Eira. And just because my real dad was here now, it hadn't stopped him from acting like a surrogate one.

The break was much needed, and I was able to prod some stories from my dad about his life with mom. He didn't tell any sad ones. Only ones that were lighthearted and made me laugh. He even got a grin out of Balwyn. *How in the world?* When I saw his thick lips turn up, I was astounded.

Mind you, to anyone else it would have looked like a snarl. But no, it was his version of a grin. It seemed that Rohn had the ability to put anyone at ease and make them laugh. It was one thing he hadn't passed down to me, but I took note. He was laid back and casual. Despite the notoriety that the Elves had spoken about him with, he was *just* a man. Just my dad.

He was kind and thoughtful. When someone else spoke, he didn't try to talk over them. He listened and then either gave thoughtful advice or praise. I hadn't heard one negative word pass his lips since I met him. I wanted to be like that.

Even though old Andie would've sneered and said she didn't care how or what anyone thought about her, new Andie did. I'd vowed to change. And now I decided to be more like him. It would only be to my benefit.

While we talked, Teagan was forgotten. Freya, the Fomori, and Helios were forgotten. We were just a dad and daughter enjoying each other's company and getting to know each other better.

I'd never had a better day.

The entire week was a whirlwind of working on sifting with my dad. He'd come early some days, and we would have breakfast together. The change in Balwyn was amazing, all thanks to Rohn.

Yeah, I know, I shouldn't call him Rohn. I'm working on it though, and I don't call him that to his face.

We'd work throughout the day only to end in the same results as the first time. He was beyond patient, assuring me that I'd get it and cheering me on every time I tried. I imagined this is what it was like for a regular kid when they competed in sports or any other extracurricular activity.

He had faith in me that I didn't know could be possible.

It wasn't until Friday when I was exhausted and being unusually hard on myself as we neared dinner time when it finally happened. I'd let my temper get the best of me, and it was then when I'd screamed in frustration that my body sifted, and before I knew it, I materialized in Celeste's kitchen, much to her, Emric and Charlie's amazement.

Emric had been so startled, that he jumped from his cozy spot on the floor up onto the kitchen counter and squealed. I couldn't help it. Between my excitement and his reaction, laughter belted out. The deep belly laughing that doubles you over and makes tears run out of your eyes. Just when I'd thought I had it under control, the picture of his face when it happened would cross my mind again and I'd start all over.

Finally, I was able to get it under control and lowered myself into a chair, wiping my eyes as he scowled at me, and Celeste smirked. My arrival didn't seem to have affected her at all. She'd known that Rohn and I were working on it, and my go-to place was her house.

"Well, I'll be hog tied." Charlie whistled, and it almost started me up again. "You did it!" He flew around me, his joy evident.

I beamed at him, nodding. "I did, didn't I!"

Dad appeared then beside me, swooping down and swinging me around in his arms. "Yes! I told you that you'd get it!" He put me down and glanced at Celeste. "You should have seen her! It was the most amazing thing to witness." He grinned from ear to ear, and Celeste chuckled.

"Why, Rohn, did you ever think it would be any different? She is yours, after all." She sipped her tea, eyes bright with merriment.

He slung his arm over my shoulder, pride lifting his chest. "No, I never doubted for a second. I just can't get over the feeling of watching her realize she had it in her, even if it took a little fury to spark it." He winked at me and chuckled. I had to admit, it seemed my magic did its best when I was mad.

Maybe that was a good thing. because I hoped the only time I'd need to use most of it was when I was in a bad situation that would most likely tick me off. "So the magic combination is me and my anger. Great."

They all laughed and shrugged.

"Whatever works, little one. Just don't be startling me like that again." Emric growled, finally making his way off the counter to rub against my calve.

Since we were already here and it was almost dinnertime, Celeste insisted that I stay. She whipped up the best pot roast and mashed potatoes with her magic after letting Balwyn and Eira know not to have food ready for me when I got back.

It was the best meal. Comfort food at its finest and Rohn regaled us with a few stories of his travels to find out what or who was behind all of this. He had a way of storytelling that drew you in, even better than Emric if I'm honest.

The time flew by, and before I knew, it was late, and I needed to get back.

"Remember, just think of the Oak and that's where you'll land. Think of something that makes you angry again," Rohn said.

While we'd eaten, I hadn't had time to think about all that had happened in this house before Celeste was taken. As I looked around now, all that anger and terror seeped back in, and I concentrated hard on it. I didn't enjoy it, but it would help with the spell.

I pictured what Freya might have done to Celeste to be able to capture her. She's still hadn't told me, but I could imagine. And the fury festered and rose. I said the spell at the same time the anger burst out, and within seconds, I was standing before the fire. Balwyn just rose his eyebrows, and Eira clapped mightily.

"Yay! You did it again! I am so proud of you!" She wrapped her small arms around my face and kissed the side of my nose. "I knew you could do it!" I smiled and twitched my nose. Her flower dress tickled my nostril.

She got the message and backed up. "Sorry! I was just excited and happy." But she wasn't sorry, and I wasn't mad. These two-well really all of my support group-were like a bunch of parents to me in a way. I couldn't have gotten where I am without them.

"I love you Eira," was all I said, smiling at the blush that took over her cheeks. And then I turned to Balwyn. "I love you too." His also turned red, and he bowed his head, nodding. To my astonishment he put his hand over his heart and thumped it twice. I knew that was his way of saying what he couldn't seem to voice.

"We love you too, Andie," Eira whispered, her eyes glistening. And I was glad I told them. I needed to do that more. I should let people know how I feel about them. Life was just too short.

Next on my to do list was to talk to Teagan. I needed to know that he was okay, and hopefully, I didn't screw it up.

The following morning, I puttered around in one of the rooms I hadn't been in before. I was nervous about sifting to Teagan's parents' house, but that was the only way I could get there without Celeste or Rohn stopping me. I imagined Eira and Balwyn wouldn't like it either, but what they didn't know wouldn't hurt them.

Before long, I made my way to the spell room and once inside I started the spell. I decided to think about how mad I'd been at Freya after Hunter was dragged away from me.

Once again, the anger bubbled up and consumed me. I let it burst forth as I felt myself shatter in that strange feeling. When I felt the tugging of my body being put back together, I opened my eyes to see Logan and Toni staring at me over their cups of coffee.

"Andie! What on earth?" Logan stood up, confusion on his face. Toni seemed more concerned as she came to me, resting her hand on my arm. "What's happened?"

I touched her back, smiling sheepishly. "I'm sorry. Everything is okay, and I apologize for startling and worrying you. I just felt like it was time I visited Teagan. I miss him and Presley."

I kicked myself for not thinking of a different room to land in where his parents wouldn't be. Now Celeste and Rohn were sure to find out.

Toni stammered and looked at her husband before looking back at me. "I should probably check with Teagan first to make sure he feels like having company." And with that, she was out the door, leaving me with Logan, who didn't look impressed.

His arms were crossed in front of him as he stared at me. Many emotions including anger flashed on his face before he sighed and dropped his arms. "I know you mean well, Andie but it might not be the best time."

I nodded and gulped. "I understand. I only want the best for him. He's my best friend, and I just can't imagine my life without him. We've been through so much together, and I don't want to lose him." I picked at my fingernail and bit my lip before looking back. "I didn't intend for any of this to happen, and I need him to know that. I need the old Teagan to come back," I said softly.

It was true. While I didn't feel quite the same for him as he did for me, I cared for him and didn't want him hurting.

At that moment Presley rushed into the kitchen, sliding on her socked feet across the floor and bumping into me with all of her weight, arms wrapping tight around my neck.

I choked a little.

"Pres-Pres! You're choking me," I managed to get out. She immediately released me and stepped back, laughing.

"I'm sorry! I was just so excited to see you! What are you doing here? How'd you get here and where's everyone else?"

Of course, she had a million questions.

"Well, I'm here by myself and I got here by sifting. Rohn, err... Dad, taught me how." I quickly looked at Logan. "They don't know I'm here by the way."

He just shook his head and looked up at the ceiling. "If they ask, you know I'll have to tell them," He turned his gaze back to me.

I was astounded that he didn't say he was going to tell them right now, and immediately I agreed. "Yes, of course."

I turned back to Pres, hugging her again. "How are you? And why didn't you return my text?" Her smile turned a little wobbly, and she had to bite her lip.

"I was going to and then I got sidetracked. You guys looked amazing and I can't believe you wore a dress! What's gotten into you?" She breathed out, masking the emotion she had just shown.

"Well, I didn't really have a choice, but it was an amazing dress," I admitted. "And Killian, I wish you could have seen him. He has changed a lot, Pres. Aine's getting him a phone if she hasn't already. You need to get his number and talk to him. He really misses you."

She looked away at a noise in the hall before turning back. "I'll do that," she said absently. But that was all. It was totally strange for her. I mean, she had a crush on Killian. What happened?

Toni walked in, looking exhausted. "Teagan will see you, Andie. But let's try to keep it short. He wears out pretty easily, and he had an awfully long rehab session this morning."

"Okay. I promise I won't stay long. I just need to speak with him for a little bit."

She nodded. "Follow me."

We went upstairs and past the room I stayed in when I had visited. She led me to the door at the very end of the hall, and I wondered why they didn't have him downstairs where it was easier to get around. It must have been a huge challenge for him to go up and down the stairs.

"He insisted that he stay in his own room. He wanted things as normal as possible," she stated, as if she read my mind. It made sense. Teagan wasn't one to do things the easy way, even in his pain.

She turned the doorknob slowly, and I followed behind her.

He sat with his back to us at a desk in front of the window that overlooked the large lake in front of the house. It was an incredible view. "Hi, Teagan," I said quietly as his mom backed out of the room, shutting the door behind her.

At first, he didn't move. He continued staring out the window, and I worried that he didn't want to talk to me. Slowly, he turned around, his gray eyes meeting mine. He tried to hide the pain, but I could still see it. Whether it was from his leg or his heart, I couldn't be sure.

"Andie." He nodded. "Have a seat." He gestured to the side of the bed closest to him and I walked around to sit down. I wanted to hug him. I wanted to pour my heart out to him about how sorry I was that he was going through all of this. But I sensed it wasn't wanted.

"How are you?" I breathed. "I mean how are you really? Please don't try to hide anything from me."

He still studied me with little to no emotion. "I'll be fine." His jaw clenched, but his eyes didn't move from mine. The steely look in them had nothing to do with their color.

I watched him, realizing that something more than his missing leg was different. His entire demeanor was changed. The caring peacekeeper of our bunch was not sitting before me. Normally, he would have smiled and tried to make me feel comfortable in an otherwise uncomfortable situation.

Not this time.

He sat in silence, and I felt that with just a look he condemned me. I *hated* it. I despised every bit of it. Rather than let the silence fester, I spoke up tentatively. " I hear Pres has been taking good care of you. I've... I've really missed you guys."

I clenched my hands together, twisting them, and looked away. While I pretended to look at the pictures on his wall, I tried to rack my brain for other topics that wouldn't cause hard feelings.

"Yes. She has. We've spent a lot of time together, and I can honestly say that I wouldn't have gotten through all this without her." My eyes swung back to his, and I nodded.

There was really no subject where we were concerned that would be comfortable, so I just bit the bullet and hoped it didn't backfire. I motioned to the injured leg that had an ace bandage wrapped around his knee where it now ended. "Does it hurt unbearably?"

He slowly shook his head, his eyes penetrating mine to the point where it had become uncomfortable. "It doesn't hurt at all anymore. Mom and Dad were able to use a spell to take the pain away. There are moments when I feel a twinge from it, but it's more like a feeling that it's still there. And then I look down, and nope. Still gone. I'm still without one whole leg. I'm still not whole."

I winced. I hated that he didn't think he was whole, and I wondered if he felt that more about his entire self than just his missing leg. At my expression, he finally dropped his gaze from mine and relief filled me. His eyes landed on my hands before traveling up to the dragonfly bracelet and then further to the unalome that rested above it.

"I heard that they found Celeste," he said quietly, his eyes not leaving the intricate symbol.

"Yes. Actually, there's so much to tell you. Rohn, well, Dad... he found her. I still don't know the extent of what she went through but she came back unhurt and well. And my dad? It seems he's back to stay, and we're just getting to know one another finally. It's all a little overwhelming, to tell you the truth."

I wasn't about to mention Hunter unless he did. Nope. I was staying far from that subject.

He snorted before looking back up at me. "You don't have any idea of what *overwhelming* is." For a moment, blue fire lit his eyes as he breathed through his nostrils heavily. It startled me, and as though realizing what he was doing, he swiveled back in his chair to face the window.

I stood up, my heart aching that I had done this to him. There was no doubt in my mind now that he blamed me. For what, I'm sure there was a long list.

"Teagan. I'm so sorry this happened. I never meant for you to be hurt. In more ways than one. You've got to know that," I said quietly behind him.

His head shook slightly as he bowed it.

"You don't get it, do you?" The tension in his voice was palpable. "I can live with my leg being like this. Heck, next week I'll have a prosthetic that the coven is working on, and it will likely be better than the leg I had before. That's not what is wrong with me." He sighed, looking up and out the window again.

"I'm sorry, Andie. I just can't do this now. I'm working out a lot of things, and seeing you again just takes me back to square one. Maybe one day, this all will change, but until then, I need time."

Until then? What did that mean?

I felt heaviness come over me. This was not at all what I expected, and now I realized why no one thought it was a good idea to see him. I only hoped I hadn't made it worse. I couldn't leave like this, though. I had to let him know how I felt. It was up to him to do with it what he wanted.

I stepped up right behind his chair and leaned over, wrapping my arms around his neck and resting the side of my face on his now much longer honey brown hair.

"For what it's worth, I love you. We've been through hell and back together, and you've been the best friend I never expected. I hope one day we can go back to how we were."

I'm not gonna cry, I told myself, but as I let go and turned to leave, I couldn't help the sniffle. "Bye, Teagan," I said as I slipped out the door.

If he responded, I didn't hear it.

It was then that the tears began to fall, and my heart felt like it was breaking. It felt final when I stepped outside, and I wondered if we would ever be able to go back to the friendship that we had before. I know it's silly; we'd only known each other a little less than a year. But we'd spent almost all of our time together. We'd laughed and cried and literally fought battles together.

Was this soul wrenching feeling due to the bond we shared? Maybe. But it hurt.

I knew I couldn't stay here any longer. I needed to get home. I wiped the tears from my cheeks and strode downstairs, finding Pres and Teagan's parents where I left them in the kitchen.

I was immediately struck by the sympathy on Tori's face. I imagine all they had to do was see my red eyes to know how it went. Pres just looked uncomfortable, and Logan, much like his son, had his back to me just staring out the window.

I didn't want to get into it with them. I wanted to mourn what felt like the death of our friendship in peace. "I'm going to go now. Thank you for letting me speak with him."

None of them moved, but they nodded in sync, as if in agreement that my leaving was the best thing.

Immediately, I pulled on my anger, wiping away any sadness that lingered. I thought about how angry I was at this situation-and at myself. It wasn't long before the kitchen before me retreated and I was back in my room at the Oak.

I didn't want to see anyone or explain anything. I wanted to wallow in my grief alone. Flinging myself to the bed, I buried my nose in the pillow and let it all out. It felt irrational and juvenile, but I couldn't help it. I couldn't stop it.

When I was drained and the sobs slowed, I rolled over and stared at the ceiling. This was stupid. I was being stupid. I should have listened to the people who told me I wouldn't help him, that it would lead to nothing good. *When* would I learn?

Despite being mentally exhausted, my body felt anxious and I couldn't lie here anymore wallowing. I blew my nose and washed my face and decided there was no time like the present to get busy. I needed to find information on Helios.

Chapter Eleven

It was late by the time I'd finished feeling sorry for myself, and when I left my room, the tree was silent. Eira and Balwyn had long since retired to their respective rooms.

I glanced up the stairwell. *So which floor do I search tonight?*

I started up and kept going until I reached the eighth floor. It was one that I had avoided all together before, and I can't really say why.

Anytime I'd passed it, I'd always get the same feeling that oozed into me now. As if something warned me away. It made goosebumps run the length of my body and the hairs on the back of my neck stand up. It wasn't an ominous feeling, just one that told me to turn around and go somewhere else.

I pushed it down.

Squaring my shoulders, I moved to the double doors that stood open, light filtering out into the hall. The closer I got to them, the stronger that strange sensation became. It felt as though I were slogging through muck and it was a huge effort to move each foot.

You know those dreams you have? Where someone is chasing you and you're in slow motion, and no matter how much you try, you don't get anywhere?

That's what this felt like, and panic surged inside me.

It's just a spell Andie. Nothing to be frightened about.

When I finally stood in the doorway, it felt electrified. I was certain that if I looked in a mirror, my hair would be standing on end.

I couldn't focus on the entirety of the room. At that point, all my focus was on breaking through the barrier that wanted to keep me out.

I chanted the same spell I had used to break the barrier outside Finias. Luckily, this one wasn't quite as strong and fell after four attempts.

Immediately, the goosebumps left, my hair fell and the pressure that had mounted left, pushing past me and down the stairs.

The magic had taken a lot out of my already exhausted body, and I slumped against the doorframe, my eyes trying to take in everything before me. It was a huge room. I couldn't figure out how it fit in the tree, but nothing about the Oak made sense.

Such was magic.

There was no furniture in here, no fireplaces. Nothing beautiful bobbed around in the air, and there were no books. None at all. But what it did have were dozens and dozens of the fairy pictures, or portals as Celeste had called them. Each one different.

The landscapes and interiors of buildings seemed to be from a myriad of places, all beautiful and other worldly. Fairies and creatures of all kinds, some I'd never seen before and had no idea what they were, moved around, going about their daily business. Unaware that someone watched them.

It was amazing.

I walked the length of the room, staring into each one, and felt like a child again.

No wonder the room had been warded so well. Any one of these could be a vessel for someone to step into and travel to places that were only meant for our eyes. I could only imagine the damage that Freya would cause if she were able to get in here.

I only hoped that once I left the room, the wards would go back up. I'd need to test it.

Halfway around the room, one of the portals caught my eye. Not because there was anything fantastical about the place it encompassed but because it, in all its natural beauty somehow spoke to me.

The side of a moss-covered mountain greeted me, stone peeking out in different places. In the crags naturally formed down it, were small waterfalls, at least five, and they emptied out at the bottom into a rocky, pebbled river. A dark cave peeked out from behind the bottom falls and mist hung in the air above the top of the mountain.

Nothing moved but the water. No one seemed to be around. It was a beautiful and lonely place. I pulled myself away from it to peruse the rest of them, but I couldn't get it off my mind and eventually went back to stand in front of it.

If I stared hard enough, it seemed as though I could hear the crashing of the water as it tumbled down against the rock face of each crag, and somewhere a seagull cawed.

My eyes ran over the picture again and again, stopping at a slight movement outside the dark cave. Something small and white moved from behind the water before hopping into the cave and disappearing, but it was too fast for me to see what it had been.

I reached forward with my pointer finger, not giving one thought to what I was actually doing and moved my finger against where the white thing had disappeared.

It all happened so fast. In zero to sixty seconds, my thoughts went from, "What is that?" To, "Oh, crap," as my finger made a ripple in the landscape before I felt the tug and I was pulled in.

The wind ripped through my hair as I found myself pressed against the side of the mountain, water rushing down beside me. The mist that hung in the air clung to my skin, making it damp and cold.

I looked down. I really shouldn't have.

The bottom seemed a million miles away. Okay, that was an exaggeration, but still. How the heck was I going to get down there? I cursed the portal. It could've put me at the bottom. But *no*. It had to put me halfway up this dang thing.

The chill in the air took my breath away as another blast of wind hit me, blowing my body back against the rock again. I needed to get down from here, and quick.

I studied the outcropping of rock that I stood on. It was maybe three feet all around. I squatted carefully and looked below me and to my surprise it seemed that there was another platform just like this one a few feet below, and another below that in haphazard fashion. As if a crude kind of staircase had been carved out of the rock a long time ago. The moss grew over spots, making it hard to realize that was what they were, but it was definitely a way down.

I straightened up and gingerly, still holding onto the rock behind me as best I could, lowered my right foot until it found purchase. I pushed a little to make sure that it was stable, and when it didn't budge, I moved my other foot down to join it.

I maneuvered like a snail down each one, afraid that if I relaxed, one of these might crumble below me, plunging me to my death. By the time I finally reached the bottom, my legs were shaking from the cold and my fingers were numb. I wasn't dressed at all for the cold. But then again, I hadn't planned to go anywhere either.

I plunged my hands into the pockets of my jeans, trying to warm them up as I looked around. Ahead of me was an ocean, the waves angry and crashing against the rocky shore. And behind me the mountain range stretched as far as I could see, and I wondered what was beyond them. Where was I?

I needed to warm up quickly, and the cave behind the last waterfall caught my eye. The fact that it was off to the side of the falls was a relief. I could make a fire in there and then figure out how the heck I was going to get back home. There was no artifact this time to take me back.

I scrambled over the small boulders until I stood looking into complete darkness. The cave looked a lot bigger in person than it did when I'd looked at it from the portal room. I only hoped that there wasn't anything living inside of it. I really wasn't in the mood to defend myself right now.

Conjuring up a ball of light, I let it float ahead of me, lighting the way. The cavern inside was too large for its glow to illuminate all of it, but from what I could see, it was an ordinary cave. Nothing unnatural or scary looked to be about, and there were no other openings leading further inside. It was just one big area with a few large rocks and driftwood littering the floor around it.

I gathered some of the rocks and placed them in a small circle away from the opening where the wind blew in and lit a fire. The magical flames helped to light the room up more, and my body began to warm.

I sat there for a while, my hands to the fire, contemplating my options when I remembered the phone in my back pocket.

Please work!

I pulled it out and saw that I was barely getting a signal and the battery was almost dead. But thank the stars I had it!

Maybe I could get a call out to Celeste and she could tell me what to do, or even better, she or Rohn would come get me.

I chewed my lip, thinking about how mad they'd be with me, but shook the thought away. Besides, Celeste was well aware of my ability to get myself into trouble. Despite the 'new Andie,' that hadn't changed.

I tapped her name, and nothing happened. I got up and raced to the cave opening, holding the phone up and to the side, trying anything for it to start dialing. It was only when I bent low to the ground with it that anything happened and after the third ring, she picked up.

I rushed on before she even got a hello out. "Celeste! I need you to help me out. I, uh... went through one of the fairy portals in the Oak and now I've no idea how to get back home."

"What? It's hard to hear you. Did you say fairy portal? Andie, which one?"

I explained what it looked like, but when she didn't answer, I looked at my phone only to see we'd been disconnected and my battery light was flashing. I only hoped she'd heard me and would be here soon.

I hurried back to the fire and huddled around it, watching the opening of the cave, and hoping Celeste would walk through any minute.

A short time later, I heard a noise, a scuffling from outside and my heart soared.

She's here!

I rushed to the entrance and looked out, but there was no one.

The noise sounded again, but this time closer, and I looked toward where it came from. There on the ground by the wall of the cave opening was a snow-white ferret scurrying inside. It had to be what I'd seen moving in the picture!

As I shifted my feet to watch, it stopped and looked at me. Its gray eyes seemed to look me over with an intelligence that most animals didn't have. Its tiny pink nose twitched in the air as if smelling it.

When it seemed satisfied with what it found, it reversed its course that would have taken it deeper into the cave, and instead marched its way over to stand beside my feet and stare up at me.

I stared back, hesitant, because I knew from past experience that not all animals were actually animals. It didn't move and continued to look up at me, and at one point turned its head to the side and made a chittering noise.

It had to just be a ferret.

"What's up, little dude? Are you as lost as I am? I can't imagine what you're doing here all alone." I blew out a breath and squatted down, putting myself closer to it, but kept my magic at the ready should I need it.

Despite some of my bone headed moves in the past, and err… just recently, I didn't plan to let this cute thing lure me in only for it to then strike.

But still it sat there, turning its head from side to side as if asking a question of me.

Slowly, I reached forward and ran a finger over its head. The fur was soft and silky. When I did, it ducked its head to rest on the toe of my shoe, and I swear it purred.

We sat like that for a few minutes before I stood back up, cold and wondering where the heck Celeste was. I hurried back to the fire and sat down close to it, trying to warm back up only to notice my little friend had followed and sat right beside me, looking into the flames.

Every so often, it would look up at me. I wasn't sure if it was a she or a he, but did it really matter?

It pushed its side up against my crossed leg, seeming to try and get as close as possible to me.

What was up with this thing?

I looked back at the entrance and still no Celeste. I began to wonder if she'd even heard half of what I told her before we got cut off.

I scooted a little further away from the creature that seemed determined to end up on my lap as it kept moving a little closer after each time it looked up at me. But it didn't matter. As soon as I moved, the thing moved with me.

I sighed. "Hey, little guy, erm… hey. You wouldn't happen to know of a way out of here would you? Don't get me wrong, you're sweet and all, but I really need to get home."

Great, here I was talking to it like it would respond. But what better things did I have to do?

It blinked at me slowly before swiveling its head around a few times. Then out of nowhere it jumped right at me, swirling its little body around mine and I waved my arms around, startled at what it was doing. I tried to grab for it but the quickness with which it moved put it beyond my grasp each time I reached for it.

When it had gotten to the top of my hair, it curled its tail around my forehead, and I felt tingling begin. Sparkles lit up the air around us, and I shook my head trying to dislodge it, but its little paws reached out, grabbing each of my ears, and held on tight.

As the vision of the surrounding cave walls disappeared, I kicked myself for not trying to sift. It seemed like the excitement from that darn ferret running up me set it in motion. I had no idea where I was headed because in my bewilderment, I hadn't pictured anywhere in my mind.

Somehow it didn't matter, though, as I reappeared in the forest with the Oak standing before me.

Pressure on my head alerted me to the fact that it seemed I also had a stowaway. I plucked the cheeky creature from my head and held it out in front of me. The innocent-looking eyes only blinked back while its tail curled around my hand.

Why does it have to be so cute?

"Come on. Guess you're here to stay until I figure out what to do with you." I walked to the door in the tree and unlocked it with one hand. "Don't you have someone who's missing you? We ought to get you back." I frowned at it while it continued to stare at me.

"What ta blaze is that?" Balwyn bellowed from in front of his hidey hole.

"Hey, calm down. You'll scare it," I admonished. Though it didn't look scared at all. It only looked around before scrabbling at my hands and squirming so much that I couldn't hold onto it anymore.

Eira appeared right as the animal hit the ground and then darted off down the hall toward my room. "Let me guess. You went on another adventure and this time brought a souvenir home." She laughed at the look on my face at her joke. "Sorry, sorry. But it was funny." She smiled.

"Balwyn, call Celeste and let her know Andie's back. Andie, you're going to be the death of us, truly," she sighed and flung herself dramatically on the couch.

"Well, I'm back now so all is okay. And it was a rather uneventful trip at that. I mean, nothing extraordinary happened."

Balwyn's face turned purple as he heard the last of what I said. "So ya think tat just amblin' wherever ya please, hangin' up in ta middle of frantic phone calls, and bringin' home a familiar is normal?"

He shook his head roughly and went to his room before I could reply.

I looked from his doorway to Eira, processing the last part of his rant.

"Wait. What? Familiar? You mean," I looked down the hall, "snowflake in there is a familiar? Like, a witch's familiar?"

Eira giggled and turned on her side, propping her head up with her hand, and she winked. "Oh yeah, that's definitely your familiar. We were beginning to wonder if you'd ever be graced with one."

Apparently, the look on my face was enough to cause her to dissolve into a fit of laughter, and I patiently waited for her to stop the rolling around and deep belly laughs.

I closed my eyes and took a deep breath. "Are you done now?"

She hiccupped and nodded, wiping her eyes before sitting up straight and trying to look properly serious. The tilt to one side of her mouth gave her away.

"Okay, so that little white thing that clung to me when I sifted back here is my familiar. What am I supposed to do with it now? I have no idea what all this entails. Scoot over." She moved over and I sat down beside her.

Balwyn's voice rang out again, yelling from his hole. "A familiar is an entity tat helps you wit your magic and powers! If ya's gifted wit one, you is blessed indeed. Even yer father and most of ta clan ain't gifted with a familiar!" he hollered. "It ain't common."

Wow. The things you learn. I figured by the time I was an old lady I might know half the stuff I should.

I rolled my eyes.

"Okay... but what do I do with it? I have no idea how to care for a ferret. What's it like to eat and drink, where will it stay, and all that jazz?" I hollered back.

Eira was enjoying our back and forth, and pretended she was eating popcorn, all into our discussion. I just shook my head at her with a smile.

"Ya's not a dimwit, but ya's acting like a dimwit!" he hollered again. "It twill go where ya go, all the time. It'll tell ya what it eats and drinks and tat's all." I heard mumbling follow and I didn't want to know what names he might have been calling me.

Eira raised her eyebrows up and down and mock frowned with her hands on her hips, imitating Balwyn's sour mood. I chuckled behind my hand and didn't respond to him. I figured he'd had enough of my obnoxiousness.

"I'm going to see if I can find the little dude, I mean 'it,' and see where it's hiding out."

I turned to walk down the hall, and Eira called out, "It's a 'she,' Andie. Hopefully, that helps."

"Okay. Thanks. Now I've got to figure out a name for her, unless she's got one already that I don't know about?"

Eira shook her head. "Nope, that's all on you. Pick a good one!"

Chapter Twelve

I found my door ajar, and when I looked inside, the little furball was curled up on my pillow fast asleep.

She really was cute. She looked like a little round snowball. I liked the idea of having another female around, even if it was a ferret. It didn't seem that she talked like Emric and Charlie, but I hoped she could give them a run for their money on personality.

I sat beside her on the bed, and she cracked an eye open. Seeing it was just me, she snuggled back in.

"Andie..." I heard my name called from the hall, and then the door opened. Celeste poked her head in, her eyes going directly to the soft animal.

"Well, I'll be," she said, coming into the room further.

"I often wondered if this day would come." She looked at me smiling. "It's not every day that you see a witch or warlock with a familiar. I've only known one other who had one, and it was an awfully long time ago."

I rubbed the soft fur and looked back at Celeste. "I guess I don't understand. From all the stories, familiars were quite common for witches. But of course, those were just books I read, and this is real life. So why is it so uncommon?"

She sat beside me, hesitantly reaching out to rub the small creature. It looked up at her for a moment as it felt her touch but seemed to give a seal of approval with the closing of her eyes.

"Well, familiars are mystical creatures, and one has to have quite a lot of magic and powers to call one to them. They have the ability to know when they're needed, so this little gal must have known that she was needed. While I don't approve of you breaking into the portal room and letting your curiosity get the better of you, it seems that she may have had a hand in it as well and compelled you to do so."

I looked at her sharply and smirked. "So maybe I'm not as impulsive as everyone thinks I am?"

She inclined her head and smirked also. "Well, you're still impulsive at times, but let's just say I think this one was out of your control." She laughed softly before hugging me to her. "I'm glad you're okay. Your father is outside, do you want to see him?"

I jumped off the bed. "Are you kidding? Yes!" And out the door I went.

He was waiting in the main room, and I'm not ashamed to say that I moved pretty fast toward him. And I'm also not ashamed to say that when he grabbed me in a tight hug, I felt like a little girl. Loved and comforted by his arms.

"I heard you went on a small adventure." He laughed, and I realized that he and Celeste hadn't really been worried. If anything, the phone call getting cut off probably worried them more.

"Yeah, an unplanned adventure which I seem to be having a lot of lately." I laughed.

He nodded and sat down. "So what's this Eira was telling me about a familiar?" Excitement lit his eyes and I realized that it had to be just as much a surprise for him as for me and everyone else.

"Well..."

A noise stopped me from continuing and I looked to see the object of our discussion sauntering in slowly. She stopped at my feet, stared at my father, and then dismissed him before hopping up to land in my lap.

"I've got to name her, but I'm not sure what yet. Eira said it needed to be something good." I frowned down at her.

"You'll think of something. And it doesn't have to be something spectacular. It's just a name. You'll want it to be something easy so that when you call for her you don't have any issues. She's a pretty little thing," he commented.

I nodded and leaned back, suddenly tired. Anytime I traveled through portals it wore me out.

I went on to tell them all about how it happened, describing the place I'd been to, but really there wasn't anything super exciting to share. I decided not to mention my visit to Teagan. If someone told them about it, then I'd discuss it, but I needed to let his parents and Pres handle him. When or if he ever decided to talk to me again, I'd broach the subject.

We chatted for a bit more until I told them I needed to get some rest. I could barely hold my eyes open. They left, and I carried my new friend back with me. We curled up on the bed and fell fast asleep.

∞

I woke up the next morning with a fluffy tail in my face, and a vague memory of stars swirling through my dreams. It had been beautiful and reminded me of the spell room. Serene and quiet.

I pushed the white tail away from my nose and looked down to see that she was gazing at me with those gray eyes, and it seemed perfect.

"What do you think about the name 'Star?' I think it fits you perfectly."

She stretched, and I swear her head nodded slightly. I scratched her head, stretching my legs out too. "Then it's set. Star it is."

At breakfast, I sat down to eggs and bacon with a side of toast. I guess Balwyn had forgiven my stupidity and was back to making sure

I ate and took care of myself. I'd gotten a bowl and filled it with water for Star, which she lapped at greedily, and afterward she'd hopped up on the table and put her paw on my toast.

Assuming this was her telling me what she wanted to eat, I tore it into small pieces and sat them on the table beside my plate. She looked at me and back at the toast.

"Go ahead. It's yours now."

She delicately snatched up each crumb, chewing slowly around each one before getting another. I was done with my food before her. She ate so *slowly*.

While I waited on her to finish, I thought about how no one had seen or heard a peep from Freya recently.

I felt like it was only a matter of time. We knew she'd been injured, so it was my opinion that she was nursing her wounds but once healed, watch out. She'd be back with a vengeance.

In no way did I think she would give up. Not until she was dead, anyway. And if Helios was pulling her and the Fomori's strings, it was going to be much worse than last time. We were only two Keys away from having them all. They couldn't be happy about that.

The next week was interesting. I didn't leave the Oak once, but Star and I practiced our magic together, in and out of the spell room. It was something to behold. The first time we'd tried, I wasn't sure how to do it. I took her to the spell room, sat her down beside me, and tried another spell from the spell book.

This one was a hearing spell. Whoever used the spell would be able to hear a conversation over a mile away.

When I began, the usual pull of magic rippled through me. But as I got to the middle part of the chant, I felt... actually *felt* another magic intertwined with mine, pushing up and out. It reminded me of all the times I'd lent my magic to Teagan when he needed it, but this was stronger.

Within one minute of completing the spell, I could hear Eira singing as if I were right beside her. I know, that's not a mile away, but really if I tried something that far, all I'd hear would be animals and bugs. So I'd focused on her, and wouldn't you know, I could hear every word that she sang as if she stood beside me.

Each day after that, we tried another, and another spell and each one worked out perfect. It was amazing.

I tried to reward Star with different goodies, but she'd always turn her nose up. Since the only thing I'd ever been able to get her to eat was toast, I had asked Balwyn to set up a table in the main room with a toaster and bread so I wouldn't have to disturb him when she was hungry.

He did so with just a little grumbling. I think he was just happy that I had her to keep me busy and out of trouble.

Halfway through the week, I'd called Killian. It had been so good to hear his voice and speak with a friend who seemed happy to talk to me. I'd told him about the visit to Teagan, and he hadn't seemed surprised. Instead, he seemed a bit jealous when talking about Pres being there with Teagan. He said that she still hadn't called him, and it just blew my mind. She had been all about Killian before and now she wouldn't even call him when she had his phone number? It didn't add up.

I'd hung up with him after getting a promise that he'd visit me very soon. Things just weren't the same without him.

A few days later, I decided to call Presley. I was a little nervous about it, seeing as she hadn't contacted me, just like she hadn't contacted Killian, but I wasn't going to be that friend who just gave up. It wasn't in my DNA.

It rang and rang forever until her voicemail came on. I was disappointed because part of me knew that she just wasn't answering me. I left a message and hoped she would call me back.

Star followed me everywhere and at first it was kind of annoying. After a couple of days, though it seemed normal, and today I decided we should get out of the Oak and go visit Celeste and Dad. I wasn't going to sift, though. I wanted to walk through the forest and get fresh air.

So off we went, my little sidekick and me.

It was fall now and the leaves had changed to oranges and browns. The forest floor littered with the crunch of them. I'd put on a sweatshirt before I left, more for Star than myself. Fall weather in Texas usually isn't too cold until you get into late November. I worried that even with her fur, due to her size, she might get chilled. And there was no way I was going to dress her up in little outfits like some people did with their dogs. If she got cold, I'd put her inside my sweatshirt to keep her warm.

Celeste's house came into view ahead, and Star pounced beside me. She seemed excited about getting out also.

Rohn was outside raking leaves into a large pile by the patio and waved when he saw me, wiping sweat from his brow. "Looks like you've been working hard out here," I noted as I walked up to him. "But wouldn't it be easier to just use your magic to get all the leaves raked up?" I scrunched my nose as I looked around.

He laughed and agreed. "Of course it would be. But Celeste has a strong 'no magic' outside rule unless it is imperative in a dangerous situation. You never know when someone might show up."

Made sense, but I still thought it was a waste of time to do all that work.

"Plus," Dad said, "it's good to get physical activity and actually feel like you're doing something and not cheating at it." He leaned against the rake.

Dang. Even though he hadn't heard my thoughts, that sure put them in their place.

"Yeah, I guess you're right."

He smiled at me and began raking again. "What's up? Feeling a little cabin fever out there?"

"It can be kind of isolating, I guess. Not a lot is going on right now and with online school... well it's just boring. Don't get me wrong, I love Balwyn and Eira, but there's only so much of their bickering that I can take." I laughed, and he did as well.

I sat down in one of the patio chairs and watched him work.

"Has there been anything new on the Freya front?" I picked at my cuticles and was surprised when he nodded.

"Actually, yes. Just yesterday, in fact, we received word from Aine that she was spotted in Spain by a shifter clan out there. We're working on getting a location and from there, we'll try to monitor her whereabouts if we can. Though as you know, if she sifts to a different location, we'll need to start all over. At least all of the different clans and packs are on the lookout more now than ever."

Great. I'd hoped for a little more time off before things started picking up again. But I guess at the same time, the sooner we got on with it, the better.

Chapter Thirteen

Over the next two weeks, there were sightings of Freya all over the globe. She was sifting all the time, as if teasing the many different groups keeping watch for her. It was only a matter of time before she showed up here, and we knew it.

Daily, I practiced my fighting moves and spells. I wanted to keep sharp and if I didn't particularly feel like working on magic, Star made sure to push me. Even though she had never spoken a word, she had a sassy way of pushing you to do things. She'd bug you relentlessly until you figured out what she wanted, but I felt like I was getting the hang of reading her.

Today, Killian was coming to visit, and I couldn't have been more excited. I finished my schoolwork early in the morning and got my spell practice out of the way. Now, Star and I sat on the couch anxiously waiting. I couldn't wait for him to see her. I knew he'd likely think she was awesome.

My leg bobbed in impatience, and my mind wandered to Hunter. I hadn't heard a word from him.

I knew he was probably terribly busy with his training and figuring everything out, but I missed the time we'd had together at the castle. I told myself that when he was done doing whatever it was he did, we'd plan to get together and work on us. I just hoped he wasn't gone long.

My thoughts were interrupted by Killian sifting in. This time, I'd warned Balwyn, and he made sure to put out the fire in the hearth.

Star stood at alert on my lap as she spied Killian kneeled before us. It was kind of hilarious. Her nose pointed down, eyes wide, and her fluffy tail stuck right out behind her. She was in full attack mode should she feel I was threatened.

Killian stood to his full height and turned around, his eyes lighting on the two of us, rounding big when he spied my new friend. She sniffed the air again, and then backed down.

I ran my hand over her back and cuddled her close as I smiled innocently at our visitor. "What? Haven't you seen a familiar before?" If his eyes could get any larger, I'd worry that they would pop right out of his head.

I chuckled and stood up, putting her down on the couch behind me as I hugged him.

"A familiar, you said?" He let me go and in shocked silence walked closer before bending down to look at her up close.

"Well, aren't you pretty," he crooned but didn't reach out. "You're going to help out Miss Andie, aren't you, little one?"

Star blinked and ducked her head, then tentatively moved closer to where his hand rested on the edge of the cushion. Killian didn't say a word and sat still as a statue. She looked up at him, blinked again and then nudged his hand with her little pink nose.

"She wants you to pet her now," I stated, and he looked back at me.

"Okay. I wasn't sure if it was all right to." He lifted his hand and ran his palm over her back, and then did it again. Star vibrated with happiness and then rolled over, giving him her stomach to pet as well.

It was amazing because she'd never acted like this with anyone but me. She must have sensed the innocence and goodness in him like I did.

"I think she likes you," I said and sat back down. "She doesn't let anyone rub her like that besides me."

He gently picked her up and sat beside me with her on his lap. "Really? Well then, I'm honored. What's her name?"

"Star. I named her that after I had a dream about stars sparkling in the sky, but now I think she somehow led me to it. Although she's kinda prissy, so it fits her in more ways than one." I laughed and she shot me a look before going back to enjoying the attention.

"Anyway, I am so glad you're here. How long can you stay?"

He looked up from Star and around the Oak. "Well, actually, I'm here to stay for a while. Think you guys can put up with me for that long?"

I was giddy with the news, and so it seemed was Eira. She must have been eavesdropping because she flew in right then and smacked right into Killian's forehead, her arms splayed to the side in a hug. It was so funny because it rather reminded me of a bug hitting a windshield.

She then proceeded to press a million tiny kisses above his eyebrows while he chuckled, and Star faintly growled. I guess she didn't like sharing.

"Ya's gonna smother ta kid if ya keep it up." Balwyn shuffled in and hopped up onto his chair, gruff like normal. Except I saw the twinkle in his eyes. I think he rather liked company more than he let on. Or maybe it was just that he liked us.

"All right, all right." She hovered in the air before us. "I'm just so happy you've come. And of course you can stay here however long you like. I'll get a room fixed up in a jiffy for you. Oh, this will be so much fun!"

Balwyn scowled at her as she flew off to presumably fix up a room.

"I guess you've heard that Freya has been sighted in different places?" I asked Killian, and he nodded. "I just think it's strange that she doesn't seem to be causing any trouble at all."

And it was true, she hadn't been. From the reports, every time she was seen, she was alone.

"Not yet," Killian said, his brows scrunched. "But that doesn't mean it's not coming."

I agreed.

"Well, we all know it's coming-it's just when. I hate surprises, and I still haven't found anything here about Helios yet. Not that I haven't tried." I frowned.

"Tat's cause you ain't searchin' in ta right places," Balwyn offered.

I turned to him with my brow raised, and patience at a minimum. "Are you telling me you know where to look? After all this time of me searching?"

He gave me a look like I was crazy. "I ain't know where ta look. I's just sayin ya have ta look in ta right places!"

I groaned. "Balwyn, that's really not much help."

He scowled, and Killian broke in. "Hey, we can both look together. That'll cut the time searching in half for you, and it'll be fun."

He grinned at me, and I patted his shoulder.

"Thanks. There's got to be something. I've just had this weird feeling lately. Maybe it's just from the news about Freya, but it's almost as if there's something in the air. It's strange."

"It's not strange at all." Killian ran his hand over Star again. "We've all felt it. In fact, I mentioned it to Aine before I left, and she agreed. She said it was time to get ready."

"Well, if anyone knows for sure when it was time, it's Aine," I said, resigning myself to the fact that I'd be donning my suit again very soon.

I wasn't sure I was ready. I mean, I was ready to take out all my anger and frustration on Freya. I hoped we could finally end her. But no one knew exactly how the Helios factor would play out. What kind of power was he giving to her? Would she be even more powerful this time?

There were so many unanswered questions, and I knew we wouldn't have answers until we were in the thick of battle. We'd need to be prepared for anything.

Killian and I trained together later that day and he certainly seemed to be impressed with my growth in performing spells. Of course, I gave a lot of credit to Star. We even worked on a few fighting moves, and it was my turn to be impressed with him. He had a graceful but deadly way to his movements. I had to commend Kitt for how well he trained Killian.

By the end of the day, we were both exhausted, and after saying goodnight, we retired to our respective rooms. His was just down the hall, and I smiled to myself as I lay in bed, Star curled up around my head. It was nice having a friend here besides Eira and Balwyn. Someone my own age who I could tell nerdy jokes with and they would actually laugh instead of rolling their eyes.

Fire raged on either side of me.

Blue waves of heat on one side and orange on the other. I strained to keep them both back. To keep them from obliterating myself and the users who wielded them. My muscles ached with the physical strain of pushing with my magic so much and my stomach ached. My head felt as though it would split open. I couldn't see who fought so hard against me and each other through the flames, no matter how hard I tried.

I woke up drenched in sweat, and Star pawed at my hair, mewling.

Breathing hard, I wiped the wetness from my face and shushed her.

It had been a while since I had a dream like that, and I hoped it wasn't a vision. It was more than likely just caused by the discussion Killian and I had yesterday and worrying about finding information on Helios. That's what it had to be.

My mind kept on, though. Going back to the blue fire, over and over. There was only one kind of fire like that, and Teagan was the only one I knew who had the power to harness it. And then I remembered the flash of blue in his gray eyes when I visited him.

I wrenched my eyes shut, telling myself it was just a dream, nothing more. I pushed that thought over the other ones that kept trying to smother it until I felt calm.

Star never stopped pawing my hair.

Chapter Fourteen

Killian and I ate breakfast together while Star had her toast. He pointed to her as he took a bite of bacon.

"Does she ever eat anything besides bread?"

I shook my head and swallowed my coffee. "Nope. I've tried, but she refuses." I shrugged. "As long as she's eating, I'm not going to worry about it. If she wants something else, she'll let me know."

He watched her a little longer before turning back to me, an excited glint in his eyes. "Hey! Rohn and Celeste want us to come over for a little bit. I meant to tell you last night but forgot," he said sheepishly.

"Okay, sounds good. I'll go change and then we can head over there."

I dressed in a sweater and jeans, pulling on a pair of comfortable boots, and then jammed my beanie on for good measure. Not that I needed it for its power right now. It didn't work outside the Fae realm anyway. It's just that it was a chilly November morning and I'd woken up cold, unable to shake the chill.

"You ready to go?" I asked as I entered the main room. He looked up at me, dressed similarly for cold weather and smiled. "Yup!"

We crunched through the brittle leaves and pine needles that littered the ground in the forest, Star hot on our heels. Killian kept looking over at me with a funny look, and after the fifth time of doing so, I sighed. "What?"

"Oh, nothing." He smiled as we exited the woods.

Smoke curled out of the chimney of Celeste's house and I walked faster, ready to enter into its warmth. Star must have been cold as well, as she flew ahead of me to wait outside the kitchen door.

"I'm coming, I'm coming," I muttered as she turned in circles.

As I opened the door, she flew into the room and I was right behind her.

"SURPRISE!"

The yells made me jump, and I instantly took up my fighting stance. That only made the people in the room laugh louder.

My eyes tracked around, taking in balloons and the cake on the counter. Amarie and the Elves stood beside Aine, Celeste, and Sari. Even Balwyn and Eira were here. Emric and Charlie sat on a counter waving at me, and I weakly waved back.

"What's going on?" I stammered.

"Why, don't tell me you forgot it was your birthday!" Celeste exclaimed, looking around at the rest of the party goers in astonishment.

My mouth dropped open and I looked again at the balloons, noticing a table off to the side with presents.

It was my birthday, and *yes*, I had forgotten it. With everything that had been going on, half the time I didn't even realize what day it was. It was a good day when I didn't wake up on the weekend to do schoolwork, only to figure out it wasn't a school day.

"Well, uh... I guess I did." I blushed and looked around at all the smiling faces. "You guys didn't have to do this. I know there are so many more important things you all probably want to be doing right now."

Aine came forward and hugged me. "There's nothing we'd rather be doing or that's more important than celebrating your seventeenth birthday with you." She kissed me on the cheek, and then everyone else moved forward to give me hugs-well except for Balwyn.

Celeste moved me around the counter to stand behind the beautiful cake. It was decorated with all different flowers and just gorgeous. Seventeen purple candles stood on top, and she used her magic to light them. As she did, Emric and Charlie broke out in a loud rendition of "Happy Birthday," throwing in some of their own funny lyrics and everyone joined in.

This was my first birthday without Nan, and my heart hurt a bit that she wasn't here. I looked around at all the singing and happy faces, and I knew that even though I'd lost her, this was my family too. My loud, sometimes obnoxious, and crazy, but loving, family.

There were a few people who I wished were here, but I wouldn't think about them now. Nothing was going to ruin this day.

I blew out the candles, and to Eira's egging, I made a quick wish. Emric tried to get me to tell him what it was, but I smarted back that if I did, it wouldn't come true.

Celeste cut the cake and handed small pieces out to everyone, along with glasses of milk. It was the best tasting cake I'd ever eaten, and when I asked her where she'd gotten it, Celeste looked at Sari, who just waved her hand in the air as if it was nothing.

"Thank you, Sari." I hugged her again. It had been a while since I'd seen her, and now her pixie hair was green instead of purple, her eyeshadow matching it.

She hugged me back tightly. "Anything for you, Andie. One of these days I'm going to get you in the café and we're going to see how you're cooking skills are." She winked at me.

"I'd love nothing more than to do that. Hopefully it won't be too much longer."

Rohn grabbed my attention then, as he held out a small box wrapped in white paper with a black bow. "What's this?" I asked taking it from him.

"Just something I've held onto for a little while. I planned to give them to you when you turned eighteen, but I think with all that's going on, now is the time." He smiled gently, gesturing for me to open it.

I slipped the bow off and peeled the paper back. It was a small velvet jewelry box, and when I opened the hinged lid, I gasped at what lay inside.

Two small diamond earrings glittered back at me.

"They were your mom's. I'd given them to her for our second wedding anniversary. They're not magical. There's no power to them, but I wanted you to have something that was hers. That you can wear every day."

My eyes welled at the thoughtfulness of the gift and that they had been Mom's. He pulled me in for a hug and held me tight before kissing my hair and letting go.

I gently took them out, and one by one put each of the glittering gems in my ears.

I'd never take them off.

"Now you've got some bling bling," Emric snorted as he hopped up onto the table that was filled with other presents. "Come here and open the rest of these. I've got a nap scheduled shortly and I don't want to be late for it." He plopped down beside a box that was wrapped in turquoise paper and had a silver bow.

Walking over to the table, I grabbed the bow off the gift and stuck it on top of his head. "There. Now you're a gift too." I chuckled at the forlorn look on his face as he tried to reach up with his paw to knock it off, and each time he failed. The sticky tape on the bottom side was stuck to his fur. He finally gave up, laying his head down on his paws with a sour face.

Everyone gathered around, and I opened up all my gifts, awed at the thought they put into each one. When there were none left, I took pity on Emric and plucked the bow from him.

He immediately jumped up and left, heading toward the sun-room for his 'nap.'

Aine made her way over to me while everyone else was chatting, a card in her hand and a smile in her eyes. "One more." She handed the card to me and then turned to find Rohn.

I looked at the card with my name scrawled across it. I knew who it was from, and my hands shook when I opened it.

The card had a beautiful picture of a butterfly on the front, and the inside was filled with a note from Hunter.

Andie,

I wish I could be there with you to celebrate your birthday. If anyone deserves a great day, it's you. I want you to know that I miss you very much. I know things are weird for you right now. I know that you're hurting not having your friends around. Hopefully having Killian there with you lessons some of that. Even though I'm far away, I can feel your pain. If there was anything I could do to make it go away, I would. I hope one day I get the chance. I want you to know that all those times in the past when I gave you a hard time, it was because I was upset that you were put in this situation. That the world has been placed on your shoulders. I'd give anything to help you hold it up.

I'm sending hugs to you in this card. Maybe one day soon I can give you a real one.

Stay safe.

Hunter.

My heart clenched as I held the card to my chest.

I wished he could be here to hug me too. The fact that he went out of his way to make sure I got this from him meant so much. I would treasure his words always.

∞

IT WAS NICE SITTING together with everyone, relaxing and chatting about lighter things for once. Laughter filled Celeste's house like it hadn't in a long while. She seemed especially happy. My gaze went over to the bookshelf where the Keys we had found resided. It would be a relief when they were all there together, tucked away to be used when needed.

Celeste's phone rang, and she went to answer it. She insisted on an old school phone still, complete with the long cord that always got twisted up. When she came back into the room, her face was pale, and I had déjà vu to another time she'd gotten a phone call and had the same look on her face.

I waited, tense, and all conversation abruptly stopped.

"Freya's here, and she's destroyed the school." Celeste put a hand to her heart and closed her eyes. "Thank god the Timmons had the foresight to close it long ago and no students were there." She sighed, opening her eyes back up and looked around the room.

Dad had stood at the news. A fierceness I had not seen before lit his eyes. "I'm going to check it out and make sure she's not still in town about to do more damage." I stood up too, Killian following. "I'll come with you. Killian, you coming?"

He had the same ferocity that my dad did in his gaze. "Yes, let's go."

Star climbed up my body and wrapped herself around my neck, her little body shaking in excitement or fear. Her power joined with mine as I watched first Rohn and then Killian sift out of the room. I looked at Celeste, and she nodded. "We'll let you know." And with that, Star and I sifted.

The sight before us was something out of a war movie.

Where the school had once stood at the end of Main street, a big black crater smoked and crackled. Nothing, and I mean, *nothing,* was left.

Store owners lined the street, many of them injured from flying debris that had hit their stores from the explosion. They were dazed and looked around in confusion. Sirens weren't far off.

Dad leaned down to me and whispered, "Call Celeste or Aine and tell them to get the coven out here asap. We need to do damage control." I nodded and pulled out my cell phone, hurrying to call them up. I relayed the request to Celeste, and she agreed to get right on it.

As I looked around, I spotted the café and breathed a sigh of relief when I saw that it was undamaged. It was one of the furthest shops from the school. Sari hadn't been happy last time Freya decided to play magical grenades with the town. I didn't want to see her wrath after this.

When I turned back around to look at the school, I noticed the coven had arrived, and witches and warlocks were moving from person to person, spelling them to forget what had really happened. Who knew what the story would be this time, but a tornado definitely wouldn't work.

Some tended to small wounds and cuts, helping out the people who had no idea what happened. Despite the carnage and terror of the situation, my heart swelled with the care that they gave the humans.

Dad walked around the large crater inspecting, and looking for something, what I didn't know. Killian did the same in the opposite direction. I ran to catch up to Killian, and by the time I reached him, I was breathing hard. "What are we doing? What can I do?"

He looked up from the ground where he studied some of the blackened earth.

"We're looking for magical traces. It will tell us what she used to do this." He shook his head, frustrated. "I'm finding some trace amounts but not enough to be conclusive. Hopefully Rohn can find more than I am. Why don't you walk around town and make sure you don't see anything suspicious? If you do, call me, and I'll be right there."

"Right. On it," I called as I backed away, hurrying back to Main Street.

I walked around, skirting debris and everyone who loitered outside. I looked down alleys and inside the shops I passed by. I didn't see anything at all to indicate Freya was still here, not yet anyway. I decided to make a loop around each block on the backside of the buildings just to be sure.

Star still clung to my neck like a soft scarf. Her head twitched this way and that as if on the lookout too. Sometimes, I wished she could speak like Emric and Charlie could. I often wondered what went through her mind. She was definitely intelligent, and of course being a familiar, she wasn't just a regular ol' animal.

I patted her and after seeing nothing amiss, headed back to my dad and Killian.

"I didn't see anything strange."

They both stood together with their hands on their hips, clearly frustrated. "Anything here?" I gestured to the still smoldering hole. They both shook their head and grimaced. Boy, if my dad had a son, Killian would've been the perfect match. Even their movements seemed to mimic each other.

I moved away from them to walk around the same paths they took, and Star moved a little on my neck, her nose pointed into the lingering smoke. "What is it, girl?" I asked her quietly but kept moving.

When I was halfway around, she slinked down my body and ran to a spot where a pile of wood sat, splintered from the blast. I hurried after her, watching her movements as she climbed onto them and tried to nudge the top piece with her nose.

"Hold on, hold on," I muttered as I caught up to her and shooed her away a little so I could move it for her. Hefting the piece up, I pushed it to the side and, not seeing anything, did it again to the remaining planks.

Once I'd moved the final one, I saw what her excitement was about. A small stone glowed green with a pulsing light, and I looked back over to where Killian and Dad still stood, watching me. I waved wildly, and they immediately sprang into a run. Once they reached me, I pointed down at the ground. "What is that? I didn't want to touch it."

Killian looked at it curiously while Dad bent down with a shocked look on his face. He looked back at me, "Can you take a sock off and let me have it? We can't touch this."

I hurried to remove my boot and slipped off the sock that was decorated in daisies, then handed it to him. He stared at it for a moment, before chuckling and shaking his head, then he slid his hand into the sock, and I vaguely hoped it didn't stink.

But hey, this was my dad. I'm certain at one point in my infant-hood he had changed a smelly diaper or too, so what's a smelly sock?

He reached out and grasped the stone that had not yet dimmed. Gently, he pulled the sock back over his hand turning it inside out with the object firmly nestled inside, then knotted it at the ankle. "We need to get this to Celeste and Aine. Killian, find Logan-he's over there somewhere-and tell him we found what was used. We'll fill him in later."

Killian nodded and took off again to the other side and headed down the street. I hadn't realized Logan was here. But of course he was. He was currently head of the coven, and I wondered if Teagan was here also. As we walked back the way we'd came, I tried to glance around for him without it being noticeable. I saw Logan and Killian speaking, and Toni was helping one of the workers from the grocery store, but no Teagan.

Dad took me around the backside of the café where no one was able to see us. "Go ahead and head back-I'm right behind you," he said. Once again, we sifted, and when we arrived back at the house, everyone sat waiting quietly until they saw us and then burst into action.

Following Rohn to the counter, they gathered around as he sat my sock up on it, untied it, and asked for a kitchen towel, which I handed to him.

He dumped the rock out onto it, and a collective gasp sounded through the room.

"So what is it?" I asked, looking at all their stunned faces. Amarie was the first to speak up. Awe and confusion lined her face.

"It is one of the stones from Helios's crown. It is said that each precious stone that lined the golden circlet he wore had different powers. That when he went to war, he had but to throw his crown in the air and they all activated at once, bringing about death and destruction like none other," she whispered, and Aine nodded before following.

"No one ever knew what became of it, but it has been long said that when he was destroyed, the crown was crushed and the stones were flung into different directions, never to be seen again. One went to the north, one to the south, and so on."

Everyone's eyes were still glued to the green light that pulsed from it, and no one seemed to want to get too close.

"So why can't you touch it?" I asked. Maybe it was a stupid question. But hey, you can't learn anything without asking questions. And I was definitely still learning. Dad looked at me then. "No one is said to be able to touch Helios's stones without his power running through their veins. Anyone who does is destroyed on the spot. No matter who they are."

So now more than ever, our suspicions were confirmed. Freya had his power running through her. That's the only way she could have survived touching the stone.

Killian spoke up then, seeming just as confused as I. "But how did she get it if no one knew where it was. If they were flung in different directions upon Helios's death, he wouldn't have even known."

Celeste had been quiet up until now.

"We know that Helios is trying to rise up, and he's using Freya and the Fomori to do so. But there must be someone else involved that we don't know about, which is rather frightful as we have our hands full enough with them. But it had to have been someone who was there all that time ago. So now on top of everything else, we have that mystery to solve." She sighed, sitting down in a chair.

"Were there any casualties or serious injuries?" Her voice sounded tired. I explained to her the scene and that luckily the worst we saw were scrapes and bruises.

Everyone was shaken up and Rohn secured the stone back inside my sock.

"Since this is property of the Titans, we need to get it into safe hands. They'll know what to do with it," he said to Celeste. She agreed, and Aine put in a call to Coeus, who appeared within moments, Rhea and, to my happy surprise, Hunter by his side.

The three of them wore bodysuits much like the ones we had worn on the journey. The men looked fierce and handsome, and Rhea looked completely badass with the top of her hair in braids that cascaded down over the back of her straight hair.

Hunters eyes immediately went to mine and as the older two spoke with our group, he pulled me into a hug, his face against the side of mine.

"I like this even better than the card," I whispered, smiling into his hair. I felt his nod against me, and he whispered back, "I'm sorry your birthday ended with this happening, but I'm not sorry that it brought me to you." He squeezed me gently and then stepped back, looking me up and down.

"Don't worry. I'm whole and okay. Except my missing sock." I pulled up my jeans to show one pulled above my boot and the other my naked skin, before casting my eyes toward the stone-wrapped package.

His lip bowed in the ghost of a smile, and he ducked his head. Clearing his throat, he looked back at me and the scrunch of his eyebrows and tension of his jaw told me that he was trying to stay in serious mode. I couldn't help it though; I'd forever try to make him smile.

Star chose that moment to fly up my body to her favorite spot around my neck, and his eyes opened wide in surprise. I was getting a lot of that lately.

"I'd heard that you got a familiar but... wow! She's beautiful." He moved closer again, his voice soft as he bent down to inspect her. And just like with Killian, she leaned into him. But unlike with Killian she hopped from me to him and nuzzled his jaw before situating herself around his neck.

I was stunned and laughed in amazement. "Never seen her do that before."

Hunter smiled at me as he nuzzled her back. "She's pretty sweet. I think she likes me."

Emric strolled by just then, and with his usual Emricky self, he sniffed and said, "she only likes you because Andie does. Oh, and you smell like Andie. You know that funny little bond you've got going on." And then he walked out, leaving me and Hunter to stare at each other, while everyone around us went silent.

I don't know why it shocked them so much. They knew about it, but I guess hearing it out loud made it more real. Frustration welled inside me again, and Hunter leaned forward, placing his hand on mine.

He had no gloves to hide the fire, and his eyes pierced mine as he made sure everyone in the room heard him. But his words were for me. "There is not one thing wrong with our bond other than the fact that I can't always be here for you when you need me. A higher power brought us together in this way, not you, Andie. This was never your doing. I know you agonized about it, still do. But this was meant to be what would happen. Regardless of what anyone else may think or believe, our bond will last forever and be one for the ages. It's powerful, it's real, and it's ours."

When he finished, the smile that lit his face was a thing of beauty. He rarely smiled anymore and to see it, especially after his powerful words, made my heart soar and a smile stretch across my face, wider than ever before.

And to think I thought that he wouldn't come back to me all those months ago. The despair was almost worth it for this moment.

Coeus interrupted, and it kinda stunk.

"Okay, you two. I'm glad you finally got that out of the way. But now," he looked at Hunter, "we've got to get this back and secure."

I wasn't ready for him to go, but I understood. I reached for him again. I really wanted him to kiss me if I was at all honest, but now wasn't the time or place. I'd settle for his strong hug, albeit a ticklish one with squirming Star between us.

Once again, he whispered in my ear. "Be safe, call if you need me, and please, please don't do anything stupid." He gave me a peck on my temple, and I laughed, grabbing Star back. "That last thing you listed might not be able to be helped."

He smirked. "Nah, you're a lot smarter than you give yourself credit for."

He went to stand beside Coeus and Rhea, who winked at me and blew a kiss. Coeus only nodded to the rest of us, and Hunter fisted his hand over his heart, his eyes blazing into mine. I did the same.

And then they were gone.

Chapter Fifteen

After they left, there was a flurry of activity. Aine and the Elves packed up and prepared to leave to go to the castle. They needed to gather the fairies to scout and the remainder of the Elves to prepare for battle. Celeste called Logan and updated him. He promised to contact all the covens around the world and the shifter packs. They would all need to prepare for what was to come, and also protect the human communities around them.

I watched from my perch on the couch as all of this was done in orderly fashion with little to no worry. My dad sat beside me doing the same. "You know I'm going to have to leave for just a little while don't, you Andie?" he said without looking at me.

I'd suspected he would. If his past were any indication, he itched to get out there and figure out what was going on, or what he could do to help behind the scenes.

"You'll be careful, won't you?" I asked, working to keep the tremor from my voice.

He looked at me then, his eyes full of love. "Always." I have someone very important who I need to make it back home to." He smiled before his eyes turned serious again.

"Promise me that if something happens and you're thrust into the next journey before I make it back... promise me you'll be careful. Use all of the things you've learned and tools at your disposal to get through it. And know that when you return, I'll be waiting."

I nodded.

"And if you don't leave before I return," he grinned with a devilish look, "promise me you'll let me go with you?"

Shock ran through me. "You mean you'd actually go with me?" I asked.

"Of course I will, if I can. I'd love nothing more than to see you through this and help as much as I can. I am your dad, you know." He pushed my shoulder playfully.

"Yes, that you are." I laughed, and Star shifted around my neck.

"I hope you'll be here. I really want us to do this together." He only nodded and pulled me in. "Me too kid, me too."

Later that night, I lay on my bed with Killian stretched out at my feet. I hadn't felt like being alone yet, and this reminded me of the time when we brought him back to Celeste's house and stayed up late talking.

He was currently using his magic to draw pictures for me on the ceiling out of light. It was like our homemade version of Pictionary. He'd draw and I'd try to guess what it was. He wasn't an especially talented artist.

"That's not a horse. C'mon, try harder."

I laughed and studied it again, turning this way and that. "Is it a cow?"

"No! Man, you're terrible at this game. It's a dog. A *dog*, Andie. How could you not see that?"

I bit my tongue, and Star chittered in my ear.

Girl, same.

"Not to be rude, Killian, but that didn't look like a dog at all."

He faked being mad and crossed his arms.

"I think you just need glasses."

"Pshh, whatever," I returned.

What I wouldn't give to have every night be like this. Regular teenagers, having normal fun. Instead, we had to worry about some evil god intent on revenge and his little lackeys who would do any-thing to carry it out for him.

"It's been a good day. Thank you for helping with the birthday surprise earlier. I never got to thank you. I especially like the onesie pajamas you got me with the fairy wings." I rolled my eyes.

Killian laughed and rolled on his side to look at me. "Hey. You're hard to buy for. Plus, it will keep you warm during the winter and re-mind you where you come from."

Again, I rolled my eyes. "As if I could forget."

"Guess who finally called me yesterday?"

I sat up straight in surprise. "Presley?"

He nodded quickly, but there was no smile on his face now. He looked serious.

This isn't good.

"She didn't really sound like herself. I don't know what's going on, and when I asked, she wouldn't say. But there is definitely some-thing." He messed with the covers, his mouth turned down and wouldn't look at me.

"I think she doesn't like me anymore. I actually think she has feelings for Teagan."

I had worried about that too from the way she acted with me, but I didn't tell him that. I bit my lip for a minute before waving my hand in his face to get him to look at me.

He did.

"You don't know that. It's really hard to gauge someone's feelings over the phone or any other way besides in person. Believe me I've had so many thoughts like that about the both of them and how they've acted toward me, but I just keep reminding myself that Tea-gan has been through a lot because of me, and Pres, well, she's trying to help him the best she can. You'd do the same for me. And after I visited him, I can see how easily his attitude would wear on a person. I'm hoping a lot of this will change with them after all of this craziness is over and done. Maybe then you and I can enjoy life like we should have been the last year."

I smiled gently at him, and he smiled back.

Good.

I hoped I had eased his mind some. Sometimes all it took was to vent to your closest friends and have them listen and offer sound advice. Our minds can be a strange place to get stuck in. I would know.

∞

I woke later that night after another horrible dream. It had been so real. I rolled back over, trying to go back to sleep, but the image of Teagan's eyes burning bright blue wouldn't go away.

Sighing, I rolled over and grabbed my phone to see that it was three in the morning. I was going to be so tired tomorrow. When I lay back against the pillow, Star was sitting up, her gray eyes staring at me.

"What? You can't sleep either?" She nudged my shoulder.

"I know, I know. We should just get up and do something then, right?"

She nudged me again. "Okay, okay. I get it."

I got up and went to wash my face, then pulled on a pair of jeans and my hoodie, throwing my hair back in a ponytail.

"So," I looked down at her, "what shall we do then?"

I hadn't expected her to answer, and she didn't really, but she took off to the door and patted it.

Okay...

I opened it, and she sped out into the hallway with me following. The only light illuminating it was the soft glow from the fireplace in the main room.

She raced to the stairs and stood on the bottom step, waiting for me. Once I got there, she raced up to the second floor, turned, and looked at me.

"Seriously?"

I wasn't really in the mood to explore, but she wouldn't leave me alone until I did. She'd badger me with her nudges and whines until I did what she wanted.

She was smart.

"Fine." I said and followed her up and up until she stopped on the eighth floor. She ran around toward the doorway to the portal room, and I groaned.

"Nope. Come on, let's go up a little more." I tried to coax her, but she didn't budge. I even went and picked her up and took her to the stairway before she scrambled back down and ran back to the same spot.

"You are going to get me into so much trouble." I sighed as I went to stand before her.

She then raced up to her normal spot, clinging to my neck, and I felt her magic tingling through me. I concentrated on it and fed mine into it too, and together we broke down the barrier faster than I ever had before.

I was impressed.

Once we crossed the threshold, she skittered back down me, running around the room like a loon, and I swear her little head was turned up and looking at each one of the fairy portals. She'd stop in front of a few different ones, look at them, then scurry away to another. I kinda thought that maybe she just wanted to go back to where she came from. Maybe she did have someone there waiting for her, but nope, she passed by that one without even a glance.

She did, however, stop and not move once she stood underneath a portal with a castle in the background and rolling green hills on either side around a small village. It looked like Ireland, and my heart leapt a little. I'd always wanted to go there, and when I was younger, I studied book upon book of Ireland's legends and even once bought a travel magazine solely devoted to the most beautiful places to visit there.

I guess I stood there too long for Star's patience, for she ran back to me, tapped my shoe, and then ran back. I slowly walked toward her, my eyes on the figures moving around the small town and castle. They looked like regular people, but I knew they weren't. Fairies also flew around the town in between the larger figures.

I bent to pick Star up and looked at her. "So what now?"

It didn't take her long to tell me. With her paw firmly hooked in the neck of my hoodie, she reached out with her other paw, touching the portal.

Here we go...

We landed on one of the grassy rolling hills, and I couldn't see anything else but the castle and town for miles. Star scrambled down from her perch, and I knew it was time to follow her. She seemed to know what she was doing, so I wasn't going to second guess it.

She headed in the direction of the town, and I followed as close as I could behind her. It was probably no larger than Junction but looked quite a bit more primeval. The roads were dirt, and the buildings were made of stone with thatched roofs. People looked up in surprise when they saw the two of us, and I felt a little uncomfortable.

They must have sensed the magic in us, or maybe they knew who I was. I didn't know, but I couldn't imagine any of the magical world not being aware of our past journeys to find the Keys.

Star wound around the ones who had stopped what they were doing to stare, and I greeted them as we passed them by. Finally, she stopped outside a smaller building that had a garden off to the side. Yellow flowers grew in pots on either side of the door. Star nudged the door with her nose, and I lifted my hand to knock.

After I did, movement sounded inside, and I could make out footsteps coming closer. The door opened, and a girl my age stood there; her mouth opened in shock. She was very pretty with honey colored skin, the slant of her eyes accentuated by pink eyeshadow. Dark black hair cascaded to her waist, shiny and sleek. She was tiny, maybe five feet if that, but she looked strong.

"Hi," I spoke up, "uh, I'm not really sure what we're doing here, but Star," I gestured toward her, "my familiar, kinda brought me to your door. So maybe you know?" I questioned with a smile. I didn't want her to think I was crazy, and I absently wondered what kind of magical powers she had.

The girl nodded slowly, looking at Star and then back at me before yelling over her shoulder to someone else inside.

"Trela, come here!"

She looked back at me and smiled, a dimple showing in her cheek when she did. She stuck her hand out and I immediately shook it. Her grip was firm, and that instantly made me like her. Nan always said you could tell a lot by a person's handshake, be it man or woman.

"I'm Bea," she said as the door opened wider and another girl came up behind her. She was the total opposite of Bea, tall, likely at least six feet. Her hair was short and in a curly mohawk on the top of her head, the sides shaved. Her dark skin glistened in the light from the sun, as did the multitude of earrings that lined one ear from bottom to top. She looked even more badass than Sari. Now I was even more intrigued to find out what they were.

"I'm Trela." The girl waved from behind Bea, her voice raspy.

"Hi, Trela. I was just telling Bea here that my familiar," I gestured again to Star, "led me here. I guess she thought I needed to meet the two of you. I'm..."

Before I could get my name out, Bea and Trela interrupted. "You're Andie."

I guess I was right; everyone did know who I was. And by the size of their smiles, they were happy to see me. I laughed. "Well, yes, I am."

They backed away from the door, and Trela headed back the way she came, calling over her shoulder, "Come on in!" Bea shut the door behind us, and I followed her into a small living room filled with all kinds of different things on the walls. It looked as if souvenir shops from all over the world threw up in here.

Trela noticed the attention that I gave to them and grinned.

"It's a bit much, yeah? We travel a lot and always seem to come back with something different from the places we visit. Seems a shame to put them in a cupboard somewhere where no one can see them. Plus, we ran out of room in our bedrooms."

It must be nice to be able to travel all around the world, I thought. "It's umm... different but has a ton of character," I said as Bea gestured for me to sit down.

Trela laughed again. "Honey, it's awful, but we don't mind."

I liked her already. She was open and honest and didn't give a crap what anyone thought.

"I hope you don't mind me prying, but I'm really curious as to what you both are. Or your magical abilities. You seem to know all about me already."

Bea nodded, throwing one leg over the arm of the chair she sat in. The chain on her combat boots caught the light and glinted.

Definitely badass.

"We're dragons," she said simply.

What the what?

I hadn't heard a word from anyone over the last year about dragon shifters.

She must've seen the cynical look on my face because she laughed again and lolled her head toward Trela. "It's true-we're dragon shifters. There's not a lot of us left, and we try to stay on the down-low. Off the radar. You know?"

"I guess so. But why wouldn't you want others to know much about you? Sorry, I'm still learning." I blushed a little.

Trela leaned forward. "Girl, no worries. Right now, I think we're all still learning a lot." She tapped her long nails together. "So here it is. When we," she gestured to herself and Bea, "were babies, most of the other dragon shifters were murdered by Freya and the Fomori. Yeah, there's still a few others left in different countries around the world, but not a lot. We've got to protect our existence as much as possible." She shrugged and sat back.

Bea nodded. "And it's just been the two of us ever since. After our families were killed, Aine took us in. She took us to Talisia where we were raised by a few Were shifters-well, really, the whole town. Once we were old enough, we took off on our adventures, usually at night so we weren't seen flying, and found this place. It works for us, so we stay here when we don't travel."

It didn't surprise me one bit when she told me that the loss of their families was all due to Freya. She'd had a hand in so many tragedies. I don't know how she could live with herself.

"What do you do on your travels around the world?" I asked, genuinely curious.

With no nonsense, Bea stated, "We search for more of our kind."

We sat there for hours talking. Besides Pres, I'd never enjoyed a conversation with other girls so much. They peppered me with questions about what was going on, what school was like-they had never been-and answered all of the questions I had as well.

At some point my stomach had rumbled and Bea laughed and went to their kitchen to scrounge up some food. I was amazed at what she brought back. This girl could cook!

She had a wooden board with different crackers and cheese laid out. Little bites of meat and olives and peppers on the side. After we snacked on that she went back and brought out chicken that she'd roasted with potatoes and broccoli. And she didn't mind at all when I asked if she had some toast for Star. She even cut it up like Star liked it.

When my stomach was full, I sat back and looked around for a clock. I had no idea if the time here was the same as back home, but I was guessing not. I pulled out my phone and figured I'd better let Killian know where I was before he began to worry.

I spoke with him for a few minutes and the girls hung on my every word. When Killian and I hung up, they both leaned forward, curious. "Who was that?" they asked in unison. If they didn't look so different, I'd have thought they were twins.

"Oh, that was my friend Killian. He's the one I told you about who's part Titan, Fae and warlock."

"Ohhhh," Trela breathed out. "I want to meet him. He sounds like fun."

Hmm...

"I'm sure he'd love to meet you too. In fact, he said as much over the call," I said innocently, but really, I had a plan.

Killian was upset because he thought Pres didn't like him anymore, and part of me agreed. What better way to take his mind off of her than to introduce him to some other girls who would love nothing better than to flirt and have fun?

The evil genius inside of me rubbed her hands together.

"Hey!" Bea suddenly yelled. "I've got an idea!"

"Oh yeah, what's that?" I asked.

"We should take you flying!" She squealed again, and Trela nodded in agreement, leaning over to high-five her. "Yes! Let's do it," she said.

I remembered my flight with the Snowflies and how awesome it had been, but I wasn't so sure about riding on a dragon.

"How would I stay on, and not fall off?" I questioned.

They both just stared at me blinking before dissolving into laughter. "You just hold onto our scales silly." Trela laughed. "And if you fall, don't worry girl, we'll swoop down to save your butt."

I looked out the window and saw that night was falling. I didn't want to look weak in front of these girls who seemed to have absolutely no fear. Plus, I was excited to see them change and what they looked like, not to mention the story I'd be able to tell Killian.

I'd made up my mind. "Okay then. Let's do it!" They both high-fived me and whooped into the air. Star just looked unimpressed.

Chapter Sixteen

When the sun was down and the moon was rising, we headed out. There were clouds covering most of the light from the moon so we wouldn't have to worry about anyone seeing. I was concerned that something might happen to Star while we flew, so Bea had fashioned a sling out of one of the sarongs she brought back with her from Tahiti, and we wrapped it around my neck, stuck Star in, and then I pulled my hoodie over it. I pulled the neckline down some so her little head could peek out if she wanted.

We trudged over the hills, away from the town that had come alive with music. Fairies and other shifters danced through the street singing. It really did seem to be a lovely place.

Once the girls were satisfied that we were far enough away, they told me to stay where I was, and then they ran off a little bit further.

The change was much like when Hunter had changed, bones snapping and bending. They'd only worn robes out there and had dropped them where they stood so when we returned, they'd have something to slip back on.

Trela was the first to turn, and as her body grew, changing shape and color, scales popped up, glistening in the waning light. From my vantage point the color of her dragon was dark blue, her scales a mixture of dark blue and silver. She was big. Bigger than I had ever imagined a dragon could be.

Bea's transformation wasn't far behind. Though smaller than Trela, her body looked more muscular. Her coloring was opposite of the other dragon., silver with just a few blue scales here and there.

They stared back at me as I walked closer, awe written all over my face.

Trela leaned her head down, and I grabbed ahold of her scales like she'd told me to and pulled myself up and over until I straddled her neck. They wouldn't be able to communicate with me in this form other than certain motions but would be perfectly able to understand anything that I said to them.

Trela gave a slight stomp, our agreed-upon motion, to let me know that she was about to take flight. I tapped her head and held tight to the scales on her neck, my legs gripping as well as I could around it.

Her wings unfurled and she gave a slow flap, picking up speed and the wind blew my ponytail back with her motions. Little by little, her body lifted up off the ground, Bea's doing the same beside us, and before long we were up high in the sky, soaring through the clouds. They flew side by side, and I squinted my eyes to keep the wind from making them water so much. It was colder up here, but Star kept me warm.

It was so dark that I couldn't really see much until we flew over towns, the lights from below looking like fairy lights they were so tiny this far away.

I thought about how lucky the girls were to be able to see different places from this view and to be able to travel so swiftly and far. Yes, I could sift, but I hadn't tried it on any long distance and wasn't even sure if it was possible.

I looked over at Bea and saw her looking at me, her dragon mouth parted in what looked to be a smile. Then she winked, before turning in a roll and shooting straight down like an arrow before arching her back and flying right back up to us.

"Whoa!" I yelled, hoping she could hear me. "That was so awesome!"

She winked again, pleased with herself, before her head turned to look at Trela, whose head was turned down as we flew, staring at something below us.

Without loosening my grip, I strained my head around to look down as well.

Below us, a fire burned and the longer I looked at the area, I could make out people running around. Wolves running, pulling injured people away, as cries rang out. Trela and Bea looked at each other and it seemed that they decided to help when they both pointed their noses down and we plunged.

I almost think that Trela forgot about me as I struggled to hang on. The deep plunge causing gravity to fling me backward, and my fingers began to lose purchase. Just as I was about to shout, the steep incline leveled out and their feet touched ground, moving quickly at a run to help slow their momentum.

Now that the wind was out of my ears, I could hear the screaming. It must have been what alerted Trela to the problem before she saw the flames.

It was startling and scary and the scene around us was total chaos. Someone on the other side of the blaze was pleading, asking someone to stop. Wait, no. They were *begging*.

There were bodies everywhere, some burned beyond recognition and long gone. Others helped the injured and wolf shifters of every size and color still pulled people from the burning structure.

Trela and Bea shifted, too worried about helping to be concerned with their nakedness. I saw a blanket on the ground nearby and used my magic to rip it in half and then ran and grabbed both sides and handed them to the girls. They thanked me and wrapped the fabric around their bodies in a toga fashion.

"What's happened?" Bea asked the nearest person who was tending to someone injured. The woman gasped and pointed to where the begging could be heard. "The devil. She came," she took a ragged breath, "she wants to kill us all."

The girls and I looked at each other. We knew who it was, and we had to do something. She couldn't get away with this. Not this time.

I don't know what I was thinking. Well, likely I wasn't thinking at all.

I didn't wait on Trela and Bea. I only saw red and all the people who Freya had hurt before flashed through my mind.

I ran. I ran as fast as I could around the blaze, my jaw set, and my magic tingling. Star beat at my neck with her paw while stuck inside the sling. I ignored her completely. Truth be told, I didn't even realize she did it until I came to a complete stop.

I was focused solely on the witch who stood in front of me.

Her hair blew back like a dark wave as the flames grew higher behind her. This time, she was by herself, but the power rolled off of her in waves. I felt more than heard the two dragon shifters fly up behind me.

Freya hadn't noticed me until that moment.

Her head snapped around, and a coy smile formed on her lips. Her blue eyes looked black and sparkled. Before I even had a chance to pull my magic to me, her hand thrust out and her lips went from a smile to a snarl. The power that hit us was indescribable.

We were thrown back at least twenty feet, and I didn't realize it was happening until I hit the ground. All of the air was forced from my lungs, and I rolled to my side gulping, trying to force air in. Trela and Bea laid still on either side of me.

With a rush, air suddenly flooded back into my lungs and I breathed deeply, scrambling to get up. As I did, the two girls groaned, and I thanked the heavens that they weren't dead.

I looked back to where Freya stood and realized that she didn't think I was a threat at all. She had actually turned her back on us to continue terrorizing the people who still ran around in fright. I didn't know what to do. My mind felt foggy from the hit I took, but we couldn't just sit here and let her do this.

Star wiggled inside of her sling, reminding me that she was there. I pulled her out, and she curled around my neck before placing one of her paws against my temple. Instantly, a vision of me in the spell room appeared. I watched my finger move in a clockwise motion before the comet streaking across the wall stopped.

The motion spell. Yes!

"Thank you, sweet girl." I rubbed her head as I got to work.

I kept my eyes on Freya, concentrating on her arms as they shot out in front of her, flames landing wherever she pointed them. My magic rose and the hair on the back of my neck stood on end as I watched Freya's back stiffen before she turned slightly, looking my way over her shoulder.

She must have felt it. I didn't have much time now.

I quickly finished the spell, turning my pointer finger in a circle at the same time that she turned to face me, fury lining her face. She didn't have time to do anything as the spell shot out like a bullet, hitting her dead center, and she froze like a statue.

Trela and Bea had stepped back when they saw what I was doing, but the moment that the spell took effect, they whooped and high-fived me.

I wasn't near as excited as they were. I didn't trust her to not break the spell. Not with the power I had felt radiating off of her. I worried that it was only a matter of time, and unfortunately, I had no weapons at all on me.

"I don't know what to do now," I admitted to the girls. "The only weapon I have is my magic. I can try, but I'm worried her power is too much and she'll break the spell she's under right now." I bit my lip, racking my brain for something that could finally end her while she was in this state.

The spell I used on the trolls where the snake went at them and turned them to stone might work.

"Okay, stand back," I told them. "Let me try something."

Again, Star began to pat my neck, but I didn't have time for it right now. I didn't feel like time was on our side. I rushed to weave the magic and sent it off to slither around Freya. As the magic turned and twisted around her, nothing happened. The ephemeral snake slithered up and down, but it was as if it couldn't penetrate her at all.

It was a huge disappointment.

"Girl, I'll just shift and bite her damn head off," Trela said, shedding the toga blanket.

I guess it was worth a try. I shrugged and nodded, my heart hammering as I stared at the devil in front of me, watching for any movement.

Trela shifted faster this time, the cracking behind me making me wince.

Bea and I moved out of the blue dragon's way as her large feet stomped over to where Freya stood still as death. Trela didn't waste a moment. I could almost see the giddiness to take out her family's murderer glisten in her dragon eyes.

She swooped her head down, jaw open wide, and sharp dagger like teeth dripping saliva. And it was as if her head hit an invisible stone, bouncing off of the top of Freya's head. She tried again and again, and her anger at not being able to crush the witch below her grew with each try until she threw her head back and let out a roar that reverberated around the countryside.

Immediately, she shifted back, slumping at Freya's feet. I rushed over to her and helped her up, slinging the blanket around her shoulder. Bea wrapped her arm around her dragon sister from the other side.

"It doesn't seem that we can do anything else right now to her." I sighed. "We need to get the people who are left somewhere else, though. If and when she's able to break the spell, she's going to be much angrier and I don't want them here to take the brunt of it. Plus, there's nothing left for them here." I gestured around us.

The girls both agreed, and we split up to find anyone we could who was still alive. Once we'd gathered them all together, there were only ten that had made it. Half of those were gravely injured.

"We're going to have to fly them out of here." Bea said. "We should just take them home with us. They're Were shifters and will be welcomed."

I nodded. It sounded like the best course of action. There, the injured could be tended to.

We all agreed, and after explaining this to them, the people were resigned to leave their dead family members behind until we were able to send someone to get them. It was high on my priority list once I got ahold of Celeste or Killian.

The girls shifted, and we hurried to get everyone situated on their backs. I had found some rope nearby and fashioned harnesses, wrapping them around the injured and uninjured so no one would slip off. Once that was done, we took flight. This time, the girls took it easy, knowing they carried precious cargo. I looked back to see the lone figure left standing, illuminated by the flames. She still hadn't moved.

Whimpers and soft cries sounded behind me the whole way back, and it broke my heart. I knew that these people were in shock, the horror of losing their loved ones just now setting in. I wished that there was some way that I could console them. But I knew it wouldn't help.

∞

When we arrived back at the town, the fairies and other shifters surged into action, taking the injured to different buildings to tend to them, and consoling the uninjured in a way that left me feeling as though this had been one hundred percent the right decision.

The whole ride back, I kept thinking about Freya. What had kept her from being harmed while the motion spell froze her in action? I couldn't figure it out, and it scared me to no end. I had no idea how we would be able to end her. Not with the power she now wielded.

It was imperative, now more than ever, that I leave to find the third Key. Then the fourth right after that. If we couldn't get rid of her with our magic, the Keys together would be our only hope.

Trela and Bea were exhausted. The flight with the extra weight had been a strain on them both, and though they smiled and acted like it was no big deal, I could tell. They collapsed onto their couch, and Bea laid her head back in Trela's lap.

They had a remarkably close bond and relied on each other so much, and they'd quickly shown me that I could trust them.

I called Celeste and explained everything to her. She wasn't upset, but at the mention of what happened when we tried to end Freya, surprise was evident in her voice. I wasn't happy about it, but at least now I knew I had done all the right things. It just hadn't worked, and Celeste knew it too.

She agreed that we needed to make arrangements to get ready for the journey, and promised she'd send someone to the ravaged and burnt town to see if Freya was still there and to bury the dead.

When I hung up, both girls stared at me with excitement in their eyes. I had heard them whispering while I was on the phone, but I hadn't paid any attention to them.

"What's wrong?" I asked.

Trela laughed softly and shook her head. "Honey, there's nothing wrong at all. We've decided that we're going to help you with this little quest to find the next Key." I was a little shocked, but the more I thought about it, the more it sounded like a great idea.

They'd proven to me that I could trust them. That they wanted Freya gone as much as the rest of us, and that they had absolutely no fear.

I was already down two people anyway from my last group, and I wasn't sure if Amarie or any of the Elves would agree to go. Not after the loss they suffered the last time. All I knew was that we'd need as many who would be willing. The more powerful the better.

I looked at Trela and Bea, their faces now set in serious lines. "It's going to be a lot more dangerous than tonight was. Each journey has gotten progressively worse the more power she's given. We try to protect each other the best we can, but there have been casualties, and I'm afraid there will be many more. You sure you're up for it?" I asked of the two.

They didn't even hesitate. They only grinned with fierceness in their eyes and simultaneously said, "We wouldn't expect anything less. We'll do it."

Chapter Seventeen

Even though we were all exhausted, I needed to get back. Since they had pledged their help, I would sift them back with me. They'd each packed a light bag, mostly clothes and I looked at Star as the two girls wrapped their arms around me.

"I'm going to need all your magic to help me get us home, okay, girl?" She patted my neck, and I looked at Trela and Bea. "It's now or never." I took a deep breath and pictured Freya in front of the fire and all the anger that I'd felt in that moment came back. It bubbled up with heat and intensity as if I still stood there, Star's magic joining in.

The trip felt a little different. Heavier, well... because it was. It's hard to explain, but it was like literally carrying two people across a room.

I collapsed in Celeste's living room, the three of us tumbling to the floor and I wacked my head against an end table. "Oww!" I cried out.

"Oh, dear, you poor girls. Are you okay?" Celeste ran around the couch and helped us up, checking us out to make sure we were uninjured.

"I'm fine." I sighed. "Just wasn't expecting that."

I slumped against the couch cushion with the girls beside me as Celeste looked us over. We made quick work of introductions, and Celeste made the girls feel welcome. "Let me run and get something sweet along with some warm tea. You girls probably need some sugar after all that exertion."

What I needed was sleep, but I figured it would be hard to come by from here on out.

"She's really something," Bea said, reaching back to gather her sleek black hair, and pull it into a ponytail. With her hair pulled back like tha,t it really accentuated her dramatic eyes.

"Yes, she is. I don't know what I'd do without her."

Celeste came back in the room with the promised treats, and while we snacked, I called Killian to tell him I was back and that I'd brought the dragon shifters with me. It wasn't a minute later that he appeared, walking from Celeste's kitchen, his eyes on Trela and Bea.

"Well, *hellooo* sunshine..." Trela called out when her eyes landed on him. His cheeks turned red, but he sauntered in the room to stand before them.

See? I knew this would happen. I bet right at this moment he wouldn't even remember Presley's name. Not that I wanted him to forget her, or that I was mad at her, just that I didn't want him hurting over her anymore.

And these girls were the perfect distraction.

He was the perfect gentleman, no matter how much Trela and Bea flirted or egged him on. Before long, it was if the four of us had known each other forever as we joked and cut up.

I left them to their fun and went to find Celeste.

She sat in the kitchen rocking chair with Emric and Charlie at her feet. I guess the two of them hadn't felt like being friendly, but I couldn't wait for them to meet my new friends. Maybe once they woke up, I'd take them in there. Emric was no fun when he was tired.

Hopping up on a barstool at the counter, I turned to my guardian. "Have you heard if she was still there or not?" I asked.

"She wasn't there, as you suspected. I imagine the spell held for a while, but if you're right about the amount of power she has now, it was probably shortly after you all left that she broke free. I'm only glad you had time to get yourself and everyone else out of there." She looked at me, pride shining in her eyes. "That was smart thinking to use that particular spell. Had you not, I hate to think of what would have happened."

I nodded and bit my lip. "I just wish we had gotten there sooner and been able to save more people." I looked down at my hands. "It made absolutely no sense what she was doing. I mean, those people didn't do anything to her. They were just going about their business and then some crazy lady comes and starts murdering everyone. One of the ladies we helped called her the devil. I'm beginning to wonder if she is."

We were too tired to do much else that evening, so Celeste got her guest rooms ready and implored us to get some rest because to-morrow was going to be a terribly busy day. I didn't argue. I simply fell into the bed and passed smooth out. I didn't dream, and I don't think I moved at all from the position I'd gone to sleep in.

I think it was the best sleep I'd had in some time.

When Star and I made our way down to the kitchen the next morning, Trela and Bea were already up and eating the breakfast Celeste had made.

Bea's eyes lit up when she saw me, and she immediately pointed to Emric and Charlie. "Why didn't you tell me about these two?" she said with her mouth full. "Oh my god, they're hilarious. You are so lucky." She put her head in one hand and smiled at Emric who stood and preened.

"She is lucky, and she knows it."

I rolled my eyes as I fixed a cup of coffee. "You are so modest," I told him, and the girls laughed. "So…" I sat down and looked at them. "I guess we need to get planning. Where's Killian?"

"He went to the Oak to gather your packs. Don't worry. He was going to get your beanie too," Celeste said. I explained to Trela and

Bea about my beanie at their questioning looks and gave them the short version of the past two journeys.

By the time I was done, Killian sifted back into the kitchen and we sat down to formulate a plan. Many cups of tea and coffee later, we'd come up with one that amazed even me.

Now that we knew the power Freya wielded, we all felt that we needed to be a little tricky. We'd decided that it would be me, Killian, Trela and Bea, along with of course, Star, Emric and Charlie. Celeste had gotten ahold of my dad and he would be along shortly as well.

That news alone put a little pep in my step. His magic was strong, and he was smart. He knew far more than I did, and I welcomed his expertise and guidance. My only worry would be his concern for me while we were there. I didn't want it to throw his concentration and cause him to get hurt or worse.

I had to trust that it would all work out.

Amarie had bowed out of it, as I had suspected she would. Not because she didn't want to help, but because of what it had cost her the last time. She did let us know that she and the Elves would be taking up position here and around town to keep it safe. You just never knew when Freya and the Fomori would strike again.

"Okay, so let's go over it again." I scrunched my eyebrows as I thought back to our plan. "The three of us and Star," I motioned to Trela and Bea, "will go through the portal to Falias. That way, if anyone is waiting or watching, they'll think it's just us. Trela and Bea will fly me to a secure location of our choosing, preferably a cave or somewhere hidden. I'll leave drops of the potion that you, Celeste, will make, as we go to said location. Then, when Rohn, Killian, Emric, and Charlie come through, they'll be able to sense the magic trail and follow it to meet up with us. Correct?"

Celeste nodded. "Yes. That's exactly it."

Something about this plan kept nagging at me, but I couldn't figure out what was wrong. It made me nervous, but it was a sound plan. I couldn't argue with it.

"Oh, I almost forgot!" exclaimed Celeste, who got up out of her chair. "Just one minute. I have something for you all." She rushed out of the room and I heard her rustling around in the sunroom. When she walked back in, she had a stack of folded clothing. Setting it down on the table, she ruffled through them.

"I called in a favor late last night when you all went to bed. You two," she nodded at the girls, "will need suits. And Andie, Killian, I had new ones made for you as well. I wanted to make sure that these had extra fire protection in them."

She handed each of our suits to us, and mine looked pretty much the same as my old one. I was glad to see it was still purple. The other suits were just black. I'd often wondered before why mine was the only one that was different. I'd never figured it out and always forgot to ask. Not that it really made a difference. A suit was a suit. All that mattered is that it helped protect our bodies where it covered them.

The girls oohed and ahhed over their suits and ran to try them on. Killian just stared after them. "Hey. You need help picking your jaw up off the floor?" I asked him, chuckling.

His cheeks turned rosy, but he shook it off, choosing to ignore my comment. I hoped that Emric didn't pop off with something that would embarrass him even more.

Celeste's phone rang, and I cringed. I hated that sound now. Anytime I heard it, there was always bad news on the other end. I could tell Celeste felt the same way as she waited for a moment before answering it.

"Hello? Okay, Presley slow down. I can't understand a word you're saying." My entire body tensed up as Killian and I both leaned forward, listening. "Okay. Yes, yes. I'll let them know. Yes. Call me if you hear anything. Anything at all. Goodbye."

Celeste hung up the phone and turned around to look at us, taking a deep breath.

"Well, as I'm sure you heard, that was Presley. She called to let us know that Teagan is missing. He received his prosthetic leg a few days ago, so he's getting around much better now. But she said that he was acting extremely strange lately. He locked her and his parents out of his room, hasn't been eating, and the last she physically saw him, he was angry and irrational. She doesn't know where he went, and neither do Logan and Toni," she sighed.

What she said scared me. It brought back all the dreams I'd had of him recently. This wasn't good,. What if he did something stupid and got hurt?

Killian stayed quiet but put his hand on my shoulder for support. Teagan was his friend as well, and I knew that despite his worry about Pres, he wouldn't wish anything bad on him.

"There's nothing we can do. I'll get in touch with Aine and Coeus and let them know about it. Maybe the Titans can help find him," Celeste said. She looked worried as she turned to go to the attic room where she practiced her magic.

Trela and Bea came into the room then, dressed in their new suits, and as I suspected, they fit them perfectly. If it was even possible, they looked fiercer than they already did.

"These are a dream!" Trela exclaimed, but her smile wavered when she saw the serious looks on our faces. "What's wrong?"

I told her about Teagan and why we were worried about him. She only shrugged. "When someone is hurting, the best you can do is let them take care of whatever they need to and be there for them when they come back."

"Yeah, but I don't have a good feeling about this. If you knew him like we do, you would know this isn't normal. I'm afraid of what he might do." I still hadn't told anyone about the hellfire. I didn't think Teagan had either. Maybe it was time, especially since the blue fire kept haunting my dreams, and it all centered around him.

I didn't want to tell the present company though; I didn't even want to tell Celeste. I needed to tell Hunter. He'd know what to do.

"Uh... I'm going to go upstairs and call Hunter. I'll be back in a little bit." I rushed upstairs to my old room and shut the door. The phone rang a few times before I heard someone pick up and noise in the background.

"Andie?" Hunter's deep voice sounded in my ear, and I about melted. "What's wrong?"

"Hi, nothing's wrong. Well, no. That's not right, everything is wrong, but right now I'm fine. I'll be leaving soon to find the Key. I wanted to call and hear your voice, and uh... there's something I need to tell you, but no one else knows."

There was silence on the other end.

"Hunter? Are you still there?"

"Yes, sorry. Okay... so lay it on me. What is it? I'm sure it'll be okay."

I loved how positive he was about it. I mean, this was a really big deal, and with Teagan's frame of mind, I wasn't sure how well he'd be able to keep the evil of the hellfire at bay.

"Well, before the last journey, I found out that Teagan had made a deal with someone. A deal for some really strong magic. And well, now he's gone missing. Pres just called and said no one knows where he is. I'm worried about the state of mind he might be in and what he might do with that magic if he completely loses it." I said in a rush.

"Hmm... Well, this doesn't sound good. What kind of magic is it and who did he get it from?" Hunter was all business and I silently thanked him for not thinking I was overreacting.

"Okay, don't freak out. He called it hellfire and said he made a deal with this weird guy named Declan. Declan would give him the power to use it if he in turn let Declan siphon some of his power every month."

I squeezed my eyes shut, waiting for him to freak out. Again, there was only silence. This time, I didn't say anything. I knew he was still on the line, probably trying to process it all.

Finally, he responded. "Hellfire? I've heard of it before, but I don't know much about it other than it's extremely deadly. And I don't know who this Declan is either. Let me do some digging and see what I can come up with? It's going to be okay Andie. We'll figure this out."

My heart melted right then and there. How was this the same Hunter I first met in the school hallway? The one who was rude and not real mature.

"You don't know how much you saying that just calmed me down," I said. "But what if you don't find anything before I leave? I'm worried what could happen."

"I doubt I'll find anything if you're leaving so soon. But don't worry, we'll help any way we can. You know I'm going to have to get Coeus involved in this too if I can't take care of it."

I gripped the phone tighter, but I knew he was right. If he couldn't take care of it on his own, and things got bad, the only thing that made sense was to involve the other Titans. Someone had to make sure that everyone back here was taken care of and safe while I was gone.

"I know, it'll probably be for the best. I just worry what that Declan guy will do. Part of me thinks he's behind all of this that has changed Teagan so much."

"He probably is. But don't worry, like I said, we'll get to the bottom of it."

There was a knock on my door then, and the little bubble I'd cocooned myself in of his voice and our conversation, burst.

"Listen, I've got to go. Someone's knocking. Thank you, Hunter. I mean it. You made me feel so much better," I said softly.

"You know I'd do anything to help you, right? I'll always be here. Just promise me you'll be careful, and hurry home." His voice was strong, but I caught a slight tremor in the last word. He was worried.

He wasn't the only one.

We hung up, and I went to the door and opened it to find my dad standing there, hand raised to knock again. "Sorry! I was on the phone with Hunter." I reached out and hugged him. "I'm so glad you're here."

He smoothed my hair back and hugged me tighter.

"Of course I'm here. I came as soon as I could after Celeste called. Oh, and guess what? I got one of those cool suits like your friends down there too. And by the way, I like them a lot. Pretty tough girls with good heads on their shoulders." He smiled as he pulled back.

"Yeah, they are. I think I was pretty lucky to find them. Well, I guess it's not really luck when you've got Star to point you in the right direction." I ran my hand over her smooth fur.

Sometimes, I forgot she was even there, so used to her being wrapped around my neck like she was. He smiled and rubbed her fur too. "She's a smart girl, isn't she? I think whoever sent her to you knew what they were doing."

I agreed.

I followed him back downstairs and we went over the plan with him. He seemed to think it was solid and I could see the excitement in his eyes. He'd been all around the world, but he'd never been on a journey like the one we were about to embark on.

Later that evening we sifted to the Oak. Trela and Bea were enamored with it, not unlike anyone else who first sees it. "We'll give you a grand tour once this is over," I said, "but for now, we need to make sure we've got everything and get going."

Balwyn and Eira made sure to load us up with food, even some toast for Star, and plenty of water. We'd all changed into our suits, and I like to think we made a pretty striking picture.

I stuffed my beanie into one pocket and the potion that Celeste made into another, then I ran to my room and grabbed a hair tie, pulling my hair back into a ponytail. It was far too long to have it all over the place. I spied the glasses that blocked auras and grabbed them just in case. You never knew what you might need, and I'd rather be prepared as much as possible.

Chapter Eighteen

Back in the main room, I looked around. Everyone seemed to be ready. "Okay, I've got the potion. I'll leave drops along the way to our meet up point, be on the lookout for them."

I hugged my dad tightly. "See you there." He smiled and nodded. "See you soon, sweetheart."

And with that, I led Trela and Bea up to the eighth floor.

"Okay, Star, let's do our thing," I whispered to her in the doorway. This time, the barrier fell even quicker than before. I had been concerned about the others getting through it, but Celeste assured me that between Killian and Rohn, they'd have no issue.

I strode into the room, the girls hot on my heels, and Star scurried down, running right to the portal we needed to get to Falias. I didn't even pay attention to what was in the picture this time. I simply turned to the girls and told them that after I went through, all they needed to do was touch the picture and they'd be transported as well.

They nodded in unison, fear and excitement glittering in their eyes.

Once Star had gotten back into her place, I reached out. The pull this time was rough. It felt like my body was being sucked up into a vacuum. Not painful, but uncomfortable.

We landed on green grass, with a small stream that glowed a strange green in front of us and trickled through an odd-looking gate. It was made of branches bent into a circle, with other branches going through the middle that formed a swirling pattern.

I looked down the stream to see if I could tell where it went, and it actually became wider and looked more like a river further down. Trees surrounded us, and it was ungodly quiet. I didn't hear any birds or even bugs. Just the sound of the water trickling.

"Look up there," Bea whispered, and I followed her gaze up into the tree.

On one of the highest branches sat a woman, her skin extremely pale, almost white. She was naked save for her long, bright red curly hair. On top of her head sat a crown of flowers and leaves of every hue, and pointed ears peeked out between her red tresses. Her eyes were ice blue, and her lips were red as if she wore the brightest lipstick. A smattering of freckles decorated her nose and cheeks.

She stared down at us, not blinking, and I wondered if she was a friend or foe. I wasn't ready to engage in battle just yet.

We didn't move, only stared back at her, silent. I began to wonder if she was even real. She hadn't moved a muscle, not even blinked.

Trela leaned into me and whispered out of the side of her mouth, "Maybe we should say something to her?"

It was as if the slight sound of her whispered voice had woken the woman, for she suddenly stood up, unfolding her pale body. She blinked then. And she smiled.

I wasn't sure if that was a good thing or not.

Gracefully, she jumped from the large branch she perched on, landing easily on both feet a few yards away. The smile was still plastered on her face, and I felt rather than saw my friends tense beside me. They were ready for anything.

Star hadn't moved from around my neck, and that gave me some comfort that our lives weren't in danger. Surely, she would've acted strange if she sensed that we were.

As the woman came to a stop a short distance in front of us, her icy eyes rose to meet mine, and she stretched out her hand. I glanced down at it and then back to her face, hesitant to reach out and take her upturned palm.

Her brows raised a bit in challenge.

Slowly, I stretched mine out, laying my palm against hers. Her fingers curled around my hand. "Welcome to Falias." Her voice was smooth and soothing. "I do not blame you for being cautious. There are many creatures here that could cause you harm. *I'm* not one of them."

She looked at Trela and Bea. "This is my home, but I am aware of what goes on around it. I felt the energy shift before you arrived, and I was curious."

She let go of my hand, and I studied her just as she did us. She wasn't at all concerned about not having clothes on while we did. I discerned that this was natural for her and who knows who else in this place. Her long hair covered the majority of her tall body, anyway.

Trela spoke up then, her voice a lot quieter than was normal for her. "What's your name?"

"I have many names, most which you wouldn't be able to pronounce. You may call me Leif. It's an abbreviation of my name." She noticed Star then and her head turned to the side with curiosity as she looked at her. "You've a spirit of your own?" Her eyes flicked up to mine.

"Uh... her name is Star. She's my familiar."

Leif straightened up and nodded. "She's a rather strong one. She told me that the two of you are a perfect fit." She looked at me again as if she were searching for something. "I can see it as well."

What did she mean that Star told her that? Could they communicate?

"Are you saying that you can talk to Star?"

She dipped her head. "Yes, I can communicate with spirits of all kinds." She gestured toward Star. "And she is powerful, as I said before. She wants you to know that she also would like her toast soon. What is toast?"

The woman's eyes blinked as I pulled my pack off and dove my hand inside pulling out one of the toasted squares from a sandwich baggie.

"This is toast. It's bread that has been cooked so it's crispy on the outside." I tore it into bite sized pieces and fed them to Star one at a time.

"Ah... I see." She backed away slightly, her red waves shifting as she did. "I must go now, but I send good tidings with you and wish you well on your journey. Watch out for the avartagh. He is a dreadful tyrant," she said as she turned to leave.

We watched as she jumped high onto the same branch she had been on before, and then continued to hop across the trees until we could no longer see her.

I turned to Bea and Trela. "What's an avartagh?"

Both of the girls shrugged. I guess that would be a question for my dad when he met up with us. I just hoped that we didn't encounter this thing before then.

"Guess we should get going or else our plan will be for nothing," I stated, my hands on my hips. They agreed and moved to either side of the stream. The area wasn't large in between all the trees, so they would need to shift one at a time.

Bea went first, discarding her suit and handed it to me. We'd agreed that I would put their suits in their packs and then hook their respective packs around their necks once they shifted.

After Bea stood tall in her dragon form, I hurried forward to sling the pack around her. She then lifted up into the air slowly, her wings causing the trees on either side of us to sway with the movements. Once she had cleared the tops of them, Trela also shifted and

I repeated the same steps with her before hopping onto her back and sliding the potion out of my pant pocket.

Trela flew up off of the ground gracefully until we hovered in the air beside Bea. Her head turned to study the surroundings. All I could see for miles around were the tops of the trees and in the far distance a tall mountain.

It was so large that the peak of it seemed to disappear into the clouds. The dragons looked at it and then at each other and shared a subtle nod between them before taking off in that direction.

I began dropping the potion little by little. My hand clenched around the dropper tightly, afraid that I might lose it with the air whipping by me. I counted to twenty between each drop and hoped that they wouldn't be too far between each other that the others would have a hard time finding them.

As I did, I surveyed the landscape below. Every so often, there would be a break in the treetops, and I would get a glimpse of a turquoise pool, or the river that snaked through.

In one clearing, I spied smoke curling from a crudely made chimney.

Ahead of us, the mountain loomed larger the closer we flew. It was enormous. There had to be some caves in it somewhere. My eyes scanned the rocky sides, and I knew that the girls were searching as well. Between the three of us, surely we would find something suitable to hide out in.

Bea flew ahead of us, her speed increasing, and I knew she must have spotted something.

I strained to see where she was going, but my eyes weren't made like a dragon's. They could see one hundred times better than I could.

Trela followed her dragon sister as she swooped further down the mountainside. It was a good thing we were so close because the potion was almost gone, and I decided to save the remainder for when we got to where we were going.

It was then I spotted the cave. It was at the base of the mountain and surrounded by a field of dandelions. The whites of them blew like a wave in the wind, back and forth.

It was mesmerizing and the thought of the dragons landing on them, crushing them with their clawed feet made me cringe. For some reason I didn't want them damaged.

The thought made absolutely *no* sense, but it was the first thing that popped into my mind.

I didn't have to worry, though. Trela and Bea must have had the same feeling, landing on the soft green grass behind the field. As soon as their feet touched down, Bea changed back and Trela patiently waited for me to disembark before she did as well.

They donned their suits and looked around, studying the area around us.

I still couldn't take my eyes from the flowers that were really weeds, but right now, they were just a beautiful, whimsical sight. "Aren't they something?" I said to the girls.

They both looked at me strangely and then at each other. "They're dandelions," Trela said.

"Well, yeah, but isn't it strange how many there are? You never see them grow like this back home. I'm so glad you guys didn't want to damage them."

"Girl, what is wrong with you? I don't care about those dandelions. I just wanted to land further away from the cave in case something's in it. Don't want to give them a heads up, ya know?"

Both of the girls' eyebrows were scrunched as they studied me, and Star patted my neck again like she does when she wants something. I rubbed her back as I took a step forward, closer to the field of white, watching as a few of the umbrella-like seeds took flight with the wind.

The touch against my neck became more frantic, and Star mewled. "Hang on, girl, just a second. I just want to pick one."

I took another step forward, closing the gap between me and the flowers, and just as I reached forward to pick one, my arm was yanked back.

Bea shook it a little and my gaze snapped to her. "What?" I felt irritated that she had interrupted. I mean, jeez, it was just a stupid flower.

She pointed at Star. "Don't you think she's trying to tell you something and maybe you should listen to her? You said it yourself-it's strange to see this many of these growing in a field like this. And they just happen to be in front of the cave we want to go into? Come on now. You're better than this."

My mind felt a little foggy, and she was right. It was pretty strange. I shook my head to clear the fog and then nodded sharply. "We need to find a way around them." They were right; the way I felt the need to get one of the flowers wasn't normal.

As I walked to the right side of the field, Star's erratic motions stopped and I realized that Bea had been right, my familiar was trying to warn me of something. What exactly? I'm not sure, and I probably didn't want to find out. From now on, if she wasn't acting weird, I'd assume all was okay. If she was, then I'd start listening to her.

The girls followed behind me, and as we rounded a curve on the white field, I saw that there was a break in it. An actual path. Though it wasn't very wide, I thought we had room to walk through it. We would just need to be cautious. And I wasn't about to touch any of them. Memories of the red field of poisonous flowers from my first journey filled my mind.

"Let's go through here," I said and dropped a small drop of the potion where I stood. Then I waited a beat to see if Star did anything strange. When she didn't, I stepped onto the path and began walking, the girls close behind me.

When I had gone about ten feet, a gust of wind hit and millions of those little seeds took flight around us. That set Star off, and I was instantly on alert. She dug her nails into my throat like she'd never done before, and I hoped that she hadn't drawn blood.

In the flowers around us, shuffling noises began, a skittering and clicking sound. I looked down to see round little black beetles scurrying toward us from both sides, instantly setting off the ick factor for me. Chills ran down my spine.

"Run!" I yelled to the girls behind me, and I took off as fast as my legs would go.

The cave entrance was just ahead, and I prayed that those beetles didn't follow us in, and even more so that there wasn't more waiting inside.

The beetles were almost to the edge of the path and I began throwing my magic at them. It would push them back a little and then they would surge forward again. We were almost to the dark opening when I pushed with my magic as hard as I could. Out of the corner of my eye, I saw the black bodies flung through the air to either side of us.

We threw ourselves through the opening, and gasping, I yelled, "Get behind me!"

Trela and Bea ran further in and I turned, shouting a spell to put up a barrier between us and the nasty bugs that once again were headed our way. They seemed manic in their quest to get to us.

"*See*! I told you that there was something about that field. And you wanted to go into it!" Bea gasped, horrified by the beetles that had come after us. She shuddered, arms wrapped around her waist.

"Hey. It's okay. They can't come in now." Trela rubbed Bea's back before looking at me. "She hates bugs, has a deathly fear of them." She said, her brows drawn in concern as she looked at Bea.

I felt for the girl, really, but right now we needed to make sure this cave was secure. And I was worried about the guys when they arrived having to get through that mess of black bodies.

I turned around to face the interior of the cave, and cast my spell for light, this time conjuring a larger ball to bounce around. I didn't want any surprises. I followed it around the interior of the cave and saw there were two tunnels that led from this one deeper into the mountain.

I had absolutely no desire to explore them or think about what might be hidden in them.

I hurried up to each one, and with Star's help, we warded them as well. Nothing would get in or out of this cave without us lowering the barriers. I walked back over to where the girls stared outside. The beetles were crawling over each other, trying to get in. In their efforts they were effectively making a wall of their squirming bodies.

"Come on." I pulled the girls away from the gross sight. "Let's not worry about them just this second. Sit down, I'll make a fire and we need to eat a snack and have some water."

Geez, I sounded like Celeste.

They both nodded, and Bea reluctantly took her frightened gaze away from the creatures. I situated her to where her back faced them. Luckily, we couldn't hear their scratching.

"Okay, so I think that my dad and Killian should be able to figure out a way to get through them. Emric and Charlie will probably just eat them, and we won't have to worry," I joked, trying to make light of the situation.

Bea's shoulders relaxed a little, and I knew it was working.

"You saved me back there Bea. I can't thank you enough. If it hadn't been for your quick thinking, I probably would have just walked right into that field." I smiled kindly at her, and she smiled a tentative smile back.

"So what do we do now? I feel like we should be doing something." Trela fidgeted and looked around the cave.

I pulled two granolas bars and handed one to her and one to Bea. At Star's mewl, I also pulled out some toast. How she was hungry so soon after her last piece, I didn't know. But she wanted what she wanted, and I wasn't about to deal with her pestering me to have it.

"We eat. We rest while we can. And we wait."

Chapter Nineteen

It must have been at least an hour later when I looked outside to see the wall of bugs disintegrating.

"Look!" I pointed to the doorway and Bea's eyes opened wide, a huge smile gracing her face. "That's what I'm talking about! Why didn't you do that?" She turned to me with curiosity.

"Uh... actually, I just didn't think about it. I was too concerned with getting in and not letting any of those suckers in here with us." She tsked and gave me a mean look before turning back to the entrance.

Killian, Dad, Emric, and Charlie stood outside looking in. I quickly dropped the barrier and rushed to them. "Thank goodness you're here!" I hugged them both and patted Emric and Charlie on the head. They were both in their panther forms.

Emric stretched and yawned. I swear he always seemed to be tired.

"We would've been here sooner, but Charlie wanted to scout. Plus, we had that little nuisance to deal with that you left us." Emric indicated the pathway outside.

"Hey, I didn't want to make it so easy for you that you didn't feel challenged enough," I quipped back. I wasn't about to let him make me feel bad. "Anyway, what'd you find, Charlie?" I turned to him and he rubbed against my leg.

"You're not going to like it. There's nothing here other than a few small homes in the wild. I'm thinking that our way to the Key is going to be through this mountain. I flew to the top of it, above the clouds and there is a marker up there. It's got the symbol on it."

Killian and I looked at each other. If the symbol was there, then I couldn't argue. Though I really, really didn't want to have to travel deeper into this mound of stone. There was no telling what lay ahead.

"Okay. Guess we need to pick a door." I waved to tunnel one and then tunnel two. "And before you say anything," I looked around at the group, "we are not splitting up."

They all agreed, and since no one knew or even had a tingle of suspicion which tunnel to go down, I headed to the one on the right, the group right behind me. Just as I was about to take down the ward, Star's paw gently tapped my neck.

"All righty then. Not this one?" I went to stand before the tunnel on the left and looked down at her. "Is this one okay?" I raised my hand to take down the ward and she tapped me again.

Seriously? If both of them weren't the right path, then where the heck were we supposed to go?

I sighed and turned around. "Apparently neither of these are the way we're supposed to go." I looked down at her again and muttered, "You'd better be right."

Dad came to stand beside me. "Why don't we search around the walls and see if the entrance is hidden? It won't take long with all of us doing it." It was sound advice, and I remembered the hidden door in the mountain cave we'd visited with Aine.

"It makes sense. The entrance wouldn't be in plain sight for just anyone to see," I said aloud, but mostly to myself. "Okay, I'm not sure what we're looking for, but everyone feel the walls. Look for spots that are weak. Push on the stone too and make sure there's not a concealed button or something."

We searched slowly and meticulously, trying to make sure we didn't miss one inch of the stone walls. I heard a soft cry from Trela over my shoulder and turned around to see her hand sticking through the stone as if it had been cut off.

We all ran to her, fearful that she had been injured, but when we approached, she pulled her hand back out, wiggled her fingers, and looked around at us before plunging it back in.

"Think I found it," she smiled. I wiped my forehead, flinging off the sweat that had gathered there.

"Please don't cry out like that again unless you're in trouble. You scared the crap out of me, especially when I couldn't see your hand."

Killian chuckled and moved beside Trela, sticking his hand through it as well. "I'll go first." He turned to Trela and Bea. "Just stay close behind me. I'll make sure it's safe before you do." He grinned at them both and stepped through the false barrier.

Trela rolled her eyes once he couldn't see her anymore, and Bea laughed. It was weird seeing half his body go through until the rest of it followed. The girls waited, then jumped as his head popped through, and only his head.

If we weren't in such an anxious situation, I would've laughed.

"We're good. Come on." He smiled and then popped his head back to the other side.

When I stepped through the false wall, my eyes lit up in amazement. What awaited us on the other side was nothing like the cave we had been in. It was still a tunnel that we were all crowded into, but veins of silver and gold threaded through the rock walls, glittering and bright against the light from mine and Dad's orbs.

Killian moved forward down the long tunnel with the girls behind him and then me, dad, Emric, and Charlie. It was slow going as Killian seemed to be super cautious of what might lie in wait.

I wished I'd taken the lead, but I knew that I needed to let him do this so he wouldn't look weak in front of Trela and Bea.

Up ahead, the tunnel curved, and once we made it around the bend, it opened up into another large cave, this one the ceiling was extremely tall and there were a few holes in it that let in light from outside. A pool of water sat in the middle, glowing cerulean blue. It reminded me of a highlighter with the glow that it gave off.

That wasn't the most fascinating thing about this room though. It was the plants that grew down from the ceiling, giving us the feeling that we were upside down.

As a child, did you ever lie on the floor and look up at the ceiling, pretending to walk on it? That topsy turvy feeling that you got when you did it? That's how I felt now. It actually made me a little dizzy.

Trees grew down, their trunks thick with roots running across the ceiling. Flowers and plants of all kinds grew amidst them.

"This is so weird!" Bea exclaimed, and I agreed. I had to look down and away from it all because it was making me my head fuzzy and my stomach roll.

While the rest of them stood there taking it all in, I trudged down the rough steps carved in the floor to the pool of water and looked in. It was clear the closer you came to it and bright green fish swam around in it and through the aquatic plants that swayed at the very bottom. Nothing seemed amiss. No strange creatures lurked in the depths. It was a relief.

But apparently that was to be short lived.

On the other side of the pool was another tunnel, the only other exit from this cave that I had seen. Shuffling and thumping came from it, and I stood still, the conversations behind me stopping. Light bounced off the walls of the tunnel, inching closer, and I put my hand to Star, hoping she was ready for whatever was about to greet us.

The first thing I saw was a foot. A big foot. It was encased in a black boot with spikes that ran down the side of it. The body that followed sent shivers down my spine as I recognized it and a promise that I'd once given.

Tinock. King of the Trolls.

I'd forgotten about him until now, and I'd also forgotten about the oath that I'd given to him. That if he let Killian go, I'd come to him when he called.

I hope now isn't that time.

He grinned when he saw the look on my face, as he came to stand across from me, the other trolls in his guard behind him. I felt my group rush to stand behind me as well, and Dad leaned in, whispering out of the side of his mouth not to do anything rash. I just nodded. This was one story I'd forgotten to tell him.

He had no idea we'd met before. But Killian did. He had flanked my other side, and as I glanced at him, his shoulders were tight but thrown back, his chest puffed up, and his jaw set in the most serious line I'd ever seen on him. Hate and disgust radiated off every inch of him, and rightly so.

Tinock looked him over and grinned, his nasty teeth brown, and white spots sat in the corners of his mouth where spittle had gathered and dried. He was just disgusting. Not to mention that it seemed as if he'd grown even more warts and pustules over his skin than he had the first time I saw him.

"Well look at you lad!" he boomed, his voice echoing across the walls. "I see ya've gotten a spine now, eh?" He laughed uproariously, and the trolls behind him followed.

None of us laughed.

When he finally shut up, I spoke out. "Tinock, what are you doing here?"

I wouldn't show any fear; he seemed to feed off of it. And I wasn't about to remind him of my promise. If that's what he wanted, he'd have to say so.

"Why am I here?" He turned to his comrades. "She asks why I'm here." They all chuckled and shook their warty heads, their horns and tusks clanking. He turned back to me, the smile dropping from his face, his beady eyes squinting at me. "Now I know ya couldn't have forgotten the promise you gave to me."

I groaned inside, and he continued. "Now I've come to cash in on that promise."

I tried to think of a suitable excuse. But he wouldn't care. I had to be clever. My thoughts were interrupted when Dad turned to me. "What is he talking about?"

Before I even had a chance to reply, Tinock laughed again and explained it to him in plain terms. I had no argument. I had promised.

I didn't have time to sit here and argue with him. I looked at my group and saw that all but Killian wore looks of surprise and fear. I turned back to the troll king and nodded. "A promise is a promise. But listen, this is going to have to be quick. We're on a mission that I can't stray from long. If I do, the consequences for even you will be dire. Freya will come for you too if we don't stop her."

He thought about it for a minute and nodded. "Yes, she is why I'm here to collect on your promise. She severely injured my wife and I need ya to come heal her. We don't have the ability."

Seriously? All of this craziness and acting like what he wanted to cash in on was something bad? I guess he had a reputation to maintain, but still.

I nodded slowly. "Give me just a moment." I turned to my team, and they huddled around me. Dad put his arm around my shoulder and drew me to him.

"You don't have to do this, Andie. I'll figure out a way to get rid of them."

I knew he meant well, but he also knew that when you made a promise, you kept it. He'd be the first to do the same. It was only because I was his daughter, and he was worried about me that he'd voiced that at all.

"No, I need to do this, and really it's a much better request than I imagined. What can it harm? I only hope that whatever is wrong with her I can fix."

Killian spoke up then. "What if I come with you?"

I shook my head. I wasn't about to put him in that position. I remembered the nightmares he had after we saved him from the trolls. "No. I'll go alone, and I'll try to hurry back." I turned quickly to stave off any other input and looked at the burly troll. "I'll help you, but I can only be gone a few hours, nothing more. Okay?"

He shook his head slowly at me, and it was strange to see what looked like relief light his eyes. "Only a few hours then. But only if you heal her. If you can't heal her, you'll stay there as long as it takes to do so." He growled.

Oh, god. I hope I can heal her.

I hugged my dad and the rest of my team, murmuring that I'd be back as soon as I could. They reassured me that they would stay right here. Tinock didn't give them an option.

"I'm leaving a few of my guards here so you don't try to follow." He looked at my team.

As I walked around the pool to stand near him, one of the guards roughly grabbed my arm and I yanked it back. "Don't touch me. I can walk just fine on my own."

Tinock chuckled. "Ach. No, we'll be blindfolding you, girl. You'll need guidance through the tunnels. I can't have you seeing how to get to our home."

Like I even want to find his home after this. "You know we're going to have to come through these tunnels to get where we're going once you bring me back, right?" I said while one of his lackeys slipped something over my head, effectively shutting me in the dark.

"I do," Tinock rasped, "But I'm not taking any chances. Besides, when you're long on your way to find the Key, you'll never find the way to my home as long as I keep you like this."

Whatever, I thought to myself. He'd be surprised what I could find when I put my mind to it.

I felt my arm grabbed again. This time, whoever held onto me was much gentler. They steered me away, and I vaguely wondered if this was a trap. It was too late now. There was nothing I could do about it.

We walked forever and I was treated to raucous laughter and lewd comments the entire way. I stayed silent, intent on remembering the path my feet took me and the sounds around me. Well, besides all of the troll's noise.

One of them farted loudly, and I about gagged. They honestly did not care how disgusting they were, and I couldn't wait until this was over with and I was away from their wretched stench.

It seemed like the time stretched on before I was stopped and the covering over my head was removed. I blinked over and over, adjusting to the brightness of the light overhead. We were in a small room with only a bed and a table inside. When I saw who lay in the bed, shock coursed through my system and I blinked again thinking that maybe I was seeing things.

The woman who lay there looked as normal as I did. I was expecting the girl version of Tinock, disgusting and covered in boils. But this woman, she had short brown hair and mocha-colored skin. Her eyelashes were long and dark against her high cheekbones.

I searched the bed to see if she was secured to it, intent to make sure she wasn't being held against her will. I didn't see anything. My eyes tracked to where Tinock went to stand beside her, and I watched him lean down and place a soft kiss to her head.

Wonders never cease.

How on earth had they come to be together? And why on earth did she want to be with him? Her eyelids fluttered open to gaze at him, and the love and pain I saw reflected there made me gasp.

She loved him. She was really his wife. This was just so strange. Tinock whispered to the woman, and her eyes shifted to look at me. She glanced at my suit and smiled gently and beckoned me to her. I hesitated, and Tinock growled at me. "Get over here. She ain't gonna bite."

Seriously? Why the heck would I think she'd bite me? Didn't he see the craziness of what he said?

The woman bit her lip, trying to contain laughter as she looked away from him. I walked to the end of the bed and nodded. "Hello. My name is Andie, and I've been told you've been injured? Can you tell me what hurts?"

She tried to push herself to sit up and winced in pain, leading Tinock to reach down and pull her gently to sitting. "Thank you, dear." Her voice rasped as she looked up at him before swinging her gaze back to me.

"Thank you for coming, Andie. Tinock told me about your promise and insisted you could help. You see, a few days ago, I happened to be in the woods looking for a particular mushroom when Freya came upon me." She coughed a few times, wincing again, then proceeded. "I was alone. I had no way of defending myself. That wicked woman just laughed as I tried to run away. She was upon me before I'd even taken ten steps, and she put something inside of me. I don't know what it is, but it burns. She whispered a spell, and black smoke flowed out of her and into me. The pain is constant. It doesn't stop."

I nodded and gestured to her feet. "May I?"

"Yes, of course. Whatever you need to do," she agreed.

I pulled the covers from her feet and laid my hands upon them. Star purred around my neck. It surprised me that she hadn't raised a stink this entire time. "What's your name?" I asked as I sent my magic into her body, searching for the cause.

"Kalie. My name is Kalie." She wheezed as another fresh pain flowed into her. I felt it now, an oily spell that curled into her stomach.

"Well, Kalie, I've found the spell, but I'm not sure how long this will take, and honestly I've never done this before alone, so I can't guarantee it won't hurt." I told her honestly.

I just hoped that whatever I did worked.

I pointed to Star and said, "This is my familiar Star. She'll help me, and I want you to focus on her as I work. Okay?" She nodded, and I got to work. Closing my eyes, I focused on my magic intertwining with Star's. I pushed it into Kalie and the exact spot where I'd felt the black spell reside.

Together, Star and I pushed and pushed until I was panting with exertion and Kalie had cried out a few times, much to Tinock's displeasure. I could feel the spell moving, dislodging from its original spot only to lodge against something different as I tried to move it up and out of her.

An hour had passed, and I wiped the sweat from my forehead, glancing up to see that Kalie had passed out at some moment before. Tinock kneeled beside her bed and now had his forehead to her shoulder, whispering to her.

The spell had finally moved up into her throat, and we needed to work fast before it somehow kept her from breathing. I took a deep breath and closed my eyes again, gathered my magic from as deep as possible, and pushed with all my might.

A wet sound came from Kalie, and my eyes popped back open to see her mouth stretch wide and a greasy black smoke billowed out, dissolving as it hit the ceiling.

Instantly, the pallor of her face lessened and Tinock let out a loud breath, slumping against the bed once more.

I wanted to do the same, I was so depleted of energy, but I needed to get back to my team. I cleared my throat, and Tinock peeked an eye open from the arm that he had slung over his head. "I think she'll be fine now. And I need to get back."

He sat up, leaning back on his knees and heels, and nodded. His fist came up to his heart and he bowed his head. I barely heard the words, but he whispered, "Thank you."

Again, my head was covered, and I was led out of their home. Tinock didn't come with me this time. He'd left the job to his soldiers, and I understood that he was afraid to leave his wife.

I so wanted to know their story, but that moment hadn't been the time to ask or get into it. Maybe I'd never know, but it sure was intriguing.

Chapter Twenty

Before long, the covering was whisked away once again, and I stood before my team.

They all rushed to me as the trolls backed into the tunnel again. One called out, "Do not follow!"

"What happened?" Dad was right to the point, and I noticed how his gaze ran over me, making sure I was unharmed. I proceeded to explain everything, and they were in just as much shock about it all as I had been.

"It's not that uncommon for different species to fall in love," Emric said, his nose held high in the air. "It doesn't matter a whit what you look like, only what is in your heart."

Killian and the girls snickered, but I thought about what he said, and he had a point. I wondered if he had ever loved someone like that. The way he'd said it made me feel as though maybe he had.

I was still exhausted, and they all begged me to take a break. We couldn't, though. I'd already set us back a few hours. "I'll just eat some of this beef jerky real quick and that will help." They looked at me skeptically but knew better than to argue.

I chewed it as fast as I could and downed it with some water before I picked up my pack and we charged on.

The tunnel that the trolls had taken me through was long and felt never-ending. Here, the silver and gold veins were gone. Instead, diamonds poked out of the rough stone everywhere you looked. Eventually, the long tunnel came to an end and branched off into ten different tunnels. I stood before each of them, letting Star tell me which ones not to go down. That left only one, and we filed in. This time I talked them into letting me lead. I argued that Star would alert us to anything and if we had to choose which way to go, she would also tell us that. They grudgingly agreed.

Now as we slogged along, the ground beneath us seemed rise at an incline and I felt as though we were heading to the top of the mountain. It was slow going and I was getting fed up with the narrow passageways and darkness that surrounded us. I'd never been very claustrophobic, but this might just make me that way.

We didn't pass by any new caves. There were no large rooms, and I heard Trela sigh more than a few times behind me. There *had* to be something ahead.

My legs were screaming at me now. On top of being exhausted, the incline was strenuous. I made a note that when working out, try running up and down the stairs.

Further ahead, I noticed a faint blue light.

"Guys, I think there's something ahead. I can see some light. Let's go!" I picked up the pace, ignoring my muscles with only the thought of fresh air screaming at me.

The light grew and grew, and I could see fluffy white clouds. It was the end of the tunnel and we'd finally get out of this dreadful mountain. I cautiously stepped up to it.

"Careful, Andie, you don't know what's on the other side," Dad cautioned behind me. He was right, and I slowly peeked out looking to either side of the doorway.

We were on top of the mountain.

Snow covered every inch of it, and the air was freezing cold.

I stepped outside, my boots crunching on the thick slush, but they didn't sink in, so that was a plus. Everyone filed out behind me and we all looked around. The mountaintop was bare besides the snow and rocks on the peak.

It wasn't an exceptionally large area, and I couldn't imagine what we were supposed to do now.

I walked to the edge of the rock and looked down, expecting to see the bottom of the mountain many miles down. I even braced myself for the dizziness that usually accompanied looking down from way up high.

What greeted me left me swaying. Not from the height, but from the lack of height. Mere feet away from where I stood was water.

I heard gasps from Trela and Bea behind me. "What is this?" Bea shrieked. "How in the heck is this possible?" Charlie stalked up to her and looked over into the water. "Anything is possible here."

Dad came to stand beside me, and I continued to stare into the water because I swear, there was something deep down in the clearness of it. Something that looked like a city. A long lost city.

Visions of the one I swam through when I retrieved the Cauldron went through my head. This wasn't the same one. "Do you see that down there?" I asked him.

He leaned further over the edge and I bit my lip to keep myself from reaching out and grabbing him, fearful he would fall. "Yes, I think I do." He straightened up and looked around. "I walked around the entirety of the top of this mountain, and there is nothing but water. That means we'll have to go in."

"Oh hell no," Trela said, overhearing him. "I am not going in there. Nu-uh." She shook her head emphatically. "I do not like the water."

Killian came up to her and put his hand on her shoulder, kindness shining in his eyes. "We'll be there with you. Besides, I thought dragons liked to swim? You could always shift and go that way, couldn't you?" She stared at him with wide eyes like he had gone and lost his mind.

"Who told you dragons like water?" She tsked and looked at Bea, who hadn't said a word about it yet. "Tell him, Bea."

She looked at Killian, with less heat than Trela had and said, "We don't like the water. But..." she looked tentatively at Trela again, "we can swim in it. Trela had a really bad experience as a kid with water. When her family was killed, Freya tossed her into the lake, and she didn't know how to swim." Trela trembled and looked at Bea as though she couldn't believe Bea had told us this. "What? They need to know, because I don't know about you, but I don't want to leave them. I don't want to have to go through all of that," she pointed at the door we'd come through, "again. Besides, we'll be here to help each other." She smiled softly and took Trela's hand.

The two were tight. And no wonder. For so long they were all each other had. I guess it was kinda the same way Teagan and I had been as well, until now.

I wondered if they'd found him yet.

"Andie," my dad interjected, cutting off my thought. "I've got a spell we can use underwater where we won't have to worry about lack of oxygen. I believe it will last as long as we need it to." He looked a little worried, but he also looked strong and sure of himself.

"Don't tell me; you'll make air bubbles for us to hold up to our mouths?" I asked, remembering that Tegan had done the same thing.

Dad laughed. "Well no, though it will keep your lungs from requiring to work."

"Won't that damage our brains somehow?" I questioned, skeptical.

He shook his head. "No, it will also trick our brains. It's really a lot to go into, but don't worry, I have used it before, and I'm fine." He smiled broadly.

"That's a matter of opinion," Emric snarked.

Dad just laughed again. "Okay, everyone come stand by me and I'll start the spell. Just remember that once we're in the water, we need to stay together, don't get far apart, and whatever you see, don't freak out. Ready?"

We all nodded, and I realized that the girls hadn't shifted. "Wait, aren't you going to change?" I asked them both.

They shook their heads and Trela's mouth was set in a grim line. "No. If I'm doing this, I'm doing it just like y'all. We can't grow if we don't try to get over our fears, right?" She shrugged and even though she looked frightened, the set of her head and the fierceness of her gaze told me that this time, she'd conquer her fears and more.

"Right," I said to her, smiling.

Dad wove the spell around us, and as soon as he did, we jumped in. I let myself slowly sink, keeping my eyes open and looked around. The others did the same, all of our hair trailing above us.

We went down further, the weight of our bodies doing all of the work, and what I saw as a city became clearer. Was I in the freaking Little Mermaid?

The city was incased in a clear dome. Inside there was grass and trees, flowers blooming, and I could see figures moving around. What in the heck was going on? I looked at my dad and with a look of surprise he kind of shrugged, like 'what can you do?'

How are we supposed to get in there? And who exactly lives there?

Oh, god, kill me now. The lyrics to "Under the Sea," began to play over and over in my mind. If I could have groaned right then, I would have.

It wasn't even one of my favorite Disney movies. Nan could never understand why I always had a deep fear of Ursula. Maybe it was some kind of premonition of Freya. I don't know. But I'd hated her and refused to finish watching the movie.

We were almost to the glass dome that spanned several miles under the water. It was amazing and beautiful. Gold spires reached almost to the top of the dome, and there were streets running through and around all of the buildings. Strange-looking animals pulled futuristic buggies around them.

As my feet hit the dome, a strange thing happened. They began to sink through the barrier with a tingle. My body kept moving down as if pulled by some unseen force, and I looked to Trela to see her struggle as she sank through. Bea grabbed a hold of her, shaking her head at Trela violently, before wrapping her arms around her in a hug as they both sank in.

Everyone else let it happen without struggle, which was good.

I had a moment of panic as my head passed through and I worried about the height we were at. I didn't want to drop and fall to my death in this undersea city. Luckily, I didn't have to worry. Whatever magic had pulled us in, guided us gently to the ground where a group of people stood staring up at us, waiting.

They looked human, but their glowing eyes were a dead giveaway that they weren't. They didn't give off any feeling of malice, though, and as I was almost to the ground, a woman with blonde hair and glowing green eyes reached up and gently grabbed my ankle, bending at the knees to guide both of my feet down until they were solidly on the grass.

The others did the same to help the rest of my team. Once our feet had made contact, the pulling feeling went away.

Dad worked to reverse the oxygen spell, and my chest expanded. Not breathing was a very weird feeling, but after the first time I'd gone through it, this felt like a breeze.

The green-eyed woman stepped up close to me. She was much taller than I was. All of the people here were. If I didn't know any better, I'd think they were some different branch of the Elves. But they weren't. The Elves' eyes didn't glow like these peoples did.

She stood so close that I could feel her breath blowing against my forehead. "You're Andie, aren't you?" she asked with a strong voice.

There was no awe, or surprise. But luckily, there was no anger either.

"Yes. That's me," I stated, backing up an inch or two. She didn't move with me, and instead she turned and waved at the rest of the group that was waiting. They walked in closer and formed a circle around the two of us, cutting my team off and leaving them on the outside of their circle.

I heard Killian protest, but I couldn't see him.

The woman turned around again to me, raising her voice so everyone could hear. "We don't mean you harm. We're honored that you are here, and we have some things to show you."

The crowd parted, and at the same time that it did, my group rushed in to surround me. All except Emric, who seemed to have caught a lot of the citizens attention. He preened and purred at their awe. He hadn't even said a word, but it was as if they recognized what he was.

They reluctantly left him to follow along on either side of us behind this woman who I assumed must be their leader.

We marched down one of the streets, only to turn onto another one. I was fascinated by the buildings. Each and every one of them had some type of artwork gracing the front, and there were statues made of gems and metal that stood along the streets. The woman stopped in front of a tall building that had a picture of tall trees painted on it, and throughout each tree, sea glass sparkled.

There was no door, only an open wide doorway, and she didn't hesitate but marched right on through. Inside was a large room that was all white. Everything inside of it, down to the tables, chairs, and even the flowers in vases, was white. It was glaringly bright, and my eyes would have sighed in relief if they could once we passed through another door into a completely blue room.

She spun around, facing us. Her bright green eyes looked over at me before she left the room. Dad, Killian, and I looked at each other like, 'what the heck.' Trela and Bea instantly sat on the blue couch and looked bored.

"What happened to all the danger and weird creatures you told me about?" Trela asked, picking at her fingernails. "I mean, I'm not wishin' for them, but dang, so far it's been pretty uneventful."

I silently agreed with her as I looked around the room wondering what we were supposed to do in here.

I didn't have to wait long. A blue door on the other side of the room opened, and a tall man walked out. He wore a blue metal circlet on his head that had a star that sat right on his forehead. The blue of the crown thing matched the glowing blue of his eyes.

He came to stand before us, and then bowed. *Were we supposed to bow back?*

None of us did.

"Welcome to our home. I'm sure you're wondering who we are." His voice was pleasant and smooth. "My name is Frost, and we are the Sea Witches."

My dad stepped up and gave me a stern look as if telling me to be quiet before he responded. "Hello, Frost. Thank you for such a warm welcome. I've heard of the Sea Witches before. Actually, it was awfully long ago. I wasn't sure if it was a story that my parents had made up or not though, as I never heard about them again. Yet here you are. We can't stay long. As you might know, we're on a quest to find a Key. But we do sincerely appreciate your hospitality."

My dad was in full Rohn mode, exuding his own kind of stature and power. He slightly bent his back but less like a bow and more of a curtsey. He wouldn't fully bow to anyone.

I wouldn't either.

Frost only rose a sharp eyebrow before continuing.

"We like to keep our anonymity. The people here are the last of the Sea Witches. While our title may sound as though we are similar to you witches and warlocks. We are not the same. We harness the power of magic and spells, but we also need the sea to do so. Water calls to our magic, fuels it even. And so, as you can see," he spread his arms out, "we stay as near to it as possible."

The thought that these people lived under the sea all their lives amazed me. I mean, if they had no outside interactions, what was their purpose in life but to live down here all by themselves? I couldn't imagine it. And I couldn't help myself from posing the question.

"So you just live down here your entire life, you don't interact with anyone but your own people?" His gaze slid from my dad to me, his green eyes seeming to burn a hole into my soul. There was something about him that gave me the heebie jeebies, I hadn't figured it out yet, though.

"We do go above the water from time to time. But we do not interact with anyone unless we must. On recent excursions, however, it has come to our attention that the things happening above may seriously affect our way of life. And we intend to keep that from happening."

It was at that moment that a group filed into the room, led by the blonde woman with the bright green eyes. The men standing behind her looked different than the people who had followed us to this building though. These guys weren't just tall; they looked like bodybuilders, their arms huge and their necks thick.

Frost moved from his spot as I glanced at the group and then back at him. He came to stand in front of me and I tilted my head back. Star bristled and I was instantly on alert.

Trela and Bea stood up, Killian right beside them. Emric and Charlie growled low in their throats as their panther forms prowled in a circle.

I stared into those blue eyes, knowing that my intuition had been correct. Something was off.

Frost looked down at me, and his eyes seemed to gleam brighter. "When we first heard about you. Do you know what stood out to me the most?" he asked softly. I slowly shook my head, not answering and a chill swept over me. "What stood out is that you saw auras. Do you know how rare that is, or what that means?"

Again, I shook my head, and my dad began to make his way to me. I could see in the set of his shoulders that he was prepared to take this guy out should he try anything. But he wouldn't have a chance to even get close to me as two of the meatheads who had come into the room rushed forward and grabbed his arms, restraining him.

"What are you doing?" I yelled. "Let him go!" I frantically looked at Frost. "Let him go right now." I demanded. I heard my dad swear under his breath and Frost smiled slightly, waving his arm at the men who my dad struggled with.

They immediately let him go, and he rushed to my side. He glared at the man before us, wrapping his arm around my shoulders, and pulled me into him. "What's the meaning of this?" he demanded.

Frost chuckled before looking at me again. "We simply want the power that resides in her. The auras. They are said to be sent from the gods. If you know how to harness them, the user is able to see the future."

What?

My mind scrambled to catch up to what he was saying. Somehow the auras must be related to my visions, my dreams. I remembered Aine saying I was a "seer." She had known about them and about the auras but neither her nor Celeste, not even Coeus had known what the auras I had were. They would have told me.

I could tell by the confusion on my dad's face that he hadn't known either.

"Okay, wait a second," I interjected. I was frustrated and confused. First, because he said they wanted my aura power. How in the heck would they even get it from me? Second, how did it tie in with the visions. I wasn't about to mention them to him.

"I don't even know how to use the auras, and I'm not about to let you experiment on me, to try and take my power. If the gods gave it to me, it's mine. I'm keeping it." I said stubbornly, crossing my arms in front of me and lifting my chin.

Dad's arm tightened around me; his fingers clenched my bicep. Frost only chuckled before the smile on his face dropped and his eyes changed, making his name very appropriate. "You will give them to us. You don't have a say. Because if you don't, we'll take them by force."

He nodded to the group behind us and the next moments were a jumble of shouts and arms grabbing each one of us. I called for my dad, for Killian, for anyone as they yanked me through the door and away from my group. Frost followed behind. Star mewled over and over, her claws digging into my neck tightly, and that was all I need-ed to know that I was in danger.

"Don't do anything, Andie! Don't give them what they want!" I heard Killian yell as I was shuffled down a bright orange hall. I vague-ly saw pictures of all kinds of creatures scrawled and painted on the walls, but my mind was struggling to keep up with what was happen-ing.

This shouldn't be happening!

The greeting we'd received had seemed genuine. But as I thought back to it, I remembered the fanatical way they all looked at me and Emric. Now I knew why.

I struggled against the arms that held me from behind, but it was no use. They were like a brick wall, unyielding and as hard as stone. I tried using my magic, but it just rushed up in me to fizzle be-fore I could force it out. Star whimpered. Something about this place dulled our spells or kept us from using them. I imagined it was the same for the rest of my crew.

We came to a stop in front of a door that looked as if it led to some medieval dungeon. It was big and wooden, with a small window at the top that had bars running through it. The meaty guy behind me leaned over and opened it. I didn't even get a glimpse of what was inside as I was shoved hard from behind, sending me to the floor face first.

My head hit the stone, and instantly pain bloomed.

Rolling over, I looked up as I saw the door shutting. Once it was completely closed, I heard a key turn in the lock and Frost's face appeared in the small window. "I'm sorry for this. You seem like a good girl, but we need your power. We care not about your journey." His eyes moved from mine, gazing above me at something that he must be imagining in his mind. "Freya has guaranteed us that we will not be harmed when she takes over, and we want the auras too much to fight her on it." He sighed and smiled, and I knew that he was insane. They all were.

How can you make a deal with the devil and not be?

He left, his footsteps receding until I couldn't hear them anymore, and I groaned at the pain that pierced through me. When I'd hit the floor, it split open my skin, and blood oozed from my temple.

What were we going to do now? I pulled my knees up against my chest, and I prayed. I prayed that they didn't harm my friends and family. I prayed that I could figure a way out of this mess.

The room I was in was small. There was no bed, no chair, not even a table. Nothing. There was only a small orb that floated on the ceiling giving light to the room, and there was absolutely no way out.

I wondered how long I'd be locked in here. All I could think about was my group. Since these people only wanted me, would they hurt them? My mind went through a myriad of possibilities, and I bit my lip to keep from crying.

No. I wouldn't let my mind go there.

You're going to get out of this Andie. You're going to get out of it and so is everyone else.

I repeated that to myself over and over and as the minutes ticked by, I realized how easy it would be for someone to go insane in a place like this.

Chapter Twenty-One

I paced. I sat. I tried my magic again and rubbed Star's back. She had calmed down for now, nuzzling against me, taking comfort that we were together as much as I did.

After the minutes turned to hours and I thought I couldn't take anymore, I heard the key turn in the door. It opened quickly and the blonde woman stood there with one of their goons. She sneered as she looked at me. "Come here."

I dutifully stood up and walked to stand in front of her.

"Give me your pet," she stated, causing Star to cling even tighter to my neck. She didn't shake, though, and I knew she wouldn't leave me without a fight.

"No," I simply said, my hand on Star's back.

"No?" the woman asked and laughed as if I had just told a hilarious joke.

She reached forward and as soon as her hand touched Star's fur, my familiar leapt into action. She turned her head and bit the woman's hand, drawing blood. It was a flurry of activity as the woman yelled and held her hand to her chest and Star jumped on her shoulder, biting her ear as hard as she could. I watched in amazement as she then scrambled onto the man quicker than my eyes could track and bit him on the face before jumping off to run down the hall and through the open doorway.

I hoped she went to find my group. I didn't think she would have left me without a plan. And really, without our magic working right now, there isn't much she could do to aid me.

The two still stood in front of me, moaning over their wounds and it was quite amusing. I could tell that they'd never been in a fight their entire life. Despite the man's muscular stature, he was a wimp.

Anger lined the woman's face. I still didn't know her name, and I couldn't care what it or anyone else's in this place was. If I had any say in it, we wouldn't be here much longer any way. My plan was simple, and much like Star's. When they least expected it, I would strike. They didn't know I had trained with the Elves. They didn't know I could fight them in other ways besides magic.

I was roughly handled again and marched down the hall in the same direction Star had gone. They'd long forgotten about her. When we entered the blue room, it was empty, and so was the white one beyond it.

They took me out onto the street again, and this time, no one was around. The streets were empty, as if they'd told everyone to hide. I was rushed to a building nearby that reminded me of a church in Junction. It was devoid of any paintings or pictures, unlike all the other buildings here. A star rested on the top of it painted blue, while the stone was bright white.

Up the stairs we went, and the door was opened just in time for us to walk through, as if they had been waiting.

Inside it was one large room, and along the walls were chairs, and in those chairs were my dad, Killian, and the girls. Emric and Charlie were chained to the legs of the chairs that Trela and Bea sat in.

They all started when they saw me, but they weren't able to talk due to material wrapped around their mouths. My gaze went over them, and from what I could tell, they all looked mostly unharmed. Killian and my dad both sported bruises on their faces. I imagine they put up a good fight, and that made me proud.

They pushed me to a long table at the back that a white sheet was draped over. And as I stared down at it, I could hear the chairs around me thumping against the ground, murmurs behind the cloth.

"Stop that now," Frost's voice sounded behind me. "Or we'll take you somewhere else and it will be the last you see of Andie." His voice was cruel and cold, but there was also a hint of glee mixed in. The dude was certifiable.

Two of the goons walked around to the backside of the table with blondie, and Frost came to stand beside me. "Lie down there now." He pointed to it. I gulped-I really didn't want to-but I did as he said. Pictures of sacrifices from old movies I'd watched filtered through my head.

"Arms down and legs straight out." Again, I complied, turning my head to look at my group.

Anguish radiated from my dad's eyes. Killian looked furious, and the girls just looked scared.

Frost began speaking in a low and monotone voice. It was a language I didn't recognize but it had to have been a spell. Why would their magic work and ours not? Blondie joined in with him, their voices beginning to mingle until they sounded as one.

As I gazed out over that room, I noticed a white blur behind my dad.

Star!

I tried to show no emotion whatsoever as she gnawed through his bindings, then she went to Killian to do the same. I couldn't see what else she did, and I had no idea how she might get the metal chains off Emric and Charlie, but we'd figure that out when the time came.

So transfixed on me were the two crazy people and their goons, that they had no idea what was going on around them. It was then that the pain hit.

It reminded me of the time that Coeus and Celeste had pulled the curse from me. My insides felt like they were being torn out, and now, my head felt as if it would burst. I tried not to scream. I really did. But it got to a point that I couldn't take it anymore and I let one loose. It reverberated across the walls, and my eyes flew open only to see dark, slimy auras covering the ones who stood around me.

No longer did their eyes glow. *No.* They actually didn't seem to have eyes any longer.

There was nothing there but empty holes. And then I realized that they were trying to pull my aura power to their own eyes. And the glowing gem-like orbs that had set in their eye sockets before, hadn't been real eyes at all but magic they had made to replace the sight they'd obviously lost in some manner.

And another thing that I realized, was that my magic was working. If I saw their auras, then it had to be. It took a lot out of me, but I turned my head toward the movement beyond this spot to see my group freed and moving toward us quick. All of their auras were white and soft. And beautiful.

They looked like fierce angels coming to my rescue. "Use your magic, Andie. Now!" Dad yelled at me, and all hell broke loose.

Frost and his people spun around, the chant dying from their mouths. The oily black substance that surrounded them seemed to writhe. Star jumped up onto the table at the same time the fighting began, and though my body felt sluggish, I swung my legs and jumped down.

Even though the auras blinded me with their white light and blackness, all I could see was red. Fury welled up in me as Trela went flying, hitting one of the walls before slumping down. She and Bea wouldn't last long in this fight.

Power like I'd never felt before radiated from me. I didn't know if it was due to whatever they had tried to do to me, but it wanted out and it was completely focused on them. They must have felt it too.

The Sea Witches turned to me as one in that moment, and I looked beyond them to my group.

"Go," I said calmly.

They had to have seen what I was going to do in my eyes, because they didn't argue, not even a little. Dad and Killian nodded quickly, backing out the door to the building.

Frost stared at me, his mouth hanging open, longing in his hollow eyes. He began to move toward me, and Star hissed at the same moment that I smiled and thrust my hands out in front of me. The enormous power I had felt gather burst forth and white light shot out in an explosion, taking the people and half of the building with it.

Smoke rose around me, but still, I didn't move. I didn't feel joy in obliterating these people, even though they hadn't second guessed doing the same to me and my family.

All I felt inside was relief. The oily black auras were no more.

I hopped down with Star purring gently in my ear and walked through the debris that my magic had caused. I didn't know where it came from, I didn't care. All I knew was that we needed to get out of here.

My team waited on the other side of the street for me. Pride shone in Dad and Killian's eyes, and the girls appeared to be in shock. Despite what had just happened, still none of the other citizens came out of the buildings. It was extremely strange, but now wasn't the time to dwell on it.

"We need to get out of here," I breathed, rubbing my head as pain began to bloom once again from the bright white that surrounded my group.

"We will," Dad said firmly, looking closer at me. "Are you okay?"

I nodded. "Yeah, but your auras are really giving me a headache. I'd forgotten how bad it could be." Whatever the Sea Witches did had activated the auras around me once again. I was not happy about it.

Emric rubbed against my leg and looked up at me when I reached down to pet him. "The auras might be painful, but I believe somehow they aided you in there. Besides, didn't you bring your glasses? Now might be the time to use them."

I patted the pocket I had stowed them in, and relief filled me. I quickly pulled them out and put them on, and the pain instantly subsided when the white light disappeared.

"Oh, god Emric. I don't know what I'd do without you sometimes." I bent down and hugged his neck tightly much to Star's dismay. He hmphed and flicked his tail out behind him as he strode away.

"I'm not quite sure what you'd do without me either." he said snootily.

Killian laughed and Charlie rolled his eyes before Dad interrupted. "Time to go." We rushed down to the area where we had entered, and I stared up at the dome.

"How are we supposed to get back up there?" Trela asked, and rightly so. There was nothing around that was even tall enough for us to stand on to reach it.

"The real question is, even if we were to get up there, where are we supposed to go next? I mean, we can't go back to the mountain, there's nothing there," I said.

Dad was lost in contemplation, so much so that I could almost see the wheels turning. He looked back at me, his eyes on Star and his forefinger to his mouth. "I don't think we're supposed to go back up. This place was here for a reason. There has to be somewhere here that'll get us back on the right path."

Star purred and reached her paw out to bat the air. "I think she agrees," I stated. "But I don't even know where to begin."

"Maybe we should search every building," Bea spoke up, seeming to have gathered her wits about her and was back to her sassy self. "I mean, if anyone tries anything, Andie can just set herself to destruction mode again and take out the lot of them."

I didn't think it was that simple, but I refrained from saying anything. I did agree that we needed to get going though, and it would probably take looking everywhere.

Dad took charge then and I can say I was extremely glad for it. "Okay then, we'll start searching each and every building, but together. We're not splitting up."

And so, we did. And it took *way* too long.

The crazy thing was that we didn't encounter another soul. No one. Every building we'd searched so far was completely empty. It was as if they had just vanished. It was very weird.

The city was shaped in a square, so we'd started off on one street and when we were done, we went to the next one, and so on. We had gotten to the very last buildings on the very last street, and my patience was beginning to wear thin.

Killian pointed to a building across from us that was covered in paintings of fairies and had symbols drawn throughout. "Let's try this one. For some reason, it sticks out to me."

I studied it and realized he was right. The building itself was just like all the other ones in size and shape, but none of the others had drawings of fairies on them. They had all been abstract or nature-inspired.

It might mean nothing, but I was game. We went inside.

In front of us stood a bare room with stairs that twisted up to the second floor. The ironwork in the stair rail was twisted into shapes of fairies, mermaids and butterflies. Seeing as there was nothing in this first-floor room, I headed to the second floor, and everyone stepped up right behind me.

When we all filed into the small room at the top, my mouth dropped open in surprise at the lone thing in the room. It was a fairy portal that hung on the far wall.

I spun to the group. "This must be how they would get from here to our world." I proceeded to tell them what Frost had said about working with Freya and how she had promised to spare them. That what had happened to us was a complete setup by her. She was using the Sea Witches to get what she wanted.

Me. Gone.

"So how do we know this portal will take us where we need to go?" Bea asked, her eyes on the picture before us. It was a strange portal, because one scene would flash by before another took its place and so on. It was many different places in one portal.

How on earth had they gotten it?

Dad answered my question as if he'd heard my thought. We were just too much alike. "There are portals throughout the world like this one. It encompasses many places and much like a fairy ring, when you step into it you think of where you want to go. Since we don't exactly know where we're going, I suppose we just need to think about continuing the quest and hope we end up where we should."

He shrugged and looked at the rest of us. I knew the look on everyone else's faces probably mirrored mine. But he was right. What other choice did we have? We would just have to have faith.

Charlie walked to the wall, his panther head turning from side to side as he studied the portal, before he reached up a paw, dipping it in. "Only one way to find out." He grinned back at us, and then he was gone. Emric growled and, not to be outdone, quickly followed.

Killian looked concerned as he walked up to it and turned around to face us. "If for some reason we don't all end up in the same place. try to sift home." And with that, he jumped in, his body disappearing from the room.

One by one, we stepped up to it. I made the girls go next, and that left my father the last behind me. I hugged him, and he brushed a stray hair back from my face. "See you soon, sweet girl."

"See you soon, Dad." I said back and kissed him on the cheek. And then I was pulled in through the space between here and wherever.

I barely blinked when my feet hit squishy green grass. All I cared about right now was making sure that my team was here too. I found them a few yards away. They'd pulled out their provisions and were having a snack. Trela waved at me, and I jogged over to them before sitting down and doing the same. Soon, my dad landed not far from us, and I think we all breathed a collective sigh of relief.

The portal had worked and brought us all together.

I studied the hill that we were on and saw that it was a large circular mound. Around it stood almost a hundred large rocks, some engraved with megalithic art on them. And around those were larger standing stones.

Charlie sauntered up from further downhill. "Newgrange," he said before plopping down.

"What's that?" I asked him. I'd never heard of it before.

"It's the Bru Na Boinne, or as some call it, Newgrange. A Neolithic monument constructed fifty-two thousand years ago here in County Meath, Ireland."

I munched on my granola bar and drank the whole bottle of water in three gulps. "So why are we here and not in Falias anymore? I don't understand how being here is going to help us," I said as I tore off bits of toast for Star.

"County Meath is in Ireland, but so is Falias, in a way. Falias is the Fae twin of County Meath. It's here-you just can't see it," Emric said like that told me everything. And it obviously didn't.

"Okay... but still, I don't understand."

He looked down his nose at me, golden eyes blinking slowly, and his whiskers twitched. As if speaking to a child he enunciated each of his words and spoke slow as molasses. "County Meath, Ireland. That's where we are. And... not far from here is the Hill of Tara and Killeen Castle. Do you not know anything about the Hill of Tara?"

I glared at him. "No. I. Don't." I used the same slow and disjointed speech that he had. He only rolled his eyes.

Dad spoke up then and tried to de-escalate the tension that Emric was causing.

"The Hill of Tara once housed the Stone of Destiny, which is now obvious to me the Key we're after. Also called Lia Fail. Long ago it stood on the hill, a large stone, and it would cry out beneath the king who took the sovereignty of Ireland. The stone was made by Morfessa of the lost city Falias, and one of the four Keys brought to Ireland by the Tuatha de Danann. Besides the fact that the stone is a Key, it's also said that the powers of the Stone rejuvenate and fit that person with a long life."

Killian spoke up once Dad had quieted. "I remember studying about this with Aine. She mentioned that even though there's a stone that still stands on the Hill, it is not the original Stone of Destiny. The original is hidden somewhere." Dad nodded in agreement.

"So now we just need to find out where," I stated, processing all this new information.

Once we were done with our snacks and rested a bit, we left the mound. There was nothing for us here.

By the light of the moon, we trudged over the land. One day when we weren't in for the fight of our lives, I promised myself that I'd come back here and explore it properly.

Fields of heather stretched across from us on both sides and swayed with the night breeze. The smell of clean air and the flowers filled my lungs, and I found myself constantly breathing deeply of it.

As we walked, I thanked the stars above for getting us out of that underwater nightmare. And I prayed that whoever watched over us continued to do so as we went on.

Star had long since left her perch around my neck, choosing to stretch her legs and, by the looks of it, lead us in the proper direction. I didn't once question that we followed a ferret. I believed she had more knowledge than all of us combined. Even Emric and Charlie seemed to have total faith in her direction.

It appeared that the rest of the group did also, though Trela and Bea seemed a bit skeptical at first.

We trudged up a large hill behind Star, and as we crested the top, a huge castle came into sight. This must be the Killeen Castle that Emric spoke of.

It wasn't a huge castle like I'd expected or imagined when I thought of them. More like a large stone mansion. From here it seemed as though it were occupied. Lights glimmered in the windows, and the surrounding landscape was heavily manicured.

"Uh, are you sure this is the right place?" I questioned aloud. "It looks like it's been modernized, and I can't imagine our group just walking up to an estate and explaining our journey to normal people."

I stopped walking. So did everyone else, even Star.

Emric sauntered back up to me and sat back on his haunches. He looked exasperated, and if a panther could sigh, he did. "Can you just have some faith?" He growled. "No, we're not going to just walk in there and tell the world what is going on. There is a veil, right up there, and when we walk through it, you'll be in Falias. That castle will be empty and there is where the true journey will begin. Because behind that veil somewhere is the Stone of Destiny, waiting for someone to claim it. And if we don't get moving, it won't be you."

It felt as though he'd slapped me with his rude words. What was his deal lately? I'd never known him to be as short with me as he had been this entire trip. And I told him so. I was not going to put up with it.

"Listen here, kitty, I can't help it if I don't know everything like you do. Cut me some slack or go home." And I flicked my fingers at him, making sparkles of glitter rain down in his fur. I knew he hated glitter.

He turned his head to look back at me. Those golden eyes seemed to have softened, but only a bit. He shook his fur out and said, "Very mature." Then he came back to stand in front of me. The rest of the group knew better than to say a word.

"I apologize for being rude to you. I just think you could have studied up a bit more for this Key. You're relying way too much on that," he nudged his head in Star's direction, "and less on your own magic and smarts." Then he marched back to stand beside Charlie before they moved together, headed toward the veil.

Maybe he was right. Maybe I *was* depending on Star too much, but there wasn't really anything I could do about how she helped me. She complimented my magic, yes, she also made it stronger, and yes, she seemed to know all the places we should go. But what did he expect me to do? Not follow? She'd gotten us this far. And she'd saved our butts back there when we were in the Sea Witches clutches.

He must have been jealous. And wasn't that strange for a Phooka?

We approached the veil side by side. From here, I could finally see what he meant. It was only a slight glimmer, and I'm sure that anyone without magic couldn't see it. It rippled from the sky all the way down to the ground.

"So we just step through it, and poof, we're in Falias?" Trela asked.

Dad nodded, sticking his hand through the veil. "It won't hurt. You won't feel it at all. Shall we?" He looked around.

I gave a sharp nod, and as one, we stepped through. And sure, enough the castle that now stood before me looked old and run-down. There were no windowpanes or lights burning from within. It was just an old dark structure with dead grass around it. Nothing more.

"I say we go inside and get some rest for tonight, or what's left of it," Killian spoke up. He was right; all of us looked and felt exhaust-ed. The strain of the long day before had worn on everyone, and it showed on their faces.

No one argued, so we trudged through the open doorway.

Inside, it was dark, so dad and I lit our light orbs and in one of the main rooms, we built a small magical fire. The floor was nothing but dirt, so we wouldn't have to worry about doing any damage. This castle was basically just a shell of its former and future self.

Emric came to curl up beside me, and I took that as an apology. Charlie did the same, and Star hopped up to rest around my neck. I leaned my head back and watched as Killian and the girls walked around the structure, looking in nooks and crannies, while Dad sat down on the other side of me, our shoulders touching.

He reached over and guided my head to rest against his broad shoulder. "Sleep. I'll keep watch, then trade with Killian."

I couldn't argue because my eyes were already closing on their own, and sleep took over.

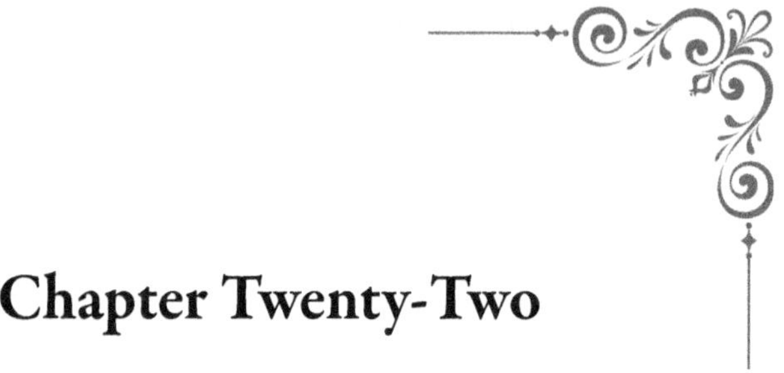

Chapter Twenty-Two

I woke a few hours later from the incessant sound of birds chirping outside and a bright burst of sunlight that glared through the window directly across from me. I pushed the glasses I'd been wearing back up onto my nose from where they'd gone askew as I slept and looked around.

Killian sat against the far wall, both Trela and Brea resting against his shoulders, mouths open and snoring. He grinned at me from his spot, and I imagined he quite enjoyed being their pillow.

Dad snoozed beside me. At some point, he had lifted me up and laid me on the floor with one of the packs under my head. Charlie and Emric had curled up on either side of me. I was thankful for their warmth throughout the night. I quietly stood and stretched, intent on letting them and my dad get some more rest before I woke them.

I looked out the window nearest to me and was stunned at what I saw. The field before me stretched for miles. The heather from last night was still there, and the purple flowers were so thick that they formed a wavy carpet. But that of course wasn't the cause of my wonder. It was who I saw marching through that beautiful heather that made my jaw drop.

It was the Titans. And they didn't look happy. Hunter was the first to see me leaning out the window, intent on their approach.

"Killian!" I whisper-yelled. "It's the Titans-they're here!" I guess I wasn't as quiet as I'd hoped because the girls and Dad stirred,

224

instantly alert. I wanted to jump out of that window and run to Hunter, but I stilled myself from doing so.

The energy that had surged into me was full of adrenaline, and I didn't want to act like a fool by throwing myself at him in front of everyone.

I still didn't understand why they were here. Whatever was wrong, it wasn't good.

Instead of coming to me in the window, the group marched around and in through the door. By then we all stood waiting. Coeus and Hunter led the group, both standing at the forefront, both serious as all get out.

A flash of sympathy shined in Hunter's eyes as he looked at me, and then his gaze went over the rest of the group. He looked every bit the leader. Strong and sure. Handsome...

Coeus spoke first, his voice strong, rousing me from my perusal of Hunter. "I'm sure you're all wondering why we're here." To which we all nodded. "We felt it imperative to bring you information that might impact your journey. It seems-and Andie," he glanced my way, "this may be hard to hear, but please don't fret."

My heart stopped. I wasn't sure I could handle any bad news they might give. But I chewed the inside of my cheek and didn't say anything.

He looked at Hunter, who then turned to look into my eyes from across the room. "We found Teagan. He's not hurt," he assured, "but you were right in your suspicions about Declan and the hellfire."

I hadn't expected this to be about Teagan; my first thought had been Celeste. But I felt no better at the news.

"Teagan is angry, and the hellfire power that he holds is seeping into him. The evil of it, that is. I tried to talk sense into him, did everything I could. But it didn't work. Declan wasn't there but I have a suspicion that he knew this would happen. That it was his plan all along. Teagan thought he was strong enough to handle it. And he may have been, but that was before he was injured."

He didn't say it, but everyone knew what he'd left out. *It was also before I broke his heart.*

Hunter took a deep breath and began again. I could see whatever he was about to say was exceedingly difficult because his hand trembled. "Teagan sifted to Virginia, to where one of the Were shifter packs live. It's a very remote place in the Shenandoah mountains. Andie... he obliterated the entire pack with the hellfire. I watched it happen and could do nothing to stop it."

His voice wavered, and Coeus put a strong hand on his shoulder, lending him strength.

I gasped and put my hand to my mouth. I felt sick to my stomach immediately. If I had told someone about this sooner, I may have been able to keep this from happening. Anger, pain, sorrow and disgust all ran through me. I rushed to the open window and leaned out, emptying the meager contents of my stomach onto the ground below me.

Warm hands soothed my back as I finished. I'd thought maybe it was my dad, but Hunter's voice sounded in my ear. "This wasn't your fault, so get that out of your head right now."

Tears dripped from the corner of my eyes to mingle with the bile and vomit below me. "Yes, it is my fault. It's totally my fault," I hissed. "If I had said something when I first found out, Celeste or Aine could've done something to help. His parents might have been able to also."

He didn't try to argue with me. I knew it wasn't because he believed what I said, but because he knew it wouldn't make a difference. I'd still feel the same regardless.

He just stayed where he was, rubbing my back, letting me know he was there and lending me his strength. At this moment, I wanted nothing more than to just disappear with him. Leave all my obligations behind and live a normal, boring life. But that would never happen.

Soft conversation rose behind me. *Get it together Andie,* I told myself and wiped the tears away.

Sniffing, I stood up, but his hand never left my back. He handed me a bottle of water, and I swished my mouth with it first, spitting it out to the ground below, before taking a deep drink and handing it back.

As I straightened up, his arms guided me around and I felt myself pulled into his embrace. "This isn't like him Hunter. Not at all. I can't imagine Teagan wanting to hurt anyone, let alone kill them. It's got to be Declan. He's got to be the one behind all of this."

I felt Hunter nod against my head, and I breathed in the calming cedarwood scent that was uniquely him.

"We've deduced that the power he has given to Teagan is more than just a regular spell. Somehow, Declan is tied to Freya, and it seems this was all a ploy from the beginning. Freya's trying to destroy you from the inside out, by getting to everyone she can inside your group. No one is immune."

He stepped back and held me at arm's length, eyes compassionate as they stared into mine. "I need the strong Andie to come out now. This is a fight she needs to be present for. Everyone here, including your father," he whispered, "needs you." He hugged me again and then turned away to stand with the other Titans who I hadn't paid any attention to.

Rhea stepped up to stand in front of me. She pointed at where the unalome graced my arm, though it was hidden by my suit right now. "Remember what that symbol on your arm means. Remember it and memorize it. You must remember that the path is sometimes filled with missteps, lessons to learn, and suffering. It will not always be rosy or straight." Her eyes were kind.

"You, my dear, have had a lot thrown at you in a short amount of time. And... you've dealt with every blow with strength and resiliency. Yes, there may have been moments when you wanted to give up, when you questioned yourself and others. But did you?"

Her eyebrow rose as she waited for me to answer. I knew she was right; I knew what she said was true, but it didn't make any of this easier.

"No," was all I said.

She smiled widely. "No. You didn't. Despite all the heartache, the injuries, the terror and the unknown, you forge ahead without hesitating. This, Andie, *this* is why you were meant to find the Keys. I personally believe there is more to you than any of us can even dare to dream of, and I look forward to seeing it all unfold."

She leaned forward and kissed me on the cheek. After her speech, one by one each of the Titans stepped forward to stand in front of me, each one giving me words that were meant to build me up.

By the time Coeus stood before me, I was speechless. I didn't know what to say to any of them, other than 'thank you.'

Coeus held up a hand to stop me. "We don't want your thanks, Andie. You have done us a huge service, whether you understand that or not. You, and of course your team," he nodded around at them all, "have done and will do far more than anyone else in this entire world. One day, you will understand this." He also kissed my cheek and stood back in line with the others.

"I'm afraid it's time for us to go now. We need to find Teagan and work on finding Declan. Finding him will be the only way to take the power away from Teagan."

"Do we even know who Declan is?" I asked, my spine straighter now.

Hunter shook his head, his mouth tight and his eyes full of determination. "No, but we're going to find out."

∞

They left then, and even though I felt stronger now after their homage to me, part of me felt as though it was leaving with them.

I'd noticed that feeling each and every time Hunter went away. I guess that was the bond working. And it might even be why sometimes I felt as though a part of me was missing when he was gone.

Trela and Bea gathered our packs together while we prepared to leave the castle. As I looked at the doorway that the Titans had exited, I wondered if part of that feeling that something was missing had to do with Teagan too.

We were also connected, though I couldn't figure out what exactly that entailed. I mean, you'd think it would be something similar to what Hunter and I had. But I'd never felt that with Teagan. Just a close friendship and pull to be around him. Nothing more.

"Ready?"

My dad pulled me from my thoughts and I absently replied, "Yeah."

And on we went.

This time, I made sure to keep Star from climbing down and leading the way. "You stay here today. We need to let Emric feel useful," I whispered to her. She seemed to understand as she settled in for the ride.

I much preferred traveling during the day. This way, at least I could see the beautiful land that surrounded us and any dangers that might lurk within it. I could see the difference between the real Ireland and Falias. Here everything seemed brighter, as if the colors and textures were turned to the sharpen focus on a camera.

As we walked through the heather, butterflies rose into the air, swirling and swooping like crackles do when they take flight. They formed patterns in the air. I had no idea if the shapes they formed meant anything at all, but it sure was a sight to see.

"Look up there, Andie!" Killian called from ahead, pointing toward a large hill that had something sticking out from the middle of it.

The Hill of Tara. It had to be.

Even though I knew the stone pointing toward the sky wasn't the real Stone of Destiny, I was in awe. I wouldn't pretend that the history lesson I'd heard earlier hadn't impressed me.

The fact that people once came to this hill to stand beside or on that stone and be pronounced the ruler of the land was intriguing. I'd studied a lot on Ireland, but somehow missed this legend.

We trudged up the hill and gathered around the stone. It wasn't nearly as tall now that we stood beside it as it had looked from far below. I felt only a slight hum of magic from the ground below the stone, not from the rock itself.

"Well, it's rather plain, isn't it?" Emric murmured.

I got the feeling that he had been just as excited to see it as I was, and now felt rather let down.

"What now?" Trela asked. I swear, it seemed like lately that was all that came out of her mouth. *But... really, what now?*

We looked around and there was nothing nearby. I don't know what I or anyone else expected to happen when we came here, but the silence from my group was palpable and we all stood there waiting. Even Dad.

We stood looking at each other with no idea what to do next. It frustrated me to no end. Something should be happening. Even Star wasn't leading us anywhere. She just sat still around my neck, calm as could be.

What the heck!?

I groaned and stomped to the stone-*that wasn't the Stone*-and bent down to look all around the base of it. For something, anything. Some magic seeped up, but not enough to make my senses tingle.

I leaned further down, hoping that maybe I'd feel more if I moved closer.

To keep myself from falling, I propped one hand on the stone, and immediately a wave of magic washed over me. I stared at my dragonfly bracelet, but it did nothing. It wasn't lit up at all. I felt disappointment because right now it seemed as though we were no closer to finding the Key than before.

The magic curled through me again, and my vision wavered, lines of the land around me moved like a tide, back and then in, and dizziness struck. I faintly heard everyone around me shout, but my mouth wasn't able to form words, much less get any words out because in that instant it felt as though my body was bent in half, sucked into a chute only to be spit out somewhere completely and utterly different.

Vibrant pink trees surrounded me, with boughs of purple flowers that looked like wisteria dripping throughout them. It was a botanist's dream.

The strange thing, though, was that I couldn't see anything else. It almost appeared as if I were in the bottom of a bottle, the picture before me had curved and blurry edges. And in the middle of this beautiful place sat none other than the red headed woman who we met when we first went through the fairy portal. Leif.

She was still wearing nothing but her long red hair and the crown of flowers. Sitting cross-legged, her hands gently rested on her knees, and she regarded me calmly.

Slowly, I walked closer to her, glancing around every so often to make sure that no one snuck up on me. She smiled at my antics before reaching out a hand to the plush grass in front of her. "Andie, please, have a seat."

I studied her a moment longer before folding my legs under myself to sit exactly like she did. "I don't understand what is going on," I said, and she nodded gently.

"No, but you will." Again, she smiled as if she had a secret. Her ice blue eyes sparkled.

"I apologize for bringing you here so suddenly, but there are things you must know if you are to continue on this journey. If you are to find the third Key."

My pulse sped up, and I leaned in closer. "Do you know where I need to go? At this point, I have no idea." I sighed.

"Yes. The place you must go to is one that was once lost. Hidden until it was time to be recovered. It's time for you to find it and what it hides. True power resides there, and only *one* is meant to reclaim it."

Her eyes glowed now, more white than blue. Through my special glasses, I could see that her aura burned brightly.

"You will be required to pass many difficult tests, and you must be prepared mentally *and* emotionally. It is not for the faint of heart. Ah... but your heart is not weak, and your mind is not dull."

I felt a slight tickle at my mind, as if she were searching it, but then it pulled away. I listened raptly. This woman had strange powers, but her words seemed honest and true.

"A great force fights against you, and before long, it will rise up and be your biggest challenge yet. You must use all of your knowledge and power. All of your resources, including your friends to defeat it. There *will* be death and destruction, but this must happen for you to overcome. Guard this," she leaned close, her dainty hand pressing against where my heart sat in my chest, "and this," her hand glided up to smooth against my forehead, "to defeat the evil that wishes to win."

I was so confused by her words of wisdom that really didn't seem to give me any new insights at all. Or maybe it did, and I just didn't understand.

She looked at me knowingly. "It will all be clear in time."

I nodded, sure that she was right. I mean, didn't everything clear up in time? I just hoped that I didn't figure it out too late. "Please, can you tell me where I need to go to find the Key? And how do you know all these things?" I breathed out.

Her eyes glowed white again.

"You must travel to Beactive Abbey along the River Boyne. There you will find a false door that lies under the stairs on the side of the Abbey. It leads to caves and there your tests will begin." The brightness of her eyes faded, and she leaned in once again, taking my hands. "And as to who I am? I am not so much a *who* as I am a *what*. I am a portal through which the gods speak to deliver messages or teachings, even prophecies. Do not take what I have told you lightly, and do not forget." Her eyes flicked up to the sky, and her body tensed before she looked back at me with fearful eyes that seemed out of place after her earlier calm.

"You must go, and hurry!" My body began to sift on its own at her words, and Star who had been quiet the entire time, shifted, tightening her hold on me. "Your friends are under attack. You must go to the Abbey!"

Her words faded as I sifted completely, and I hoped I hadn't missed anything else that she said. I was thrust back to the hill beside the stone, and the sight that greeted me made me stare in terror.

The sky was no longer bright, and the sun no longer shone.

Dark storm clouds rolled across the sky, and my eyes immediately went to the crowd below the hill.

Freya and the Fomori.

There had to be at least one hundred of them spread out down there. The most I'd ever seen at one time. My group was spread out, their eyes on the evil that waited below them. Killian's eyes startled me; an orange glow like fire lit them as he stared. Trela and Bea had shifted and stood proud in their dragon forms.

I had to get to that Abbey. I shook away the feeling that I needed to rush at Freya right this minute as she stared daggers at me. I'd love nothing more than to stab one-or two-into her eyes this very second.

Rushing to my dad, I grabbed his arm to get his attention. The wind whipped around us, and lightening crackled in the air. "I've got to go to Beactive Abbey! I was taken to someone who told me where to go and that I need to hurry!"

His eyes widened, and he immediately nodded. "I know where it is. Go with Charlie! We'll keep them from following if we can."

A cry sounded behind me, and he grabbed me in a strong hug. "Be careful Andie. I love you."

He let me go, and I turned to run to Charlie, shouting behind me, "I love you too Dad!"

Charlie ran beside me in his panther form, the black hair on his back stood on end, and he yelled to me, "When I change, jump on and hold on tight. I'll get you where you need to go!" I looked at him, and his form shifted to the Peryton that had flown me to Finias to retrieve the Sword of Light.

Once his transformation was complete, I ran as close to him as I could and leapt. My hands connected with his side and I yelled an apology as I pulled on his large wing to help swing myself over. He didn't wince or cry out. I knew he was made of strong stuff, and I thanked the gods for that.

He lifted off the ground and into the air, soaring off in the opposite direction than we had come. His wings strained against the strong wind, and I glanced back to see that the battle had begun. My dragon friends' large bodies were silhouetted against the lightening that flashed around them, and my body tensed as I saw the mass of Fomori surge forward toward my small group.

And I prayed.

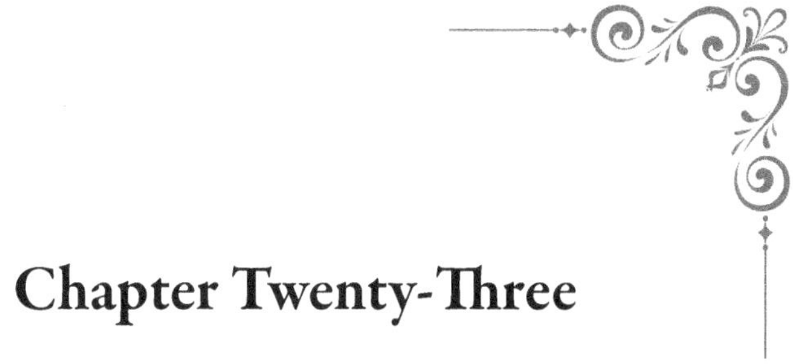

Chapter Twenty-Three

Charlie dodged bolt after bolt of the lightning that seemed to flash directly at us. Fingers of fire rippled across the sky from them as if they were reaching out to scorch us.

My fingers ached and my legs were locked so tightly around Charlie's back that the muscles bulged with strain. He'd already maneuvered two impressive rolls as he swept through the sky, working to outrun the storm that chased us.

Ahead the dark clouds seemed to give way to sunshine, and his wings pumped with extra effort. Somehow, he and I both knew that if we could get into that daylight, reach that normal atmosphere that didn't scream of evil like the one we were in, we'd be okay. At least for a little while.

When we finally reached the strip of sky where the dark and light met, I allowed myself to relax a little. Charlie soared majestically through the bright cloudless sky like an arrow, straight and true.

"Do you know where you're going?" I shouted over the wind that whipped against my face.

"Beactive Abbey, right? Yes, I know exactly where it is. I have a bit of history there."

"What?" I responded, shocked.

"That is a story for another time. It was *my* beginning. Where I rose from the ashes... I'll tell you all about it once you get us out of this mess." He chuckled, trying to lighten the mood.

I'd forever wondered what his background was. Where he came from, what he'd been through. *What he was...*

I couldn't wait to hear his tale. But he was right. We had a job to do. Stories could be told afterward.

"There it is, straight ahead. I can't go in with you, but I'll stand guard outside."

He swooped down over the treetops, and I spotted a large stone building with ramparts that had long crumbled in places. It was deserted, and really old. Arches lined the different walls, and the stone was dark in places as if a fire had ravaged it.

Charlie's hooves touched down, and he ran a short distance before his speed slowed and he came to a final stop beside stairs that led up to a catwalk. Below the stairs was an open doorway, and darkness seemed to yawn from it.

I hopped down and stretched my sore legs before turning to Charlie and wrapping my arms around his neck. "Thank you for getting me where I needed to go. If something happens..."

Charlie nudged my head with his own, interrupting me. "Nothing will happen to you. Believe in yourself and you'll get this done and come right back to us. All of us have so much faith in you. It's time for you to have that faith too."

I sighed and pressed my forehead to his. "I'll do my best." I pushed away from him, and with one last look, I turned and walked into the darkness.

The light from outside didn't reach very far inside, but I could make out a trap door in the floor at the back of the small room. Goosebumps pimpled my arms as I remembered the last trap door that I'd gone through, and the spider I'd encountered.

No matter what's down there, you'll get through this.

I'd found that my internal pep talks helped some.

Tentatively, I stepped down the first crumbling step into the dark abyss. There was absolutely no light ahead. The only faint light that I saw came from my arm where my bracelet lay. I was definitely headed in the right direction. Immediately, I cast my orb to light the way. It barely made a dent in the dark, but at least I could see where I was putting my feet.

It was slow going, the steps curving the further I descended, and the silence was deafening. Not even Star made a peep.

The steps ended abruptly, causing me to feel disoriented in the dark, and the orb bounced ahead through an arched doorway. I strained to hear if anything was hiding in the darkness, and the only noise heard was a slight dripping. The air was colder down here, and I imagined it was due to being so deep in the earth. I thought back to the stairs I had walked down, and I had to be at least three floors down from the abbey.

I inched my way into the interior room ahead of me, and a soft breeze caressed my cheek, ruffling my hair.

Where had a breeze come from?

Again, I shuffled across the worn stones at my feet, relying on the small light, following it as closely as I could. It was too quiet, and that made me nervous. My heart pounded with anxiety.

Taking deep breaths, I moved on.

My foot crunched down on something, the noise startling me in the silence. I jumped back and glanced down, but there was nothing there. My eyes scanned the floor illuminated by the globe, and there was absolutely nothing. Maybe I had kicked it into the darkness around me, but whatever it had been wasn't there any longer.

I looked back up and screeched at what stood not even a foot away. Star growled softly once before settling back down. I didn't know what I was looking at. It hovered in the air, like a fine mist but had the shape of a man, without a face. I could see right through him.

My shoulders tensed as I waited because something was about to happen. I didn't know what, but I knew it was inevitable. And I was right.

The silence that had filled the cavern was smothered by the sound of multiple voices speaking as one. It was a mixture of male and female voices, soft in timbre and smooth in tone. They spoke in another language and I had no idea what they were saying. Panicking, I hoped that it wasn't imperative that I understood.

Just as I was about to speak up, to let them know that I didn't understand, a flash hit my eyes and a vision struck.

I stared in horror at Teagan as he stood on the mountain, blue fire raining down on the wolves below. The evil that lit his eyes was palpable, and I felt terror. Terror that this was my best friend. Terror that he was causing death and destruction, and terror that he would never be the same.

His gaze caught mine and I shivered. This was exactly like the previous vision I had. It was what Hunter told me had come to pass, but this time, he saw me. And this time, his evil was directed at me.

He yelled down to me from the top of that mountain. Shivers racked my body, and his words shook me to my core.

"You think that you're winning in this fight. You are not! You don't understand. How could you? You're nothing. You're not powerful." He sneered. "You don't deserve to live!"

And with that, he began his assault, throwing hellfire that seemed all too real as it hit beside me. There was no heat, strangely enough, but coldness radiated from the flames that licked the ground beside me, inching closer to my boots.

I looked back at him as he laughed. The look in his eyes showed me that he wasn't playing around. And I ran, dodging the volley of fire balls that hit everywhere I'd previously been.

But I didn't run away from him. I ran *at* him. I had to stop him.

A fireball flew by my arm as I got closer, and if he was surprised that I didn't run away, he didn't show it. Maniacal light gleamed in his eyes, and I realized that he might not even know what he was doing. The evil had taken over fully.

Twenty feet. Ten feet. Five feet.

And then I was running him over with all the strength I had.

He fought against me, but I held on tight, shouting the spell to freeze his actions. As I turned my finger clockwise, I realized that Star was not with me.

Why wasn't she?

Teagan growled below me, shouting obscenities and filth that I'd never witnessed him say before. They were abruptly cut off as his mouth and body were stopped with the end of my spell. And then I was falling down the mountain, darkness surrounding me.

My vision returned, and I still stood in the underground room, Star nestled around my neck, pawing me softly. My body tingled, and the apparition in front of me moved to the side with its arm out, motioning me to move on.

My legs felt stiff, but I pushed them to move on. The voices still spoke softly, and this time, it sounded as though they spoke French. I still didn't understand.

Ahead, my orb lowered to knee height and bounced through a small opening in the wall.

I was supposed to go through there? It looked like a Hobbit door it was so low to the ground. Sighing, I got down on my knees and crawled through, my eyes darting around the new room. There was a slight red glow by the wall, and I cautiously stepped toward it.

"What would you do if you had to choose between Celeste's life and the lives of one thousand people?" the voices intoned, stopping me in my tracks. The red light was another apparition, this one the size of a child that sat on the floor in front of me.

I stared at it.

What kind of question was that? I bit my lip, working out different answers in my mind, with no idea what might be wrong or right in these people's-or thing's-minds.

So I just answered honestly.

"I'd do all that I could to save Celeste *and* the one thousand people, but if there was absolutely no way to save them all, then I would save the thousand." My mind rebelled at the thought that I wouldn't be able to save her too if I had to, but my conscience would never let me choose to save only one person over that many others. No matter how much I loved her. And in my heart, I knew she would be disappointed if I did.

The voices were quiet now, and I worried that somehow I hadn't passed their test. Because there was no mistake about what they were having me do. These were tests. Strange ones, but tests nevertheless.

A sigh rolled through the room, echoing the many disembodied voices, and relief washed over me when I realized that I must have answered correctly. Across the room twinkling fairy lights appeared along a corridor that I hadn't seen before.

I took it as a cue to move forward.

I strode toward it, ready for this all to be over and tense at what lay ahead. I'd be lying if I said that I thought the rest would be easy. It never was. But this time, everything felt out of whack and strange. I had expected monsters and fighting for my life. Not this.

Star shivered a little around my neck, and I instinctively reached up to stroke her fur. She nestled in closer, and comfort that I wasn't actually alone in this rippled through me.

The stone hall seemed to stretch forever, and the sparkling lights danced near the ceiling. When I thought the path would never end, it did. Abruptly. Like a picture shifting, a new cavern now stood before me, brightly lit and warm. The stone walls changed to my bedroom in the Oak. All the familiar things were there. Not a detail had been missed.

Was I really back in the Oak? Or was this another illusion?

"You cannot leave this room. You are trapped here forever unless you harness the magical ability to escape," the eerie voices intoned.

So it wasn't really my room. I don't know why I'd even entertained the thought that it could be.

But what did they mean, I couldn't leave? I searched the room, I even tried the door, and it wouldn't budge one inch.

Star bristled and mewled, and my chest rose faster as anxiety set in. Breathing deeply, I shut my eyes and racked my brain for ways to get out of this. Why would they put me through all of those tests only to trap me here? This had to be a test also; I just needed to figure out how to pass it.

I sat on the edge of the fake bed, gathering my wits, and worked on trying to calm my mind. I thought about my friends, and my mind once again wandered to Teagan and the guilt I felt for not doing something to help him sooner. I should have known what was going to happen when I sifted to his house the last time...

Wait...

I can sift out of here! My guilt dissipated, and I shot to my feet.

"Star, girl, we're going to have to put all our magic into this and hope it works." I scratched her head, and she purred.

Again, I closed my eyes and thought about Freya. I thought about all the people she had killed for no reason, and I felt our power build. It swirled through my body and Star's; her hair stood on end from the amount we had conjured. It went up and up, to the top of my head and I waited for my body to sift. And waited.

Then our power slammed back into me, sending me flying back onto the bed and bouncing off of it to land on the other side. My head hit the nightstand, and Star howled as she scrabbled underneath me.

I grabbed her and held her to my chest, murmuring soft words, comforting her and feeling to make sure she hadn't been injured. Slowly, her cries melted away, and she tentatively wound herself around my neck once again.

"Well, that didn't work," I said to the empty room around us. The voices had long since been silent.

Frustration built the longer I stood there looking around, having absolutely no idea what to do now. Star kept pawing at my necklace, and I swatted at it. "Stop playing. We've got to figure out how to get out of here." I scowled as I looked down when her paw pushed at my necklace again, sending it swinging. My eyes landed on the locket, and I swear if a lightbulb could actually appear above my head, it would have. It wasn't the photos inside that piqued my interest, but the feather that my father had told me about. I remembered his words:

"The feather is spelled so that should you ever need to sift, which is what I did just now to transport here, and you're stuck in a magically warded place, all you'll need to do is take it out. Then blow on it and as it drifts away in the air, you'll be taken where you want to go, even if you're in a place where your magic has been warded. The magic in it will be stronger."

This had to work. If it didn't, we were screwed. There were no other options.

I opened the locket and caught the feather as it drifted out of the metal disc. It was so tiny, maybe the size of the end of my pinky finger. I held it tightly, bringing it up close to my mouth and thought about getting out of this room. Over and over, until it was all I could think about. Then I let the feather go and blew softly at the same time. I felt Star's magic mingle with mine, and the air shifted around us. The feather floated up toward the ceiling, falling apart as it did until it disappeared into thin air. When it did, a percussion rippled through me, and I was pulled backward, my body disintegrating like the feather and the bedroom around me faded away.

With a rush, we were spit out of the in between into a new room. My breath puffed out in front of me, frozen in the air, and immediately my body started shaking from the cold. Star snuggled in tighter, shivering as we looked around. It was as if we were inside of an igloo, ice covered the walls and floor, sparkling in the light from an overhead orb. I felt my eyes water, the tears turning to crystals at the corners.

This wasn't good. It would only be a matter of time before I couldn't take this cold anymore, and my body would freeze and shut down, or get frostbite.

It was a small room, maybe a ten by ten in size, and through the ice that surrounded us, I could see an open doorway. We needed to get through to it, and fast.

"You're going to have to help me get through this, Star. We need to melt it with fire. That's the only way." Every hair on my body was raised with the goosebumps that puckered my skin, and my teeth chattered uncontrollably.

I struggled to think of the spell that I needed as I felt my body quickly becoming numb from the icy air. Star must have felt what was happening as she lifted her paw up to my temple, placing it gently against my skin, and the spell I needed ran through my mind, along with the words and motions. I'd thank her later; right now, we needed to get to work.

Shouting with a raspy voice, I chanted the spell, watching fire pour forth like a flame thrower from my hands.

The fire hit the wall of ice, and for minutes it didn't seem that anything was happening. My body strained to hold itself up; the coldness had set in and was beginning to shut it down. Star kept her paw against the side of my face, and I knew somehow that she was holding my mind together, for it surely would have shut down totally by now.

The sound of drips perked me up, and as the moments wore on, the drips sped up and I watched as water began to surround us, the thick sheet of ice finally beginning to melt.

I was weary. I could no longer feel my feet, and I didn't think my suit was working anymore, this freezing room defeating even it.

Stars paw rapped me upside my head, and my eyes shot open as the fire from my hands began to dim. I bit my lip and shook my head, it felt full of cobwebs and my eyes didn't want to cooperate.

A fresh burst of magic ran through me as Star pressed her face to mine, and determination pushed me harder. I ground my teeth and pulled the magic from deep down, making the fire burn brighter and faster than before until I heard a chunk of ice break and watched it fall through into the other room.

That was all the incentive I needed. The hole was large enough for me to squeeze through, and I wasn't about to freeze to death. Pulling myself across to the other side, my body slipped against the wetness and I melted onto the floor, my breathing hard and labored. My lungs struggled to adjust to the warmer air and my hair and skin was now damp as the frost that had covered it melted.

I lay on my back staring up into the darkness as Star pushed her face into my hair as far as she could. I'd always thought it would be cool to visit Alaska, or Iceland. I didn't think I wanted to anymore. We couldn't have been in that room for more than twenty minutes, but it was enough cold and ice to last me a lifetime.

My body groaned as I rolled to my side, sitting up and taking stock of what was around me. Again, it was total darkness beside a hovering apparition. This time it was the figure of a petite woman, her red dress floating around her.

Her hands were held out before her, holding two objects but from my place on the ground, I couldn't make out what they were. She hadn't moved, but patiently waited for me.

Slowly, I stood up, brushing the rest of the moisture from my suit and made my way closer. Her eyes were hollow, her body see-through, but the objects in her hand were real and whole.

In one hand, she held a dark red, shiny apple. Perfect in every way down to the stem with a small leaf attached to it. In her other hand was also an apple, but this one was rotting, with chunks missing and a worm slid through a hole in it. It was disgusting.

"Choose," the woman spoke finally, her feminine voice one among many that rang out. Once again, I got the feeling that there were many of these things watching me as they spoke as one. It was creepy.

I looked at the small woman, but she gave no clues as to which one I should choose, or why. My eyes scanned over each apple, hoping that somehow one of them would give me an indication, but they hadn't changed. They remained the same.

Of course I wanted to choose the perfect red one. Who wouldn't? No one would want the rotten one. Not ever. And for this reason alone, I reached for it. I mean, I was kind of like that disgusting thing. I wasn't perfect-I had flaws-and even through all my bad attitudes and immaturity, my friends and family had picked me. I knew they always would.

My hand connected with the apple, and I could feel that it was slightly mushy as I wrapped my fingers around it, plucking it slowly from the ghostly hand.

"Eat," the voices intoned again, and I visibly recoiled.

Eat this? With the worm crawling through it and who knew what else? They've got to be kidding. I felt a gag rise in the back of my throat as I stared at it. I couldn't do it. My stomach rolled and squeezed itself at the thought of putting this thing into my mouth.

Star purred by my ear, but it didn't calm the cement mixer that was now my stomach.

The woman stayed quiet, her empty eyes watching.

I had to do this, whether I liked it or not. If I got sick afterward, it would be fine. At least then the nasty contents would no longer be inside me, and I'd still have accomplished what they expected of me.

I brought the apple closer to my face, and the putrid smell of it engulfed my nose. I swallowed another gag. I had to get this over with fast. I was only delaying the inevitable and making it worse.

My mouth opened wide, my tongue moving as far back into my mouth to keep from touching the apple as possible, and I bit down, eyes closed. Juice poured out of it, and my stomach rolled again. But... it tasted sweet, not gross. It tasted like an apple should, like the sweetest apple I'd ever eaten. The flesh hit my tongue as I moved it forward in my mouth again, finding that the apple was firm and crunchy. My eyes flew open to see that the fruit in my hand was just as red and beautiful as the one I hadn't picked.

Looking back at the apparition, I saw that the hand that had held the red apple, now held one that was even more disgusting looking than the one I had chosen, the core practically falling through the mush.

"You have chosen well." The woman's head bowed, and her arm swung toward a wall of stone that disappeared with her movement, revealing a large room with soaring ceilings. A glint of light from outside, way up high, poured down to illuminate a stone below it.

The Stone of Destiny.

"You have done well and passed our tests. Move forward to your destiny..."

What does she mean-my destiny?

Chapter Twenty-Four

I stared at the stone as I walked into yet another room. It was smaller than the one on the Hill of Tara, about half its size and crumbling in places. The Celtic symbol etched into the rough stone glowed softly the closer I came.

My bracelet pulsed with light, and the voices surrounded me, whispering over and over for me to touch the stone. Power emanated from it, much the same as the other Keys that I'd found had, though this one seemed to be much stronger, more powerful than the others. I felt pulled to it, and I couldn't take my eyes off it.

When I stood directly before it, magic swirled around it and me. Visible trails of pink and silver, changing to blue and gold, and then every color of the rainbow. The voices didn't let up and their chant became a humming in my blood as I felt it turn cold, then hot, and my hand reached up on its own accord, my palm laying gently against the hardness of the old rock.

As soon as the connection was made, golden light seeped out through the cracks in the stone and into my body. Magic like I've never felt or imagined before consumed me, and lilting music rushed out of the Stone, along with the light.

It's singing!

The beauty of it took my breath away and the voices that hadn't let up before, quieted in a rush. Burning consumed my body, but even though there was pain, somehow the music kept me from screaming, and in the pain, I felt content. Though my blood burned, happiness and an ancient power devoured me, and I knew that all is how it should be. I don't know how I knew this, but it was a knowledge that I felt deep inside my bones.

"You are the ruler of the Fae kingdom," a single voice intoned, strong, deep and mighty. And the multitude of voices struck up again, but nothing of what they said made any sense. It was all hurried and excited, so rushed that all the words and sentences were garbled and sounded like gibberish.

It said I was the ruler of the Fae kingdom... And in my brain, it sounded unreal. A joke that was being played on me. It had to be another one of these things' tests or mind games.

But in my heart, and in my blood. I felt the truth.

I didn't know what to do with it all. The knowledge was too much.

I stared at the Stone of Destiny, the third key and apparently much more than that. I didn't have long to wonder more though as a rumble sounded around me, and the stones that made up this underground cave began to shake, small rocks crumbling from the ceiling.

The Abbey was falling, and we needed to get out.

As I pulled my hand away from the Stone, it changed into the small book that they always did, and I gently picked it up from the ground and slid it into the zipper pocket over my chest. Star laid her paw against it as I turned to find the way out.

I ran.

I ran like my life depended on it while Star hung on tight. We flew through all the previous caverns we'd been in and they were now dark, all the apparitions gone. Even though it took me hours before to get through the path I now took back, this time, it took but a few minutes.

Hunks of stone, small and big, thunked against my body as the ceilings and walls crumbled around me. I knew I'd be black and blue by the time this was done, but all I could picture was the fresh air and beautiful sky that would greet me once I fought my way out.

I tore through the last hall and up the stone stairs as I heard the crash of the Abbey behind me. I barely made it out of the little cubby under the catwalk before it all fell. Jumping through the door, I rolled on the ground and back up to a standing position, facing the rubble behind me. A dust cloud covered the air and the stones groaned as they settled.

"I'm surprised you made it out," a cold voice sounded behind me, causing my body to tense as I turned around.

Freya stood before me alone, her eyes glittering in the light from the sun. "You didn't think that I would bother with fighting the group you left me with, did you?" Her eyebrow went up, and that stupid evil smile showed her white teeth. She would have been beautiful if she weren't so much like the devil. I stared at her silently, not giving her any ammo to use against me.

"I couldn't care less what they do, and I didn't have time to worry about them. You see, I knew you'd lead me right to the Key." She laughed as she nodded to the rubble behind me. "I knew that you'd do all the work for me, and all I'd have to do is wait right here for you to deliver it into my hands." She laughed, then her smile dropped along with her eyebrows. "Now. Give it to me."

She stood there looking regal, her hand held out as if she expected me to give it right over. She was nuts if she thought I would do that. But then again, she knew she held a lot of power that wasn't hers,. She was high on that knowledge and felt as if she could beat anyone that stood against her.

It wouldn't be me though.

Once again, knowledge that I'd never had before flowed through me. The whispers of a million spells, visions of the past... and also visions of the future. Power roared within me, and I knew that whatever the Stone had done to me, it had given me it all.

In the air behind Freya, Trela and Bea flew, their great wings flapping against the horizon, my dad and Killian riding on either one. I could see that they shouted toward where Charlie now stood by a tree, yelling at him to help me.

But he knew. I could see it in his eyes, that he knew now what I was. I smiled at him, and he smiled back. His eye winked before he sailed up to meet them.

My eyes found Freya's again. She was furious that I'd taken my attention from whatever she was spewing now. But I didn't care. I reveled in the knowledge of what I was about to do. Once and for all, Freya's evil was about to be done forever.

She threw some ungodly power at me then. It pushed me back against the stones behind me, stinging a little, but I stood back up and dusted myself off.

Her eyes widened, and fury twisted her face. It didn't help that I beamed as I looked back at her.

"What did you do?" she hissed, throwing spell after spell at me. I easily pushed them away as I walked closer to her. The deflected spells hit whatever was nearest to where I had flung them, and I heard explosions and fire erupt around us. Somewhere in the distance, I knew that my team hovered, watching, but I couldn't afford to take my eyes off of Freya now.

By the time I'd made my way to stand before her, that face that had been the last one so many people saw when she destroyed them was now pale, her smirk long gone.

"I didn't do anything. All you need to know is that now... now your hatred and destruction comes to an end. Your murdering and lust for power will be no more." I laughed as she cringed, looking around for someone, anyone to help her.

"No one is going to come to your aid. Do you really think that after everything you've done in your lifetime, that anyone would want to help you? Well, other than Helios that is."

Surprise and confusion at how I knew about him washed over her face, but I continued.

"Yes, we know about that little fun fact. And guess what? Where is he to help you? Not here. You're just a pawn in his game. You always have been. Do you seriously think that if you had gotten him back in power, that he would let you keep all of this up? He's using you, you dimwit!" I roared. The hate for her rose with each word I spoke until I couldn't take it anymore.

I reached out and grabbed her magic. I didn't even have to touch her. I didn't want to.

Curling my fingers into a fist around the magic inside her, I pulled with all of my might. The power that the Stone had given me soaked it up, pulled it into me and out of her. It felt like there was a straw attached between the two of us as it was sucked inside my body.

As it was, I watched her change. It was subtle, but I realized that when the last of her powers had flowed into me, she was left a weak useless creature.

And she knew it too.

She crumpled on the ground before me, railing and slamming her fists into the dirt.

I stepped closer again, squatting so I was at eye level. I hated being cruel to anyone, but she was the exception.

"How does it feel to be powerless and at your enemy's mercy? You never gave anyone mercy, not even people who did nothing to you. You killed people who had nothing in this fight and left so many children without their families. I should end you now. Yes, I really should. But... you know what? I think leaving you alive, without magic or power of any kind, tossed in a cell to rot away the rest of your days is the vengeance all of your victims would want. Not quick and easy, no, we won't be putting you out of your misery. You're going to swim and wallow in it for the rest of your miserable life." I spat on the ground beside her and walked toward my team, who had now landed behind Freya.

Anticipation, worry, and wonderment lit all of their faces in a myriad of emotions. I was exhausted, and as the events of what had happened just now and in the Abbey hit me anew, my body began to shake and my breathing became erratic. Dad jumped down from Trela and ran to me. I crumpled in his arms.

"Andie, sweetie, are you okay?" His voice was filled with concern and anxiousness. I nodded into his chest, and the emotions I held in before all spilled forward.

He held me as I cried, and I felt Killian come up behind me, leaning in to hug me too. Star snuggled into him, purring, before doing the same with Dad. I laughed a little once the waterworks had ended, and Emric twisted around my legs.

Both dad and Killian pulled back, and I shook my head in mirth. "Star really likes you two. Hunter is the only other one she does that too." Dad smiled, and relief crossed his eyes as he took me in.

"She has good taste." He joked and ran his hands down my arms. "Are you okay? You're unhurt?" His brows scrunched as he looked into my eyes.

"I'm sure I'll hurt more later, but probably just bruising. Nothing a little time won't heal," I quietly stated, remembering that what I was now wasn't what had left my team earlier in the day.

I didn't know how to tell them the news. I was barely able to comprehend what it meant myself, or what would be expected of me. And how on earth I would add this to finding the remaining Key.

Shouting sounded behind me, and Dad's eyes lifted over my shoulder, his body tense. Killian had started stalking toward Freya, his hands out and his eyes glowing. "Killian!" I yelled toward him. "Leave her. She has no powers anymore. She's only yelling because she's angry about it."

He stopped in his tracks, head swinging to stare at me, at the same time my dad did too.

I shrugged and looked at them both. "It's a long story." I sighed, my shoulders sagging. "Can I tell you all about it when we get home, please? But first, we need to tie her up and get her on Trela or Bea. She's going back with us, and we're locking her up and throwing away the key."

I could feel their eyes on me as I stalked back to Charlie, Emric pouncing along beside me. "You'll have to tell them soon," he stated, and I stopped to look down at him.

"You know then?" I asked. Of course he did. When did he and Charlie not know everything?

He dipped his head in my direction before taking up his prancing again, and I hurried to catch up to him. "I do, but not until I got close to you. That was when your power hit me and I realized it all."

We reached Charlie and he lowered his front legs, still in his Peryton form. I climbed onto him, my body aching and sore now that the adrenaline had worn off.

His deep voice vibrated through my body as I hugged his neck and Emric sauntered off. "Don't let this new development in your story shake you. It is all a part of your journey and will only help you and now your people. But you do have much to learn." He laughed as he lifted off into the air, and I gazed down at my team as Dad hauled Freya onto Bea's back and Killian hopped up behind her. They'd be close behind, and I would take these next moments to collect myself.

Something inside me felt off. I wasn't sure if it was just all of this new power, but there was an oiliness to it, curling its way through me. I pushed it down, and stared ahead, the Hill of Tara was approaching.

Charlie landed, and I heard the swoosh of the dragons coming in fast. Slowly I slid off his back, watching out for his wings.

He nudged me with his nose. "Just remember that you're still you. You haven't changed. You're only... more."

I thought about what he said as Trela and Bea landed below the hill. He was right. I'm still me. Still the nerdy, goofy girl trying to find her way in this magical world. My thoughts went to Hunter.

What would he think about all of this?

I still didn't know what to think about it. What it entailed, what would come with this newfound title and power. But right now? Right now, it was time to celebrate the fact that we had found the third Key and eliminated Freya from the equation. For now, I'd enjoy those accomplishments and be just plain old Andie again.

Chapter Twenty-Five

I ran down the hill and right up to Trela and Bea. They hadn't changed back from their dragon forms as first we needed to know where to go to find a portal back home. Regardless, I threw my arms around their necks, one by one, taking stock of gashes and cuts they had sustained during their fight with the Fomori.

"Thank you both so much for your help. We couldn't have done this without you, and I'm so proud that you're on our team." I smiled at them both, and knew that if they could respond, they would have.

Both dipped their heads in response, and Trela winked her big blue eye at me. They were both beautiful creatures. I had never thought a dragon could have been so gorgeous.

Then I turned to Dad and Killian, who stood watching me. I walked up to them and did the same, kissing them both on the cheek. "And I don't know what I'd ever do without you two either. Now, can we go home?"

They chuckled and agreed.

"There's a fairy circle not far from here," Charlie said, turning toward the east where trees grew in the distance. "We need to get to those woods, and from there I'll lead you to it."

Once again, we hopped on our rides, and I glanced at Freya flung over Trela's back. At some point, Killian had shoved a piece of fabric into her mouth to shut up her insistent ranting, but her eyes still spit fire as they stared into mine.

I just waved as Charlie and I took flight. I couldn't wait to lock her up where she belonged.

Once in the forest, we trudged through, Freya slung over Killian's shoulder. A clearing appeared before us with a small waterfall tucked in below a short drop. And there, in front of the waterfall, was a fairy circle made out of grapevines twined together. I'd never been so ready to be home in my life.

Again, I slid off of Charlie and in my peripheral vision, I saw him change into his parrot form, the girls had long since changed back before we entered the trees. I think that they had sensed that something had changed with me but couldn't yet figure out what it was. Their lack of chatter on our hike confirmed my suspicions.

I practically ran up to the circle, knowing that my team wouldn't be far behind me, thinking about Celeste and then I stepped through.

Her kitchen was warm and smelled like snickerdoodles. How that woman knew what I needed the exact moment I needed it, I'd never understand. But she did, and as soon as my feet hit her tile floor, she turned around and walked straight to me, gathering me in her arms. It was what I needed. *She* was what I needed.

Somehow, she had become my surrogate grandmother and I loved her. Don't get me wrong, my team and my dad also meant the world to me, but there was nothing like the love of a grandmother. In Celeste's hug, I felt my Nan. Her essence surrounded me, wrapping me in love too.

"She's always with you, my dear," Celeste whispered, and I cuddled in closer.

She stroked my hair and rubbed my back. I wasn't emotional, but I craved the compassion that she gave me.

The air shifted behind me as the others appeared, and gently she released me.

I glanced at my team as they filed in and felt her eyes on my back. I knew she felt that something had changed. How could she not? But I wanted everyone here before I began to tell them all about the trials I had endured and the power I had gained.

But I also needed someone else.

Hunter.

Turning to Celeste again, I knew it was a lot to ask, but I couldn't help myself and knew she'd understand. "I have a lot to tell all of you, but first, can you please call Aine and Coeus and see if they can come and bring Hunter too? They really need to be here for this as well."

She must have sensed the gravity of it all and nodded before turning to go to her spell room.

I sat at the kitchen table, exhausted but restless. It wasn't until a cup of coffee floated into my vision to land in front of me that I looked up to see Dad smiling, and the others gathered around, watching me as if I might explode.

Sighing deeply, I picked up the mug and raised it to him. "Thank you. I needed this." And as I looked at my friends, I snorted. "Would you all sit down and relax? Please don't treat me like this. Everything is okay. I promise."

They all visibly relaxed, and Trela leaned forward, eyes bright and curls bouncing. "Girl, I don't know what you did, but something is different." She clucked her tongue, and I just nodded. Bea nudged her as she continued to study me. "Leave her alone, Tre. She's been through a lot. We just need to be patient. She'll tell us everything." She nodded to herself, confident that it was settled.

Celeste came back into the kitchen, letting us know that Aine, Coeus, and Hunter should be here any moment.

And my heart sped up again. I felt like a kid on Christmas morning, antsy and excited. And the cause for that excitement appeared right beside me, leaning down and swooping me up into his arms.

He nuzzled my ear, and I felt Star stir with jealousy. "You're unharmed?" he immediately asked, and I nodded. Lifting his head up, his dark eyes pierced mine, and before I could even get another word out, he was kissing me.

Everyone else faded, and I was lost in the intensity of it. His worry, his love and his relief all poured into me.

"Get a room!" Trela's voice broke through the fog that had filled my brain as Hunter kissed me silly. I don't think he would have pulled back if I hadn't, so intent on only me he had been.

Reluctantly, he sat me down, but his hand slid down my arm, grasping my hand tightly. I smiled up at him, only to see his brows scrunched down as he studied me.

I knew he must feel the new power. And it was time to tell them all about it.

"Hey," I shook his hand a little, "it's okay. Let's sit down and I'll tell you guys all about it." He agreed, but I could tell something was really bothering him, but he'd let me say my piece before he said anything.

∞

Hours later, I looked around at everyone. I had told them everything, not leaving out a single detail. I told them as if I were back there in the Abbey, and when I said what the Stone had done, what the voices said, it had been shocked silence ever since.

Hunter, though, shocked by this turn of events like the others, had recoiled when I explained what I did to Freya. I don't know why, or what he thought he knew, but the way he'd acted after that, dropping my hand suddenly and standing up to look out the kitchen window.

That had scared me.

"Somebody say something. Please. I mean, I'm still me... I haven't changed," I pleaded.

Trela and Bea avoided my eyes, and Killian just stared at me, clearly at a loss for words.

Of course Emric and Charlie sat at my feet, Star at my neck, all three of them lending me comfort and supporting me.

Celeste cleared her throat. She, Aine and Coeus had looked the least surprised, and I'd yet to look at my dad, but when I did? All I saw was a mix of fear and pride warring with each other in his eyes.

"Of course we know you haven't changed," Celeste stated, smiling gently at me. "But you have to understand that it is a lot to take in. We haven't had a Fae ruler in thousands of years, not since Nemid died. And you have a lot on your plate already. We'll need to get with the heads of each faction and come up with an action plan to guide you. But... the Stone chose you, Andie. It wasn't an accident, a fluke. Somehow this has been destined from your very start. You were meant to find the Keys, and in turn, also for the Stone to call you out as ruler."

Coeus nodded, agreeing with her. "And what a grand ruler you shall be." He grinned. "I cannot wait to see what you accomplish, because I may not know much about what lies ahead for you, but I do know that you will rule for a very long time."

He glanced at Hunter's back which straightened up taller at Coeus' words, and then back at me, waiting on my reaction.

Does he mean what I think he meant? Giddiness bubbled up in me.

"Uh... like how long would that be?" I questioned him, not willing to let myself get excited without his confirmation.

Instead of Coeus answering, Aine finally spoke up, a twinkle glittering in her eyes. "Why, you'll live forever, or until someone more powerful is able to take over."

Shock reverberated through me, and I felt it roll off of Hunter's shoulders. He turned slowly, his eyes meeting mine, and I could see jubilance in them, along with a lingering uncertainty.

What did this mean for us now? It had been his concern previously when it came to a relationship between us. Would this knowledge cancel that out and we could be together? I knew my smile had to have lit up the entire room as I beamed it toward him. Eventually, he couldn't hold back, and the side of his lips tilted up.

"Whoa. Like *forever*, forever?" Bea asked, her eyes wide as I looked at her.

Aine simply nodded.

"We've got a lot of work to do, but first, we need to get the Key put safely away," Celeste said sternly and held out her hand. How I'd forgotten about it, I don't know, but I unzipped my pocket and pulled the small book out. Power zipped between it and my fingers, and I hurried to hand it over. She took it into the other room, to join it with the other two.

My dad had been silent the entire time, but I had watched his eyes bounce between Hunter and me. He hadn't looked worried, but rather satisfied at how all this turned out.

Killian stood, and cleared his throat, looking at everyone but me and Hunter. "Let's go help Celeste." He motioned them out of the room.

"But she can do it on her own, can't she?" whined Trela, still watching the two of us as if we were some show she was currently binging on Netflix. Killian just cleared his throat harder and yanked his head toward the living room.

"All right, all right," she grumbled, getting up and grabbing Bea. Dad followed their lead but smiled at us before he exited.

I stood up and walked over to Hunter, and he reached out grabbing both of my hands in his, squeezing them softly as the fire lit up inside him. I looked at the gold running through his veins and then up into his eyes. "Now that I won't get old and gray, can we be together?"

I bit my lip and stared into his molten eyes, hoping with everything inside of me that he would say yes. That this was the start of the rest of our lives.

He smiled gently at me, and brushed a hair back over my ear, pulling me into his arms to hold me tightly.

"Til the stars go dark and the rivers run dry, you will be mine."

My heart skipped a beat, and I'd never felt so at home as I did in his arms. I closed my eyes and the darkness inside me crept back up, twining through everything inside of me.

My eyes flew open, and I gazed at the silver toaster on the counter beside me. My reflection stared back with eyes so dark that not even the white showed.

And it was at that moment I feared the darkness that had found its way inside of me.

I hope you've enjoyed Cauldron of Hope and Sorrows. Thank you so much for reading! I would love if you left an honest review for Cauldron of Hope and Sorrows on Amazon, Goodreads, or Book-bub! Reviews help authors more than you know.

As always, thank you so much for your support and enjoying Andie's journey with me.

Love,

J.C.

ALSO AVAILABLE BY J.C. LUCAS

The Four Keys – The Beginning (Prequel to The Four Keys series)

https://www.amazon.com/gp/product/B08H1CXTKL

Sword of Light (#1 The Four Keys series)

https://www.amazon.com/gp/product/B088DKTL4C

Pre-order coming soon! Available June 30, 2021

Spear of Victory – United in Magic (#4 The Four Keys series)

IF YOU'D LIKE TO BE one of the first to know about new releases or sales, click below to sign up for J.C.'s newsletter. You'll also get a digital copy of The Four Keys – The Beginning (Prequel to The Four Keys series) for free, just for signing up!

https://landing.mailerlite.com/webforms/landing/h1f5i7

Let's be friends! I'd love to connect with you!

Instagram: @j.c.lucas_author

Twitter: @lucas_author

Facebook: https://www.facebook.com/j.c.lucas.author

Goodreads: https://www.goodreads.com/author/show/20415558.J_C_Lucas

Bookbub: https://www.bookbub.com/profile/j-c-lucas-7fadf941-1617-4680-b878-53409fa91e17

Pinterest: https://www.pinterest.com/jclucas20/

If you have any questions or just want to give me a shout, email me! I'd love to hear from you. And as always, thank you so much for your support!

jclucas78@lucasjc.com

Acknowledgements

Thank you so much to you, the readers. I couldn't do this without you all. Thank you to my ARC readers. I love sharing my stories with you, and your feedback is appreciated more than you know! A huge thank you to my author friends who have been such an inspiration and wonderful support group. You understand me, help me grow and lift me up so much! To my editor Lindsay York, for doing such a fabulous job perfecting my manuscripts as much as possible, and for always being so patient. To my cover artist, Maria Spada for weaving crazy magic to make my covers so beautiful! Both of these ladies are so talented, and I am eternally grateful to them.

Thank you to all my friends and family who have encouraged and supported me. It means the world! Thank you to my Mom as always, for her endless enthusiasm, beta reading and cheering me on. You are the BEST cheerleader, and I love you. Thank you to my husband and children for always being patient while I write. For forgiving me when I am not paying attention because I'm lost in my world building, and for sharing every little accomplishment with enthusiasm and encouragement. I love you so much!